THICKER THAN WATER

A TOM GRANT NOVEL
BOOK 5

SAMANTHA ADAIR

Publishing Assistance:

Michelle Morrow, M.S. publishology.net

CONTENTS

THICKER THAN WATER

1

ISABELLA

Isabella's left cheek burns as the man watches her from the other side of the hotel bar. Soft piano music plays from overhead and the lighting makes everything glow with a tinge of yellow. She sips her virgin gin and tonic and tucks a strand of hair behind her ear, letting her hand drift softly down her neck past the gaping red silk of her dress. She puts the glass on the bar and traces the rim with her finger.

Come and say hello for goodness sake.

She keeps her eyes trained straight ahead and reads the various labels of the bottles behind the bar while sliding her hand down her leg to caress her calf. She picks up her glass to take another sip. The man leans against the bar next to her. His aftershave wafts up to her nostrils.

She smiles without looking at him. "About time."

"This is your third evening sitting at this bar sipping gin and tonic."

She spins on her stool, her leg brushes against his. "It is." She twists the strand of hair from behind her ear around her finger.

The man smiles, and his eyes crinkle at the edges. Handsome is an understatement. His dark hair and grey eyes match his perfectly straight teeth and dimple nicely.

"So, are you staying here?" he asks.

"Perhaps. Or maybe I just like the clientele." She raises her eyebrows and squeezes the last of her lime into her drink.

He holds a hand out. "Aaron."

Isabella puts her hand in his and he raises it to his lips and kisses it before she can introduce herself.

Isabella smiles at Aaron. "Emily Maguire."

"Tell me Emily Maguire. Why have you been frequenting this bar for the past three nights?"

"Waiting to be noticed."

Aaron downs the last of his drink and motions to the bartender. "Another for me and one for Emily."

The barman nods and starts pouring.

Aaron leans in to Isabella's ear. "Consider yourself noticed."

Isabella picks up her fresh drink and holds it near her mouth. "To answer your earlier question... Yes, I'm staying here." She sips and waits.

"Visiting from out of town?"

She drops her eyes to the bar and swipes at the condensation on her glass. "You might say that."

"Well, I have been known to be quite the tour guide." Aaron perches on the stool beside Isabella and smiles at her as he picks up his drink.

Isabella leans in to him and smooths his tie. "What sights might you want to show me Aaron?"

"What's on your list?"

"A few things... but maybe I need to rearrange them now."

Aaron sips, his eyes stuck on Isabella's. "Maybe you should." He nods towards her. "That's a beautiful necklace."

Isabella fingers the pink crystal nestled against the dip in her throat and squeezes it. "It's a rose quartz."

"Is that so?"

She leans forward. "It means love," she whispers.

"Fascinating."

A woman shrieks with laughter a few tables away as a man in a suit sits back, looking proud of himself before motioning to the bar for more drinks.

"What is it you do, Aaron?"

"On a date with a beautiful woman?"

"Well, as intrigued as I am by that, I meant for work."

"Ah." Aaron nods. "What do I look like to you, Emily?"

Isabella tilts her head and pokes a finger into her cheek. "Let's see. Expensive suit, clean hands, perfectly styled hair. I'm going with finance?"

Aaron smiles, and his dimple deepens. "Finance?"

"No?"

"No." Aaron looks around the bar before fixing his gaze back on Isabella. "I'm in importing and exporting."

Isabella's eyes widen, and she leans forward. "Interesting. And what is it you import and export?"

Aaron's eyes harden for a second before he clears his throat. "Let's just say the merchandise is high class and expensive."

Isabella moves forward again, her mouth almost touching his. "I do like the sound of expensive," she whispers.

"Most ladies do."

Isabella runs her hand down his tie again and brushes her nose against his. "Why don't you order me another drink while I freshen up?" She arches her brow.

"Another gin and tonic and I'll have another scotch. Make it a double." Aaron holds her gaze the entire time.

Isabella lifts one corner of her mouth and moves off the barstool. "Be right back." She turns and walks away, making sure her hips keep him watching.

Once around the corner, Isabella blows a long breath out and shoves open the door to the ladies. The scent of pine and lavender surrounds her as she walks along the stalls, banging each one open to make sure the room is empty. She walks to the sink and peers into the mirror to freshen her mascara. "Go on. Say it."

"That was nauseating." Tom's voice rumbles in her ear.

"Nauseating?"

"Completely. But I do have one question."

"Only one?"

"Why didn't you flirt like that when you first met me?"

"I didn't?"

"You know you didn't. You were a clumsy mess."

Isabella huffs and shoves her mascara back into her clutch. "I had been informed that you were dangerous."

"I *am* dangerous."

Isabella rolls her eyes. "I thought you were going to kidnap me and kill me."

"Hmmm."

"Anyway—" The ladies room door slams open and a woman in two-inch heels stumbles in. She sees Isabella and straightens up.

The pair nod at one another before the woman disappears into a stall, slamming the door.

"Just get him upstairs. I'm bored."

"I'm doing my best," Isabella hisses as she walks back into the bar.

"Iz. Please. He's already pictured all the ways he's gonna—"

"*Thank you* for your input."

He snorts in her ear before falling silent.

Seconds later, Isabella perches herself back on the barstool and Aaron hands her a drink. "For you."

"Thank you." She smiles and sips.

"Thank you, sir," a familiar voice interrupts them, and Isabella looks up at James, behind the bar in a waistcoat and bowtie. He nods at Isabella while sliding a card reader towards Aaron.

Aaron keys his pin and shoves it back at James. "I took the liberty of settling the tab."

"Thank you so much." Isabella sips her drink.

Aaron leans towards her, takes the drink out of her hand and puts it on the bar. "The only question left is... your room or mine?" He takes her hand and rubs her knuckles over his lips.

Isabella lets a smile spread across her face. "Well, I happen to have the penthouse."

He grins. "Of course you do."

———

Isabella slides the keycard into the door and reaches behind, grabbing Aaron by the shirt. She kicks her heels off, digs her toes into the plush carpet and turns to face him, walking backwards into the main lounge of the penthouse. She pushes him onto the leather sofa and stands in front of him.

"Why don't you pour some champagne?" She nods to the bucket on the table. "And I'll get comfortable." She winks and walks backwards towards the hall leading to the main bedroom and bathroom.

Aaron smiles. "You look rather comfortable already." His eyes slide down her silky red dress to the slit up the side and the lace at the top of her stocking.

"Imagine how much more comfortable I can get." She puckers her mouth and gives him an air kiss before moving into the hall. Once out of sight, she hitches the dress up and runs to the bathroom, opening the door and slipping inside.

"Seriously." Tom is sitting on the edge of the bath. He holds both hands out, palms up. "How come you didn't flirt like that with me?"

"Impressed, are you?" Isabella yanks the dress off and throws it in the bath before peeling the stockings down and throwing them on top.

Tom shrugs and stands. "A little."

Isabella rolls her eyes and takes the earwig out of her ear, throwing it in the bathtub with the discarded evening wear. She grabs the jeans, black t-shirt and well-worn chucks from the floor and throws them on.

Tom puts his hand on the handle of the door and raises both brows. "Shall we?"

Isabella grabs her knife from the vanity drawer and spins it in her palm. "Let's go." She walks out ahead of Tom down the hallway and rounds the corner.

Aaron's back greets her as he peers out the window at the London skyline and sips champagne.

Perfect.

She sidles up behind him and holds her knife against the side of his neck, right against his jugular.

Aaron drops his glass, and it spills over his shoes. He doesn't turn around. "Either you play rough, or I'm fucked."

"She definitely plays rough. But you're also fucked." Tom's voice has an amused edge to it and Isabella grins.

"Turn around Aaron... let's have a chat," she whispers into his ear.

Isabella lowers her knife from his neck and moves back while Tom covers Aaron with his pistol.

Aaron looks Isabella up and down. "You weren't lying about being comfortable."

"I take comfort very seriously."

Aaron nods and looks at Tom. "Who are you?"

"The maid."

"Interesting. The room looks immaculate to me."

"I'll take that as a compliment." Tom flicks his pistol towards the sofa. "Sit."

Aaron sits and shakes his head, staring at the ceiling. "I *cannot* believe this."

Isabella sighs. "Not quite the night you had planned, huh?"

Tom sits on the coffee table in front of Aaron, training the pistol in the middle of Aaron's chest.

Aaron looks at the pistol before raising his eyes to Isabella, ignoring Tom. "What do you want? Money? Drugs?" His eyes slide back to Tom. "Girls?"

Tom smiles. "Generous."

"Well, which is it?"

Isabella tucks her knife into her waistband. "None of them."

"Excuse me?"

Tom leans forward. "She said, none of them." He gives Aaron a slight nod and wink.

"Then?" He holds both palms up in question.

"Have we ordered the room service yet, Nathan?" Isabella's eyes stay on Aaron while she speaks to Tom.

"Should be here any moment."

"Wonderful." Isabella sits on the arm of the sofa, next to Aaron. "I can't wait for you to see what we ordered."

A knock at the door sounds, and without turning around, Tom calls over his shoulder. "Come in."

James walks into the room carrying a laptop and a folder full of papers. "Hey Em, Nath." He sits on the opposing sofa and sets the laptop up. "Oh, hey Aaron. Good to meet you."

"You're the barman." Aaron wrinkles his forehead up.

"I'm not, but it's flattering you believed I was." James gives Tom a pointed look. "I told you I was getting better."

"What's all this about?" Aaron clenches his hands into fists alongside his legs and glares between the three of them.

"The girls." Tom lowers the pistol to rest, though it remains pointing at Aaron's crotch.

"What girls?"

Isabella's pulse quickens, and she yanks her knife out of her waistband. She straddles Aaron's lap, kneeling either side of him on the sofa and holds the blade against his neck again. "The girls you buy and sell, Aaron. The girls you abduct and force into prostitution. The girls whose lives you ruin after stealing them from their families."

Aaron's breath comes out in sharp bursts as he stares at Isabella and says nothing.

"Ring any bells?"

Aaron's eyes slide from Isabella to James and back again. "I've no idea what you're talking about."

"No? So your expensive, high-class imports aren't teenage girls from somewhere in Eastern Europe? Your expensive, high-class exports aren't girls you've snatched off the street or lured into your car here in the UK?"

"We've been watching you for three months. We have footage, photographs, and miles of phone records, emails, chat transcripts." Isabella nods to James and his laptop and folder.

"It's all right here." Tom gestures to James.

Aaron swallows against Isabella's knife and she pushes it harder against his throat. "Now you remember?" She blinks and holds his wide-eyed stare for a few more seconds before climbing off him. She grips the knife in her hand and takes a few deep breaths before she can put it back in her waistband.

"Em?" Tom doesn't turn around.

"I'm good."

Tom nods once.

"Right. Ready?" James looks up and smiles at Aaron as though he's about to show him a slideshow of his latest trip to Greece.

"He's ready." Tom hasn't moved from the coffee table. He raises the pistol to Aaron's chest again. "Aren't you?"

"Do I have a choice?"

Tom grins. "No."

2

TOM

Aaron reaches across the coffee table and slams the laptop shut. "I've seen enough."

"Hey careful. That's a snazzy piece of equipment." Tom tutts and shakes his head. "And we were just getting to the good part." *You make me sick.*

James snorts, pulls the plug from the wall, and slides the laptop into its case.

Isabella paces behind Aaron, her knuckles turning white as she grips her knife.

"So. Have we convinced you that you're fucked?" Tom raises his chin, staring at Aaron.

"I already had an idea."

"Might I say…" Tom leans forward and glares at Aaron. "Sampling the merchandise is only gonna make Emily angrier at you. That was uncalled for. And unsettling to witness, frankly. Foggy car windows are just sleazy."

"I'm only human," Aaron says.

Isabella spins from her pacing and kicks Aaron to the jaw. He falls across the sofa and groans, grasping his face.

That's my girl. Tom pulls a breath through his teeth. "Like I said…"

Isabella grabs Aaron's shirtfront and yanks him into a sitting position again. "You are disgusting. And if I didn't have any class, I'd spit in your filthy face."

Noticing the shake in her knees, Tom stands and puts his hand on Isabella's shoulder. She drops Aaron's shirt and stalks to the other side of the penthouse.

"As I was saying… Emily doesn't take too kindly to your behaviour. So how about you make amends?"

Aaron glares at Tom as he holds his face. "How?"

"Who's your boss?"

Aaron rolls his eyes. "Next?"

Tom raises his pistol to Aaron's chest. "Who's your boss?"

"I don't know."

"Excuse me?"

"I don't know. I've never met him. He just pays me a lot of cash."

James opens the bar fridge and grabs a bottle of water. "He might be telling the truth."

Tom keeps his eyes on Aaron but addresses James. "Go on."

"Well, he calls a number that always gets rerouted to burn phones, different burn phones. So whoever he's calling wants to remain anonymous. And the number he's calling has no identifier. They know how to hide."

Aaron juts his chin forward and smirks at Tom. "Like I said.

Plus, they use a voice disguise. It could be my own father for all I know."

"Is it?"

"He's dead."

"My condolences."

Isabella clears her throat and Tom turns to find her back in the red dress and stockings. Stilettos dangle from her left index finger. Her knife artfully lodged in the top of the stocking and secured with a piece of torn bath towel, just visible through the thigh high slit.

Tom frowns at the knife. "I have a few questions, but my most burning one at the moment is… how do you not tear your stocking?"

"Practice."

"Hmm." Tom turns back to Aaron. "Seems Em has a plan."

Isabella sits next to Tom on the coffee table and smoulders with dangerous intent at Aaron. "Yeah. She does."

"We finish what we came up here for?" Aaron smirks again.

Isabella whips her stilettos at his face and one of the heels cuts his cheek.

Tom grits his teeth. "Ouch."

Aaron dabs at his cheek. "What is it?"

"We're going to your shady little brothel and I'm your newest find."

Aaron freezes. "What?"

Excusé moi? Tom grips the handle of the pistol so hard his fingers go numb. "What?"

"I'm his newest—"

"I heard that part." *Are you fucking insane?* Tom swallows any more words threatening to leap from his mouth.

Aaron chuckles, and both Isabella and Tom peer at him.

"Something funny?" Isabella raises an eyebrow.

"Yeah. You're too old, for starters."

James lets out a low whistle and backs away from the three of them.

Isabella leans forward and squints at Aaron. "What did you say?" She slides her hand to her knife and rests it on the handle.

"No. I mean… you aren't old. You're stunning to be fair. But… well, you're too old for… my requirements." He holds both hands up in a weak surrender. "No offence."

Tom stands. "Right. So that's a torpedo through that plan." *Thank Christ.*

"No. I'll be something else. A receptionist or whatever."

Tom pinches the bridge of his nose and holds his pistol out towards James. "Take this, will you?"

James takes the pistol and Tom slides an arm around Isabella's shoulders. "Excuse us a moment." He goes to walk with Isabella, and she doesn't move. "Emily?" Heat rises up his neck and he shakes his shoulders to ease the irritation.

She looks up at him. "Yes, Nathan?"

Tom imagines tiny daggers shooting out of his eyeballs at Isabella's frosty glare. She doesn't flinch. "A moment?" Tom jerks his head towards the bathroom and intensifies his daggers.

Isabella says nothing but stalks towards the bathroom.

Tom blows a long breath out and turns to James. "If he moves an inch, shoot him in the knee."

"Fun." James sits where Tom vacated and grins at Aaron.

Tom walks down the hall, into the bathroom and Isabella marches at him, backing him up against the vanity. "What the hell are you doing?"

Tom's ears thunder, and he grips the vanity. "Me? What the hell are *you* doing?"

"Being creative."

"Well, stop it. You're putting yourself in danger."

"Stop it? Did you seriously just tell me to stop it, like I'm a naughty kid who keeps whining in Tescos?"

"Yes. Because you're acting like a silly kid. You go with Aaron, and you'll be dead by morning."

"I won't."

"You will. We aren't set up for this. This is a bigger operation than getting him upstairs from the bar. We're talking full scale… undercover…" Tom looks around the bathroom for inspiration. "The whole shebang." *Convincing.*

Isabella taps her ear. "I put my earpiece back in."

Tom drops his head and massages his forehead. "Iz. Listen… we need time to set something like this up. We need cameras in the location, microphones, a surveillance nest… you can't just take off with him to somewhere he stashes illegals until he can get rid of them."

Isabella holds a finger up. "We don't know that. For all we know, it might really be a brothel with underage girls in it."

"Except we know they go missing from there and never get found so…" He raises his shoulders and gives her his best patronising pout. "Not to mention he could have a whole hit squad waiting inside. You have no idea what to expect."

"Can't you just trust me?"

Something in Tom's head explodes, and he grabs both of Isabella's shoulders. "Can't *you* trust *me*?"

Isabella gently pries his fingers from her shoulders and holds his hands in both of hers. "Another two girls disappeared last night."

"And?"

"And… it's disturbing."

"I agree. But… haven't we been through this? Tonight is step one. We'll find the girls and stop the kidnaps. It's more involved than a *creative* off-the-cuff decision."

"Yes, but… they're so young."

"Okay listen. I don't know how to say this tactfully, so I apologise, but… It's not the same as what happened to you."

Isabella drops his hands and looks down at her feet. "I know that."

"Do you?"

She nods. "It just… it hits close to home." She peeks up through her hair. "I know you're scared but—"

"Scared? Scared of what?"

"Something bad happening to me."

Tom huffs and scrubs his face with both hands.

"But I'll be fine. I can look after myself. And you guys will get everything we need mobilised. What else are we gonna do, Tom? Take him back and make him sit in an interrogation room while we figure it out?"

"Yes. That's how it's done."

"And you follow rules since… when?"

Tom stares back at her, an answer not forthcoming. *Well, shit.*

Isabella's lips form a sly grin, and she nods once. "Exactly."

"Fine, I'm coming with you."

Isabella laughs as Tom moves towards the door. "No, you aren't."

"Why not?"

"First of all, you won't pass as a woman. No matter how pretty you are. Second, I don't need you around twenty-four-seven to protect me. In case you forgot, I used to hunt people down and knife them to death. Remember?"

"That's beside the point."

"Is it?"

"Yes."

"I'm going with Aaron. I've got you in my ear." She taps her ear again. "I want him to intro me, that's it. I won't stay all night. But it'll give us something to work from."

"We *have* something to work from. This is pointless and dangerous."

Isabella pushes past Tom and leans against the doorframe. "I'm going."

Tom follows her into the hall. "Martha will chop my head off for this."

Isabella giggles. "Tell her it was my idea."

"Like that'll make a difference."

They walk back into the lounge, and James stands up. "He's not much for conversation." He holds Tom's pistol out to him. Tom takes it and flicks it in a stand up motion to Aaron. "Get up."

Aaron rises from the sofa and grins at Isabella. "Did you win?"

She steps forward and smiles as though they're best friends. "I always win, Aaron."

"I have no doubt."

She tilts her head. "Tell me... you seem rather jovial for someone who had a gun pointed at his groin for the best part of half an hour."

"Because you won't pin anything on me." He nods towards the laptop bag. "Regardless of what's on that laptop. I'm just a street level... shall we say... entrepreneur?"

"Call it whatever you want. You're disgusting."

"And when we get to the *massage* parlour, you'll see it's completely legit. Sleazy I'll admit, but legit." He waves a hand out towards the door. "Shall we?"

Tom's gut clenches, and he steps in front of Aaron. "Wait a minute."

Aaron tilts his head and the smugness in his face makes Tom's fingers claw into a fist. "Problem?"

Tom swings and lands a right hook on Aaron's chin, and he drops to the ground as though he's a hessian sack full of sand. Tom peers down at him. "No problem." He glances at Isabella and gives her an imperceptible eyebrow raise as Aaron scrambles off the floor.

"Emily..."

Isabella turns and looks at Tom while James follows Aaron to the lift.

"I'm staying with you."

"No, you're not."

"My gut isn't happy."

"Then get yourself some ginger tea and calm down."

Tom grits his teeth. "That's not what I meant, and you know it."

The elevator dings, and Isabella huffs at him before striding to the lift.

Dammit, Iz.

3

ISABELLA

Aaron opens an innocuous door in the side of a dirty shop front, and holds a hand out for Isabella to walk inside. A worn red lamp dangles above her head and it creaks as the wind catches it. *Sleazy as hell.*

"In and out, Iz. I swear to God." Tom's voice sounds in her ear. She knows he's already found a vantage point to watch the building. "Just find out the lay of the land. Do you understand?"

She gives her shoulder a little shake and smiles at Aaron, mustering the sultriness of earlier that evening. "Thank you." She walks past him into a room comprising of a laminate timber front service desk and purple velvet armchairs with stuffing coming out of the cushions. "Hmmm. I expected something a little classier."

"We're all class here." Aaron puts his hand on the small of her back and it takes all Isabella's inner fortitude not to turn around and slap his face. "Hello, Melody."

A young girl pops up from behind the high counter and straightens her dress. Her hair is a brilliant fire engine red, and a ring hangs from her septum. "Sir. I did not know you would be here tonight." Her accent is Eastern European and Isabella's heart jolts. *Ukrainian.*

Melody peers at Isabella. "You brought friend?"

Isabella swans across the floor and leans on the desk, reaching both arms out across the peeling laminate. "I am Serena." She slips effortlessly into her Russian lilt.

"It freaks me out when you talk like that." Tom's voice is reminiscent of a whining child and Isabella makes a note to tease him later.

"Serena will share your job," Aaron says.

Melody raises her chin and looks down her nose at Isabella. "I do not need your help."

"I tell you what you need and don't need." Aaron's slams his hand on the counter. "Understood?"

Tom chuckles. "He knows he's in the shit."

Isabella puts a hand on Aaron's arm. "Do not shout at pretty young girl. She will teach me. Yes, Melody?"

Melody folds her arms and plonks down into her chair.

Aaron leans across the counter and glares at the girl. "I can always find somewhere else for you to work?" He raises both eyebrows.

Melody's face freezes and fear washes across her eyes. "No, Sir. I will show her. Please accept my apologies."

Isabella moves in front of Aaron, blocking Melody. "You were going to show me around?"

Aaron forces a smile and straightens his tie. "You need to learn some manners."

Isabella smirks. "Maybe you teach me?"

"I can teach you all sorts of things, Serena."

"Jesus." Tom's voice comes alive in Isabella's ear again. "Just get the tour and get out. Or I'm coming in. You know what that means."

"Thank you Aaron," Isabella says. "The quicker we do this, the quicker we can go back to my place?"

Aaron shows Isabella into the long hallway behind the reception area before slamming the door behind them and dropping the controlled pretense. He grabs Isabella and pushes her against the wall. "You're in my house now, Petal. No big strong offsider here to save you… or is he a partner in more than that?"

The silence in Isabella's ear is unsettling, but she appreciates it. *I can do this.*

Isabella smiles, keeping eye contact with Aaron. She slides her knife from her stocking and holds it against his throat. "Let me go or I'll slit your throat."

Isabella keeps the knife at his throat and pushes slightly, making Aaron step backwards. She walks him against the opposite wall and pushes her face to within a millimetre of his. "You try anything fancy and I'll slice your heart in half. Are we clear?"

Aaron smirks and says nothing.

Isabella pushes the knife harder against his throat, drawing a sliver of blood. "Pardon?"

He swallows against the blade. "Why don't I show you around?"

Isabella pulls away, wipes her knife clean on Aaron's tie and slides it back into her stocking. "Excellent idea." She nods towards his throat. "Careful there, you don't want to get bloodstains on your white collar."

Aaron dabs his throat. "It's just a scratch."

"This time." Isabella winks and sweeps a hand towards the end of the hallway. "After you."

She lets Aaron walk slightly ahead and lingers near the closed door to the reception area. "Tom?" she whispers.

Nothing.

Not good.

Aaron turns from halfway down the hall. "Something the matter?"

"Should there be?" Isabella glances around the hallway and up to the ceiling. She pushes against her ear as though she has an itch and looks back at the closed door they came through. *Steel plate?* "You pretend the door is wooden on the outside, but you have a steel plate covering this side?"

"Why? Trying to call someone?"

"No. It's just interesting." She walks along the hallway and counts the doors. *Ten.* She notices another door at the very end of the hallway, painted the same colour as the walls. *Eleven.* She opens the door nearest her and looks in to a seedy bedroom. A queen-size bed with a ratty lace comforter, a threadbare rug and a plastic chair in the corner. "God, this is disgusting."

"Were you expecting Shangri-La?" Aaron leans against the

wall beside the door and grins at Isabella. "Open all the doors. They're all the same."

She nods at the door at the end of the hall. "What about that one?"

Aaron straightens up, and his face darkens for a moment before he shrugs. "It's locked. We don't go in there."

"We don't?"

"Sorry. *You* don't."

"Why not?"

"It's a storeroom. Lots of nasty chemicals and whatnot. It's locked for safety. I'm sure you understand?"

"Not really. Open it."

"I don't have the key." Aaron turns and strides away down the hall. He runs a hand over the peeling wallpaper and mutters to himself.

"Tom?" Isabella whispers, turning her face away from Aaron.

Nothing. *He's gonna have a conniption.*

"Is something wrong?" Aaron's voice is in her ear where Tom's should be, and before Isabella can move, Aaron has his forearm against her throat and yanks the knife from her stocking. "Why don't we continue this in my office, Petal?"

Her blood slows and panic unravels in her belly. *Shit.*

Aaron swings her around so she's in front of him and gives her a push down the hallway. "Last door on your left. Walk."

All or nothing.

Isabella takes a step before spinning and kicking Aaron in the face. He falls against the wall and the knife slides out of his hand. Isabella jumps on top of him and punches him on the jaw.

He grips both her hips, throws her to the floor beside him, and clambers onto her waist. *"That* was uncalled for."

Isabella ignores him and jerks her head up to find where her knife went. Before she can spot it, Aaron pulls her from the floor and drags her down the hall. She kicks and twists, but his arms are stronger. She tries to bite his fingers and clamps down on his thumb.

"You feral little..." He slaps her across the cheek, and the sting envelops her entire face. Her eyes squeeze closed of their own volition and Aaron bends down to her as he opens the office door. "Behave yourself." He throws her onto the floor in the office and kicks the door shut behind them. He pulls a pistol from his desk before Isabella can get up, exertion slowing her reaction time.

He points the pistol at her face and nods to the chair in front of him. "Sit."

Isabella stands slowly, catching her breath. She peers around the office and moves towards the chair Aaron gestured to. He takes his eyes off her for a moment to adjust his seat and Isabella leaps onto the desk, hitches her dress and kicks him under the chin.

He grunts as his head snaps back, and he falls against the bookcase behind the desk. His gun drops from his hand. He scrambles to pick it up and Isabella jumps from the desk onto his back. They fall to the floor and Aaron reaches behind, grasping for a part of Isabella to grab while getting to his knees. She slides her forearm around his throat and squeezes.

Aaron grabs her arm and digs his fingers into her flesh. She squeezes tighter as he shifts all his body weight to the right and they fall onto the floor again. Aaron's shoulder digs into her solar plexus, knocking the breath from her lungs. She gasps for oxygen, and he gets to his feet, pulling her from the floor by the back of her dress.

She pulls in air, her stomach and lungs squeeze and contract, making it impossible to stand upright. He throws her into the chair and waits, pointing his gun at her again.

"Well, that was fun."

She glares at him, wiping the blood from her lip where she bit it in the struggle. "I want my knife."

Aaron sits behind the desk and laughs. "Aren't you a firecracker?"

"I want my knife."

"I bet you do. Well, don't worry your pretty little head. No-one is working tonight. The place is empty apart from Melody and… us."

"Interesting. How do you make money if no-one is working?"

"One or two side hustles. You know how it is these days." Aaron shrugs.

"Or, this whole place is a front for what you're really doing. Just like we said."

Aaron watches her for a moment before nodding to himself. "Wanna take your earwig out? It must be uncomfortable."

Isabella crosses her arms over her chest and keeps her glare on Aaron.

"Fair enough. Though, as you've no doubt gathered, it's useless in this part of the building."

"Which means this isn't your office."

Aaron sweeps a hand out. "It certainly looks like an office."

"A dodgy filing cabinet, old desk and ancient computer doesn't seem like a productive workspace. Not to mention that dinosaur of a telephone." She nods at the old rotary phone on the desk.

Aaron smiles and says nothing. He leans back in the chair, keeping the gun trained on Isabella. "How the worm turns."

"You think the footage and chat transcripts we have will disappear if you shoot me?"

"I'll be on a plane and out of here before anyone knows you're dead, Petal. Good luck extraditing me from the sunny Caribbean."

"Nathan knows where I am."

"You think the front door is the only way in and out?"

Isabella swallows and tries a new tack. "So why have you jammed all the signals back here?"

"Privacy. Like I said… we're all class here. Though I have cameras in every room… just in case." He winks.

Bile rises in Isabella's throat. "For the record. I'm not afraid of you."

Aaron chuckles, lifts the receiver of the phone, and dials. He waits, tapping his index finger against the slide of his pistol. "It's me. I have a situation."

Isabella stares down the barrel of the pistol.

"I'd like it taken care of tonight, if you don't mind?" He grins at Isabella. "Wonderful. We'll be in the office playing Scrabble." He puts the receiver down and pulls a Scrabble board from under the desk.

"You were serious about the Scrabble?"

"I like to pass time productively."

"But… Scrabble?"

Aaron opens the board and slides a letter stand across to Isabella. "Forgive me, but you don't seem too concerned about your impending fate." The pistol remains pointed at her, and he does everything one handed.

"Because I'm not."

"He can't hear you now." Aaron holds the bag of letters out to her.

Isabella smiles and takes a letter. "E."

Aaron picks one. "A."

Isabella takes a handful of letters and props them onto her stand while Aaron rubs his chin and rearranges his own letters. "Squeeze. Not unlike what I did to your neck in the hallway." He drops all his letters onto the board and arranges the word. "Double word score plus fifty points for using all my letters." Aaron grins. "It just isn't your da—"

The door to the office flies open and Tom barges in. Aaron swings his gun around and Tom meets it with his own.

They stand eyeing each other.

Tom lets out a chuckle and puts both hands up, still holding his pistol. "Your house, your rules."

Aaron smiles. "And you turned up uninvited."

Tom drops both hands to his side. "I'm inconsiderate that way."

Aaron tilts his head towards Isabella. "Why don't you go join your partner in crime and stop trying to be a hero?"

"Sure. One more thing, though?"

"What's that?"

Tom swings his arm and smashes his pistol into the side of

Aaron's head. Aaron's gun flies out of his hand and Isabella scrambles across the floor and picks it up.

"You played Scrabble and didn't invite me?" Tom holds Isabella's knife out.

She takes it and slips it back into her stocking.

"It's only my favourite board game."

"Fuck." Aaron pushes a hand against his temple where Tom hit him with the pistol.

Tom tosses cable ties to Isabella and throws Aaron over onto his stomach.

Isabella ties his wrists together. "See what happens when you take my knife from me?"

Aaron spits blood from his mouth. "Fuck you."

Isabella stands and finds Tom arranging letters on the scrabble board. "Fucked. Triple letter score and the K is on a double word score... I believe that's sixty three?"

"You can't put the letters anywhere you like if they aren't connected to the rest of the words." Aaron huffs at Tom.

"You take Scrabble very seriously, Aaron." Isabella hitches her dress up and squats next to him. "That's cute."

Aaron's eyes drift down her thighs, and she slaps him across the face. "Eyes up."

Tom grins and hauls Aaron from the floor, pushing his already bound hands into a gooseneck.

"Fuck!"

Tom messes Aaron's hair and winks. "I should have mentioned... I don't play by the rules."

4

TOM

Tom wiggles against the back of the lumpy sofa, staring straight ahead at the door he knows will open any second. *I'm done with this sofa.*

Isabella is next to him, tapping the nails of one hand against the nails of the other and chewing on the inside of her mouth. Her legs are crossed and she bounces the top leg continuously. Her head remains turned away from him.

He sighs and rubs his face.

The meticulously clean office hasn't changed in all the time Tom has been there. Nothing about Martha is a surprise. And when she walks into the office in a few minutes, he knows steam will emanate from her ears. *Predictable but deadly.* He concentrates on Isabella in his peripheral vision and sighs. "Iz. I know you're angry but—"

"I'm not angry." She keeps her face turned away from him.

"You're not?"

Her head drops, and she rubs her hands over her face. "No," she says through her fingers. "But I was handling the situation myself." She drops her hands into her lap and looks at him. "I'm not stupid, Tom."

Tom slides an arm around her shoulders and pulls her into him. He kisses the top of her head. "No, you aren't stupid. But you've had your baptism of fire now."

She sits up. "Baptism of fire?"

"Yeah. Your first time in battle, learning the hard way... you've never heard the term?"

Isabella taps her fingernails together again. "You knew he'd turn on me?"

"I had an idea."

She gives him a lopsided grin. "How far away were you?"

"At the edge of the building. When we lost comms I came inside and chatted with the young girl at the desk... pretended I was there to... use the facilities."

"I see."

Tom twists a strand of her hair before letting it fall and picking up another one. "I think she was a little shocked when I pulled a gun on her and made her unlock the door to where you were."

"You pulled a gun on her? She's a child!" Isabella's eyes drill through his own, a fire rages in her pupils.

"I wasn't going to shoot her. Anyway, she's with James now, having a chat. She's fine. Stop looking at me like that."

"Having a chat?"

"We'll find her family and send her home. James found her missing person report on Interpol."

The door to the office opens and Martha strolls in. She goes straight to her desk and sits her handbag on top. She takes her coat off and lays it over the back of her chair before looking up at Tom and Isabella.

"Take your time," Tom says before giving her a grin.

Martha glares back at him.

No dice. He stops grinning. "Let us have it."

"You."

Tom's eyes widen. "Me?"

"You should never have let this happen."

He nods once. "Agreed."

Martha blinks but carries on. "You should have brought him straight back here and into questioning."

"Again. I agree. But—"

"It was my fault Martha," Isabella says. "I wouldn't take no for an answer."

"Which usually I quite enjoy." Tom holds both hands up, palms to the ceiling.

Martha glares at him and Isabella huffs.

"Still not finding any of this funny? Okay then," Tom says.

Martha sits on an armchair across from them both. "It was Tom's responsibility to run this job properly. And it's your responsibility to do as you're told. This isn't like being at home where I'm sure you're in charge." She gives Isabella a dry smirk.

Isabella lifts the corner of her mouth into a sly smile. "Fair assumption."

Tom snorts.

Martha takes her glasses off and rubs her eyes. "He's waiting for you in interrogation. James has frozen all his assets. Do be sure to let him know."

Tom jerks an eyebrow. "That's it?"

"For now. It's been a long night and I know you too well to bother persisting."

Tom stands. *Let me at him.* He looks at Isabella. "Are you joining me?"

"Can I bring my knife?"

"No," Martha and Tom say at the same time.

She slides it out of her stocking and puts it on the coffee table. "Just a thought."

As they reach the door, Martha clears her throat. "Sign him up as an official informant. Do you understand? That means paperwork, Tom."

Tom winces. "Fine."

————

Tom walks into the interrogation room and slaps a Scrabble box onto the table. It makes a loud crack and the tiles jiggle inside. Tom grins as Aaron's eyes pop open at the sound.

"Taking forty winks?" Tom turns a chair around and straddles it.

Isabella sits on the other chair, folds her hands on the table and stares at Aaron.

Aaron shrugs, and his cuffed hands jangle slightly at the movement. "It's been a long evening." He looks at the Scrabble box. "What's that for?"

"I thought we could spell out all the ways you're over a barrel."

"Not much in the mood for a game."

"No?" Tom opens the board and shakes the bag of tiles.

Aaron narrows his eyes at Tom. "No."

"Well," Isabella says, leaning forward. "I wasn't much in the mood for a game earlier, but I humoured you."

Aaron grins. "I had a gun pointed at you."

"And yet here we are. You're cuffed and I'm alive." She breathes a long breath through her nose and sighs it out.

"Scrabble is my relaxation. I'm not feeling too relaxed right now."

Tom nods once. "That's fair. You shouldn't be." He drops the bag of tiles into the upturned lid of the box and swipes the entire game off the table and onto the floor. "Did I mention your assets are now frozen?"

Aaron's shoulders slump. "I figured as much. I'm fucked."

Tom grins. "Exactly. So I guess you have two choices. One… we can lock you up, build a brief for all the things you've done, and put you away for years. Two, you work with us and help undo the harm you've facilitated, all in the name of owning a yacht and a penthouse in Knightsbridge."

Aaron swallows and his Adam's apple bobs as sweat glistens on his neck. He looks down at the table he's cuffed to and Tom leans back, stretching at arms length from the back of the turned chair.

"Take your time. We get paid to sit here so…"

Aaron lets out a moan, almost as though he's a child being refused a new computer game. "They'll kill me."

Tom lurches forward to rest his forearms on the chair back again. "They?"

"The syndicate, the boss, whoever bankrolls it. All of them. Do you realise the danger I'm in if I cooperate with you?"

"Can you imagine the six by five cell you'll be sharing with another person for the next fifteen odd years?"

"At least I won't be dead."

"You don't think they can get to you in there?" Tom shakes his head and stands up. "Are you as stupid as you sound?"

Isabella clears her throat.

Tom retreats to the wall and leans against it.

Isabella steeples her index fingers under her nose. "Aaron. You really have no choices left here. We can protect you. And make sure you don't end up dead. But you have to work with us for that to happen."

"And then what?"

Isabella's head tilts. "Then what?"

Tom pushes himself off the wall with one foot and walks to the table. He leans on it, resting on both fists. "Then we can make you disappear. New name. New life. New everything." He keeps his eyes fixed on Aaron's as comprehension dawns across his face. "Yes. You'll no longer live in Knightsbridge or have a seven million pound yacht but... them's the breaks."

"How do I know I can trust you?"

Tom shrugs. "We don't know if we can trust you, either. It's a two-way street."

"Aaron." Isabella clicks her fingers at him, and he slides his eyes from Tom to her. "I'll be honest with you. I couldn't give a toss about you. You're nothing but a criminal, abusive piece of shit. But I care about the girls. And I care about what happens to them. And if working with you and protecting you is the only way to stop them being snatched, raped, beaten and sold, then it's a sacrifice I'm willing to make."

Silence descends on the room; thick and heavy.

"I've never raped or beaten anyone," Aaron whispers, staring down at the tabletop.

"But you facilitate it," Tom says.

Aaron refuses to make eye contact with either of them.

Tom's leg is against Isabella's under the table and the tremble in her body can't be hidden from him.

She stands up, sending her chair toppling backwards. "I need some air."

Tom stands and looks into her eyes.

She slowly meets his gaze. "I'm fine. I'll go prepare that paperwork we need." She leaves the room and Tom turns back to Aaron. He hasn't shifted, continuing to stare down at the table and his cuffed hands.

Tom resumes straddling his chair. "So?"

Aaron doesn't register being spoken to; his eyes fixed on the grey laminate of the table.

Tom clicks his fingers. "Hey. Over here."

Aaron blinks and looks up, his eyes appear unfocused, and he blinks again. "Sorry what?" He looks around the small room. "Where did Emily go? Although I'm quite sure that isn't her real name."

"No, it isn't."

"So what do I call her?"

"You need to make a decision before you get our names. It better be the right one."

Aaron looks at Tom before jerking his top lip and staring up at the ceiling. "Fine. But I have stipulations."

Tom grins. "From where I'm sitting, you don't seem to be in a position to be making demands."

Aaron lowers his gaze from the ceiling to Tom. "Funny. From where I sit, you aren't in much of a position to refuse them."

"We have Melody."

"She can't get you the information I can. She can't do anything. She's there for appearances."

"Appearances?"

Aaron taps his fingers on the table and squeezes his eyes shut. "It's a front."

"No shit."

"It's a part-time brothel. It only works when we have girls in transition."

"Transition?"

"Do I have to spell it out for you?" Aaron snorts.

"No. But I'd like to hear it from your mouth. And before Emily comes back. So spill."

"Why can't she hear it?"

"She doesn't need to. Talk."

"It's a holding facility. Before auctions are organised and they're transported away. While they're there, they work. Call it a side hustle. But if we have none for a few days... Melody picks up the slack."

Tom curls his lip. "How old is that poor girl?"

"Seventeen."

Tom glares at him and says nothing.

"You want more from me, you'll make sure I have a chalet in the Swiss alps and private security for the rest of my life. If they find me, I'm dead. And I quite like living."

"A chalet?" Tom scoffs. "Skier are you?"

"I have a thing for snow bunnies and Swiss chocolate."

5

ISABELLA

Isabella rounds the carpark for her fourth lap and sits on the steps leading into the warehouse. She covers her mouth and nose with her hands. Her heart beat reminds her of those cartoon characters when they're in love and their heart pounds out of their chest. She takes a breath through her hands and slowly lets it out. "Calm down," she whispers and closes her eyes.

A hand on her shoulder makes her jump and she looks up at Martha. "Are you alright?"

"Yes."

Martha moves her head the tiniest amount and purses her lips. "Shall I ask again?"

Isabella stands up and leans against the outside of the building. "I don't know what's wrong with me. It just got so claustrophobic in there. I needed to get out."

"You needed to run."

"I'm not running."

"I didn't say it was a bad thing, my dear." Martha opens the door and flicks her head towards inside. "There's a hot cup of tea on my desk for you. Let's have a chat."

"No but... Martha, have I failed already?"

"Tea." Martha smiles. "After you." She ushers Isabella inside.

James looks up from his desk and smiles as they pass. "Alright Iz?"

"Yep. Great. Is Tom still in there?"

"Yeah I took him the informant stuff." James winks. "He'll be done soon I reckon."

Isabella nods and walks on to Martha's office, where she is already behind her desk sipping her own tea. "Close the door my dear and sit down."

Exhaustion washes over Isabella as she sits and picks up the tea. She sips, avoiding Martha's eyes.

"I had reservations about you being involved in this job when you presented it to me three months ago."

Isabella nods. "And you were right to. Obviously."

"I understand why this job stirs emotion in you."

Isabella squeezes her mug and sets it down on the desk. "I wasn't sold into sexual slavery, Martha."

"No. You weren't. But you *were* regarded as property. Made to do and endure things way beyond your years."

"Yes," Isabella whispers and closes her eyes as though it will shield the images of beatings and sexual assaults. It doesn't. Tears warm the back of her eyelids and she keeps her eyes shut until they disappear.

"My dear?"

She opens her eyes and though tears don't fall, they're wet. "I need to keep going. I need to help them."

"Of course you do. I have no intention of taking you off this job. If anything, you've shown me why you need to be on it."

"I have?"

"What happens when you're passionate about something?"

Isabella blinks. "Umm…"

"You don't give up. You keep going until you win. Correct?"

"Yes."

"Those girls and their families need you. And with Tom and James alongside you, I know they'll have your back." Martha leans forward. "You can do this, my dear."

"If Tom lets me do things my way." She smiles and rolls her eyes.

"He will. Tom won't admit it but he gets scared."

"Scared of what?"

"As you know, he lost his mother at eleven, and then he was completely in love with Claire. She was ripped away from him and he couldn't stop it. Blames himself."

"Yes."

"And now he's completely in love with *you*. And though he won't admit it. He's scared something or someone will take you away too."

Isabella's mind flits back to the bathroom of the penthouse when she told him the same thing. And then to their conversation about him *letting* her do it her way.

"Is that why you recruited me?"

Martha jerks an eyebrow. "My dear?"

Isabella's skin heats up. "So he could keep an eye on me?" Her hands clench into fists.

"Isabella…" Martha leans forward and locks her eyes on Isabella's. "Tom doesn't tell me what to do. He *thinks* he does… but he does not. I recruited you because your skills are unparalleled. And I recruit people I trust. In fact, Tom was resistant to the idea of you being part of my team."

Her ears ring. "Why?"

"Well… for the reasons you just stated. He thinks it's too dangerous and doesn't want you getting hurt."

"I can look after myse—"

"Yes. You can. Which is exactly what I said to him."

Isabella's nose tingles and tears come this time, despite her trying to hold them in. She drops her face and sniffles as Martha pushes a box of tissues towards her. She takes one. "Thank you."

The door to the office opens. "They need to make those forms shorter and simpler. Honestly… how the hell do I know if—" He drops to his knees in front of Isabella. "Iz?"

"I'm fine. Just tired."

His eyes remain stuck on hers. "You aren't fine." He grabs her hand and stands, pulling her into him. "You want to go home?"

She nods against his chest.

"Twenty four hours," Martha's voice cuts through Tom's heart beat and the warmth of his arms. "Get some rest. You'll both need it."

———

Tom and Isabella trudge up the stairs towards their flat. A door down the hall opens and Edward walks out. Tom steps back behind the wall, pulling Isabella with him.

"What are you—?"

"Shhhh. He'll hear us."

Isabella sighs. "What's your issue with him? He's our neighbour."

"He irks me."

Isabella sighs but peeks around the wall to watch anyway.

Edward stands in the middle of the hallway, prods the screen on his phone with both thumbs before nodding once and shoving it into his back pocket. He starts towards the stairs and Tom steps out.

"Visiting a hooker, Ed?" Tom raises his chin. "Doubt it's the first time," he whispers under his breath.

"Tom!" Isabella slaps his arm.

Edward's face snaps up and his eyes widen momentarily before he gives a forced chuckle. "Tom. No. I... I like walking at night. Hello Isabella." He gives her a slight nod.

"At quarter to one?" Isabella can't help but ask.

"No one around." He jams his hands into his pockets and smiles. "I like the quiet."

"Right." She nods.

"Anyway, what about both of you?"

"We have jobs, Edward. We worked late." Tom rests his arm above his head on the wall and leans against it. "Actual jobs we have to leave the flat for."

Edward puffs his chest and grimaces. "I have a job too, you know. I just work from home."

"Yeah. Of course." Tom bites his lip. "Pharmaceuticals or something?"

"That's right."

"And you work from home for that?"

"Jesus Christ, Tom," Isabella whispers but she knows he heard it because he drops his arm from the wall and grabs her hand.

"Well, sometimes I have to go into the office. In London." Edward rolls his shoulders and clears his throat. "Anyway, I'll be off..." He walks around Tom, who doesn't move.

"Enjoy your... walk." Tom narrows his eyes.

Edward waves and continues down the stairs.

Tom watches until he walks out the front door. "Weirdo."

"Tom!" Isabella huffs. "Are we doing this again?"

"No. It's just... something else that makes him weird." Tom closes the flat door behind them. "I mean... if I go out at quarter to one, it's to shoot someone. Let's be honest."

"Yes, well. That's different. He's not so bad, remember he fixed our tv cable for us."

"How could I forget? Not all heroes wear capes."

Isabella shakes her head but grins.

Tom walks to her and kisses her forehead. "You okay?"

She snuggles against him. "Yeah. I ... I let things get to me and I shouldn't have."

"Nothing wrong with that, Iz. As long as you don't make snap decisions that could get you hurt."

"Like I did tonight?"

"Well, I wasn't going to bring it up. But... yeah."

She moves away from him and bites her bottom lip. "I don't need a personal bodyguard."

"I know that."

"You need to trust that I can look after myself."

Tom flops into the armchair and drops his head against the headrest. "Are we gonna do this now? At one in the morning?"

"I'm feeling really unsure of myself after tonight, Tom. I need to know that you believe in me and my ability." She sits on the sofa.

"I do." He folds his hands behind his head. "If it was the other way around Iz, you would cut my head off if I knowingly put myself in immediate danger."

"It's not the same." *It's the same.*

"It's completely the same."

"I'll be answering phones, Tom. And the only one that knows that I know, is Aaron. You know?" She grins. "And we have him by the balls. But it does feel weird using my accent again."

"It's danger—"

"Don't do that. I'm a big girl." *And those girls need me.*

Tom stares at the coffee table before nodding once. "You are. But you need to understand I can't just stand by while you're in such a dangerous position."

"What's dangerous about being a receptionist and gathering intel?"

"In a brothel full of illegally trafficked women, no... girls. Dangerous." He stands and stretches. "Not to mention the fact you don't see how dangerous it is. That's... dangerous."

Isabella holds her breath and lets it out slowly, counting to ten in her head. Martha's words from earlier echo in her ears. *He's afraid something will take you away too.*

She massages her temples. "I'll have you or James in my ear. I'll be fine."

"In your ear isn't exactly covering your back—"

"I can handle myself, Tom. Don't." *He's afraid something will take you away too.* Isabella inhales and holds it a moment while Tom stares across the room. She goes to him, puts her hand on his arm.

He drags his gaze to her face.

"Have faith in me." She slides her hand down his arm and grasps his hand. "Please. This job is important to me."

"I know. I trust you. I believe in you." He squeezes her hand. "I'm afraid something will happen and there'll be no one there to back you up."

"You will. I'm not afraid because I know you'll be right where I need you."

Tom chews his lip. "Okay."

"Okay?"

"Okay."

6

TOM

The thick aroma of black coffee and buttered toast fills the kitchen and Isabella sits across from Tom at the worktop island.

Tom licks his hand where marmalade has dribbled down. He catches Isabella gazing at him. He grins and licks his bottom lip. "Busted."

Isabella puts her mug down, leans across the worktop and kisses him. "I'm very fond of marmalade."

He cups her jaw with his free hand. "Isn't that lucky." Tom's phone goes off and he drops his head. "I swear the woman has a radar."

Isabella laughs and picks her tea up again. "You don't know it's her."

Tom grabs his phone off the coffee table and shows Isabella the screen. **Judith** flashes. He raises his brow. "You were saying?"

He slaps the phone to his ear and picks his toast up again. "What's up?"

"Ah… Tom I need. Well no. It's fine I… Nevermind—"

"What's going on? Are you hurt?" He drops his crust onto the plate.

"No.. Nevermind. I'll see you—"

"Don't you dare. What's going on?"

A silence extends for too long before Martha clears her throat, back to business. "I have a job. Should be fairly simple. And it will be a good one for Perkins to cut her teeth."

"A job? I'm already on a job."

"This needs to be you. You can handle both. This is only small."

"Why me? What's the job?"

"I am."

Tom slams his coffee mug down to the worktop and coffee slops over the side. "Pardon?"

Isabella scurries to get a dishcloth.

"I'm the charge."

"You're the…?" He stops and pinches the bridge of his nose. "Please explain this to me as if I'm James."

"I will when you get here."

"I'm on my way." Tom huffs and drops the phone on the worktop.

"What's going on?" Isabella walks to the sink and puts her empty mug in it.

"I have another job." Tom stalks to the bathroom. Isabella follows and leans on the door frame. Tom pulls his tracks off and turns the shower on. "It's Martha." He gets in and doesn't bother pulling the curtain across.

"Martha?" Isabella frowns. "What do you mean Martha?"

"No idea. To be honest I feel like she changed her mind and had I not got to the phone when I did she would have hung up." Tom's words muffle as he washes his face.

"Are you kidding?" Isabella drops her arms and steps into the bathroom as Tom looks around for shampoo. She grabs a new bottle out of the cupboard and hands it to him. "What's happened?"

Tom lathers his hair and sticks his head under the water. "I don't know. But for her to involve me..."

Isabella lets out a low breath. "Well *I* want to help."

"Martha wants Abbie on it."

"Abbie?" Isabella grins. "Wow. Awkward." She giggles. "We can exchange notes. Maybe you've learned new moves since you guys were a thing."

Tom stills and gives her a look. "Please don't."

"I wouldn't. Tempting...but..." She sits on the closed toilet. "I want to help with Martha though."

"Iz. You can't. You need to be one hundred percent focused on your job. Didn't we talk about this last night?"

"Well, yes but... it's Martha. She's part of the reason I'm not dead."

"I'll fix whatever has her in a tizz. It'll be done by tomorrow. You need to be on guard for people figuring out you're a plant and killing you." *As if I'm not stressed enough.*

"Stop, Tom."

"Not to mention, creeps go to places like that. You might not be hooking but they'll still slime all over you."

"Have you forgotten my former... *profession*?"

"I have not. But, it's not like you can just knife every Edward that walks in there." Tom turns the water off and grabs a towel.

"You're a hoot."

Twenty minutes later Tom sits in the chair across from Martha's desk and stares at her. Martha folds her hands on her ledger and rubs both her thumbs together.

He holds both palms out and tilts his head. "Are you going to fill me in?"

"Someone keeps sending me notes. I'm fairly sure I was followed home a week ago, and last night someone hacked all of my roses."

Tom's pulse beats against his neck and he grinds his teeth. "How long has this been going on?"

"Around three months."

Tom nods his head slowly and peers at Martha. "And I'm only hearing about it... now?"

"Yes."

"And do you remember what happened last time a psychopath came to your home Martha? Has that little experience slipped your mind?"

"It has not."

"And yet you wait three fucking months to enlighten me that you are being fucking stalked?" *Fucking fuck fuck!*

"I didn't think it was anything to be concerned about." Martha stands and walks around her desk. "I can handle myself. And I'm not being stalked."

"Handle yourse..." Tom stands. "No offence Martha but you're a sixty year old woman. Who *may* carry two pistols everywhere she goes, and have an arsenal of weapons in the hallway cupboard but come on!"

"You know about the hallway cupboard?"

"Please. I found them when I was fourteen. But that's not the point."

"No. It isn't."

"I'm pissed off Martha!"

"Yes, I knew you would be."

Tom scrubs at his face with both hands. "Okay, so who is it?"

"Well if I knew that—"

"Don't get sassy. I'm not in the mood."

Martha widens her eyes and purses her lips.

"I'm waiting." Tom drops back into his chair and folds his arms. The heat rising up the back of his neck irritates him and he pulls his collar away from his skin.

Martha walks around her desk and perches on her chair. She opens her desk drawer and pulls out a manilla envelope and slides it across to Tom. "These are the notes."

Tom opens the envelope and pulls out the papers. "You'll pay for what you did... Fuck you and your family, family is in inverted commas."

"Yes."

"That's weird."

"Yes." Martha's voice is husky and Tom looks up.

"Martha?"

She clears her throat. "Well it's obviously someone who wants to scare me."

"Well spotted." He shoves the papers back into the envelope. *I get the picture.*

Martha pours some water for herself and drinks, avoiding Tom's eyes.

He leans forward. "Is there more?"

"Well, early this morning, around two am, a man called me and told me my garden was beautiful and hung up. That's when I went outside to find my entire rose garden had been hacked away. The flowers were left lying on the ground and the plants were nothing but sticks."

Tom pours himself some water so he doesn't say something he shouldn't. He gestures for Martha to keep talking while he gulps.

"But the thing is, I had arrived home no more than an hour earlier and my roses were intact." Martha takes a breath.

Tom stands up. "Right. We're going to your house, you're packing a bag and coming back to my place."

"No I'm not."

"Yes. You fucking are."

"Tom. I will not be run out of my own home by... a disgruntled sailor no doubt."

"So are we going to wait until he slits your throat? Would that be a better time to act?"

"There's no room at your place."

"We'll make room."

"No."

Tom curls his lip and shakes his head. "You're impossible."

"Fine. I'll stay here."

"Here?"

"Yes. Security patrols the building all day and night." She nods to the other side of the office. "There's a sofa over there."

"Well, take it from someone who's slept on it. It's lumpy as hell."

"It will do."

"Martha—"

"All I need you to do is find them and make this stop." Her voice takes on a hard edge.

Tom chews on the inside of his mouth and taps his foot. *I'll shoot them dead.*

"I have already asked James to set up in the house across the street from mine. It's currently empty. He sorted it with the estate agent."

"Right."

"Stop sulking."

"I'm not sulking. I'm annoyed. I can't believe you left it this long to tell me."

"And use this as a training job for Perkins. I suspect this will be easy for her. She is rather impressive."

Tom rolls his eyes. *Stop avoiding my wrath.* "You are aware no doubt about this *huge* job I started yesterday? A job that happens to involve my…"

Martha raises her eyebrows. "Your?"

"Isabella. It involves Isabella."

"Yes. I simply want you to oversee this. Train Abbie to take lead. But I need you on it. It makes me feel... safer." Her eyes drop to the table.

Tom's chest squeezes. "Fuck," he whispers.

"I should have told you. I know. I'm sorry Tom."

Tom nods. "Where's Abbie?"

"Down on the range."

He spins and stalks from the office.

————

Tom slams out the back doors and heads towards the range. Dull pops sound through the reinforced structure. He presses the door button and waits for the range master to let him in.

He leans against the wall and grinds his teeth. *Three months. Fucks sake Martha.*

The pops stop. Moments later the door opens and a fifty year old man with a missing front tooth grins at Tom. The ear muffs around his stubbly neck are a permanent fixture.

"Hey, Howard." Tom walks in and peers through the glass booth at Abbie on the range, fiddling with her holster. "How's she doing?"

"She's a natural."

"She is." Tom nods once and grabs some earmuffs. "I'm going in."

"Sure, Tom." He leans into his microphone to speak to Abbie. "Firearms away. Eyes and ears off." Abbie looks up and Tom waves. "Tom's coming in Ms Perkins."

Abbie nods and grins as Tom opens the door. She leans

against the booth she's shooting from. "Come to check up on me?"

"Do I need to?"

Abbie snorts. "No."

"Are you shooting, Tom?" Howard's voice crackles into the range.

"Go on," Abbie taunts, turning back to the target and putting her eyes and ears on. "If you think you're good enough."

Tom puts his earmuffs on and grabs a pair or protective glasses. He stands in the booth next to Abbie and takes his gun out of his waistband.

"You know, one day Tom, you might get a decent holster." Howard's voice comes through, dulled by the earmuffs.

Tom grins at the target in front of him and shakes his head.

Howard laughs and both targets shoot backwards down the track. "Here we go. Twelve metres. Eyes and ears on across the range. In your own time."

Tom squeezes the trigger and fires off a magazine, seeing a nameless face with garden shears in his mind's eye. *I will fucking end you.* He presses the release, the spent magazine drops out and he replaces it with a fresh one and lines up his sights. He fires off the second, as Abbie does the same thing—albeit not as fast.

He fires the last shot and lowers his weapon to rest. He shifts his eyes to Abbie's target as her last shots blow the paper apart.

A silence falls across the range before Howard's voice crackles through the microphone.

"Reholster. All firearms away, targets returning. Remove eyes and ears."

Tom takes the glasses off and drops his earmuffs around his

neck. He unclips his target and studies the peppered hole in the centre of the target's chest. *Thirty rounds into the one spot will do that.*

"What was that about being good enough?" He slides his eyes to Abbie and grins.

"Yeah well. You look angry and tense. So of course you're gonna smash it."

"Well spotted." He tears the target in half and shoves it in the bin behind him. "Although you didn't do too bad. Except for one or two in his head." Tom nods at the target as Abbie tears it down.

"Maybe I did that on purpose."

"You didn't." Tom leans against the reloading dock and folds his arms. "Perfectionist."

Abbie shrugs and scrunches the target up, throwing it in on top of Tom's. "So, what's going on?"

"We have a job." He jerks his head towards the door and walks.

"Already? You don't want to test my defensive tactics? Wrestle with me on the mats?"

Tom stops and turns as they walk into the sunlight. "From memory your wrestling techniques are adequate."

"I may have lost my edge."

"Doubt it." Tom raises a brow as Abbie grins.

"So… what's the job?"

"Martha's being stalked."

"What? So where are we going?"

"Martha's house. Well… across the road anyway."

"She lives in a house? Interesting."

Tom snorts. "Where else would she live?"

"I pictured her living in some sort of fort with a drawbridge, you know, like the mysterious vampiress in one of those novels.."

Tom laughs. "Listen, this is your job. I'm helping you, but I'm already on another job starting tonight. Okay?"

"With Isabella." Abbie nods as they walk back into the warehouse.

"Yes."

Abbie says nothing.

The weird silence unsettles Tom. "Abs—"

"No, I mean… that should absolutely be your focus." She smiles. "Let me get my kit."

Tom winces as she darts between desks and chairs to get her things.

Minutes later, Tom stomps across the carpark with Abbie trailing behind him. He stops and scans before finding the car he's after. He clicks the unlock and flicks his head towards it. "The black Audi."

"Fancy."

Tom grunts as he pulls open the driver's side door. "I'm not gonna drive around in a heap of shit." He pokes his head into the car. "Fuck's sake."

Abbie fiddles with her seatbelt. "What's wrong?"

He reaches across and grabs an empty takeaway coffee cup and scrap of paper from the drink holders. "Can't anyone fucking clean up after themselves around here?" He slams the door shut and stalks across the carpark before hurling the rubbish into the bin. He stops and closes his eyes briefly. *Take a breath.*

"So," Abbie says as he gets back in the car. "Did you enjoy your little walk?"

"I don't understand why people can't clean up after themselves. Are we in primary school?"

"There should really be a national enquiry." Abbie nods.

"Abs—"

"Are you still seeing that ex Navy psych?"

"What has that got to do with anything?"

"You seem rather angry about a coffee cup and scrap of paper."

"Like I said, we aren't—"

"Quit the bullshit Tom. It's never worked on me before and it won't work on me now. What's got you in a flap?"

Tom clamps his mouth shut and drives.

"Fine. Be that way. But I never put up with your bullshit… and I won't now. So talk to me or get over it."

"I see him once a month." Tom grips the wheel tighter and keeps his eyes straight ahead.

"Who?"

"Mike. The Navy psych."

"And?"

"It's… fine."

Abbie snorts. "Okay."

———

Tom walks into the house diagonally across the road from the one he grew up in, sits on the sofa and dumps his gun on the coffee table.

Abbie sits on the other armchair and looks around the room. "Cute place. Though the overload of doilies on every surface is a bit off putting."

"A woman called Mavis used to live here. I'd say her family rents it out as fully furnished these days so they didn't have to bother getting rid of everything."

Abbie peers at Tom. "How do you know that?"

Fuck. "Martha told me in my briefing."

"Oh." Abbie stands and looks out the front window. "Now what?"

"We pretend we're the new tenants living in Mavis's old place." Tom shrugs.

"Okay. But tell me. If we're going undercover, why don't we just live here during the job?"

"We aren't undercover. It's just a base. But, we have to be careful no one cottons on."

"And you don't want to be away from Isabella."

"That has nothing to do with it."

"Is that right?"

"Yes."

"If you say so." .

Tom watches her for a few seconds before nodding. "Okay, you're right. I don't want to be away from her. She's on a job that makes me nervous. One I should be on with her."

"You don't think she's capable?"

"Don't you start."

Abbie holds both hands up in mock surrender. "Sorry."

James appears in the hall arch and grins at Tom. "Someone's in a foul mood."

Tom grunts. "Where are we at?"

"The house is set up. The tech is in the master bedroom that looks to the front of the house." He jerks his head back towards where he came from. "I've got surveillance all over her house. Except… you know. Inside. That'd be weird."

"That's not necessary," Tom says.

"For now." James shrugs.

Tom gives him a side eye glance. "It won't be necessary." *Stay out of her house.*

"Okay. Whatever you say." He holds his hands up in a mirror of Abbie moments before.

"Don't you have Iz's job to set up?" Tom folds his arms over his chest.

"Yes." James moves towards the front door. "And don't stress. She'll be fine."

"Cheers Nostradamus."

James snorts. "Right." James opens the door. "I'm off to watch Isabella."

"Don't fuck up."

"Give me some credit, Tom."

Tom squints at the door as it slams shut behind James.

"Who's that?" Abbie points out the window and Tom hurdles the sofa and lands next to her.

"Where?"

"Nothing… a pamphlet drop. Sorry."

He glares at Abbie. "Really?"

"Sorry. I thought he looked suss."

Tom holds his breath and cracks his neck. "It's fine. Just... you can't jump at every tiny thing. Okay?"

"Rookie error." Abbie puts her hand on his arm. "Sorry."

Tom looks up and down the street and huffs. "I'm going for a walk."

"Alone?"

"We aren't in Brixton." He leaves before Abbie can say anything and paces out the front gate. He crosses the road to Martha's front garden. The rose bed is nothing but sticks and hacked leaves with a few petals scattered around. Blood simmers in Tom's veins and he glares down the street.

Brixton would be preferable.

7

ISABELLA

Isabella walks into the warehouse and is immediately accosted by Penny.

"Iz! Hey." She waddles around her desk and stands in front of Isabella with her hands clasped. "Alright?"

"Um. Yes? Why wouldn't I be?"

"No… no reason. I thought…"

Gossip Queen Penny.

"You thought I'd be on edge because Tom's working with an ex… fling?"

"Well I… fling you say?"

"Don't pretend you didn't know, Penny." Isabella grins. "No, it doesn't bother me." She looks beyond Penny onto the floor. "And you know what Tom will do if he finds out there's gossiping about him going on?"

"No?"

"He'll shoot you, Penny." Isabella winks and walks towards Martha's office. She knocks and waits.

"Come in, Isabella."

Isabella sits and before Martha can say anything she leans forward. "Why are you being stalked?"

Martha blinks once but keeps her stiff composure. "Because felons always think they've been wronged, Isabella. They don't think they deserve to go to prison for their crimes." Martha stops and takes a breath, tapping her finger on her desk.

"So it's someone you've caught before?"

"Tom thinks so. And he's rarely wrong. Which is irritating at the best of times." She gives Isabella a tight smile. "He's going to be in a right mood for being taken off your job and onto this one. Sorry about that."

"Nothing I can't handle." Isabella stands. "I'm gonna go get changed. But Martha?"

Martha raises her eyebrows.

"He's angry at you for the same reasons he's protective of me." Isabella smiles.

Martha picks up a paper and fixes her eyes on it. "He's a pain in the neck."

———

Isabella wiggles her hips as she pulls her black fishnet tights up to her waist. She grabs the red vinyl miniskirt off the bed and steps into it. The aroma of overused cooking oil and fish wafts through the vents from the shop downstairs. Isabella wrinkles her nose up.

"So, Tom's in a sunny mood today." James' voice floats in from down the hall.

"Yeah… This Martha job won't be sitting well with him. You know what he's like." She walks into the lounge of the surveillance flat, careful not to trip on the threadbare carpet and throws a pair of knee high boots onto the floor.

"I told him I'd be here watching everything so you're safe. Surely he's comforted by that fact?" Amusement tinges the end of James' words. "Not to mention I'm also required in the house Tom's working out of. You two owe me. I'm only one person."

Isabella watches James for a few seconds. "Tom's right you know."

"About?"

"It really *is* annoying when you make sense."

James laughs and swigs from his bottle of Coke. "Sorry."

"And listen, I have a Mischa shaped bone to pick with you."

James' cheeks deepen in colour and he puts his coke down. "She's just a mate."

"Fair enough. And I'm just pretending that working in a brothel is so wholesome."

"So why are you really doing it?"

Isabella pauses as she zips her boot up. "What do you mean?"

James leans forward and rests his elbows on his knees. "I'm thick at times but I'm not completely stupid. There's something about this job that gets to you."

Isabella gives James an eyebrow quirk, hoping it's convincing. "It's a brothel, James. The whole thing is unsavoury."

"That's not what I mean. It's the fact that most of the girls who go through there are Eastern European. Right?"

Isabella zips her other boot and chews on her lip. "You don't know how Tom and I met. Do you?"

"Something to do with Paris? And killing Jack?"

"I was in hiding in the UK for ten years before Tom was assigned to protect me. And we didn't kill Jack. You know that."

"I do. Sorry that was insensitive." There's a long pause while James sits with his forehead wrinkled. "So the Russians eventually came looking for you?"

"Yes. I was dangerous to them. I knew about the Blood Orphans." She raises her eyes to James. "I was one of them. But I ran. And Jack protected me so I wouldn't kill him." Jack's face glides through her mind and she closes her eyes for a second to savour his kind face.

She opens her eyes.

James stares at her with his mouth open and gestures with his hand for her to go on."

"They looked for me for years. To be honest I'm surprised it took them so long to realise I hadn't killed Jack like I was assigned to."

"They didn't know?"

"After I went into hiding, so did Jack for a period of time. They must have looked for him and figured I got to him first."

"Maybe they thought you were dead too?."

"Maybe. Anyway, one of them spotted me years later, realised we are both alive and they threatened Jack. They said they would keep him alive in exchange for me. He held out and they threatened his daughter's life. He had Tom tail the Russians all those years ago but never told him about me. They killed Claire in her and Tom's bedroom—

"Whoa. Their bedroom? Tom was with Jack's daughter?"

"They were engaged."

"What? Tom was engaged? Really?" James quirks a brow.

"Yes." Her throat constricts at the reason Claire is dead. "Anyway… Jack had a lot of guilt about Claire's death and sold me back to the Russians and… well you know the rest."

"That's when they assigned Tom to protect you?"

"Martha did. Tom had the Russian history. She didn't know it was Jack who sold me back to start with. But when she found out she went bananas." Isabella grins at the memory of Martha berating Jack like a schoolboy in the old French farmhouse. "But eventually Kat murdered Jack."

James gazes at Isabella while he runs his finger around the rim of his coke bottle.

"Are you perving on me in my hooker get-up? Or are you a bit shell shocked?"

James startles and blinks. "I'm not perving. God. Don't say that in front of Tom he'll have my head on a pike."

Isabella laughs. "I was kidding."

"It's all such a huge can of worms, isn't it? I mean… wow."

"Okay, I need to get across the road." Isabella opens the door to leave.

"Okay. I'm right in your ear." James taps a couple of keys on his laptop. "And I'm in Aaron's cameras." He leans closer to the screen and wrinkles up his nose. "Sleazy."

Isabella cocks her head to the side. "Hey James?"

"Yeah?"

"I haven't forgotten about Mischa." She winks and walks out the door.

———

The buzzer next to Isabella's ear sounds and she glances up at the fuzzy camera footage of the doorstep. A scruffy bloke wearing nylon track pants and a crumpled hoodie with 'Get It Here' printed on the front, stands on the other side.

"Classy," Isabella mumbles to herself pressing the intercom. "Hey you," she coos in her Russian accent. "Do you have appointment?"

"Yep. Jason Smith."

That's the best you could come up with? Isabella rolls her eyes and presses the door release. She checks the open spreadsheet on the screen in front of her and finds Jason's name as he lopes towards the desk. He leans on it and leers at Isabella. She makes an effort not to wrinkle her nose up at Jason's odour.

"Good afternoon Sir."

"It's about to be." He grins and taps his fingers on the desk.

Ugh.

Isabella pastes on her smile and sweeps a hand towards the hallway. "Let me show you to your room."

"Delighted," Justin says and walks into the hallway past her.

Creep. Her skin crawls and she makes a note to bathe in disinfectant later on.

She knocks on a door. The girl inside opens it and ushers Justin inside. Isabella gives her a smile, and the girl returns it with a depth of pain in her eyes that pierces Isabella's heart.

She closes the door and turns to go back to the reception desk when she hears a scuffle from behind a door across the hall. She moves across and pushes her ear against it. All is quiet and Isabella is about to go back to the front desk before a faint sniffle stops her. She opens the door. Two girls are huddled together on the floor in the corner of the room.

Oh my God. Isabella's chest squeezes. "Are you okay?"

The girls stare at her with wide eyes. Something about the way they are huddled together makes Isabella's stomach contort. She walks into the room, shooting a quick glance over her shoulder. "English?"

The dark haired girl looks to the blonde who nods. "I do. A little." Her accent is thick but Isabella recognises it. *Romanian.*

"Have you been here a long time?"

"We arrive yesterday."

"Arrive? From where?"

"Big truck bring us."

A door down the hall slams open and Aaron flashes past the open gap of the door. Isabella clenches her jaw and looks back at the girls. "I have to go. But…" She lowers her voice. "I can help you. Yes?"

The blonde grabs her arm, digging her fingernails into Isabella's flesh. Her piercing clear green eyes dive into Isabella's. "Please…"

"Yes. I promise." Isabella waits for James to get angry at her for making promises she can't keep, but hears nothing. *Jammed.*

The bell on her desk dings repeatedly. "Serena?"

Isabella stands despite wanting to stay and comfort the girls. "I have to go," she whispers. "I'll come back."

The blonde girl whimpers and lurches forward to grab Isabella's hand again. Isabella's heart leaps to her throat and tears sting the corners of her eyes. She backs to the door and slips through.

Isabella walks into the reception area and Aaron is leaning on the desk checking his phone.

"What is it?" Isabella asks as she stalks behind the desk and sits.

Aaron puts his phone inside his jacket and leans over the desk, his face within a breath of hers. "Where exactly did you disappear to?"

"The toilet. I hope that's okay with you?"

"I just had a phone call."

"How lovely. Did you talk about the weather?"

Aaron's hand shoots out and he grabs Isabella's hair, tugging her head to the side. "You're mine in here. You do as you're told and you treat me like a fucking king. Do you understand?"

Isabella covers his hand with hers and yanks it from her hair. "I know how undercover works, thanks for the tip."

"I have to go to a meeting. Don't let anyone in or out while I'm gone. Do you understand?"

"There's a bloke in room two. What if he finishes?"

Aaron leans further over the desk and peers at the computer screen. "Jason? He'll be here all night. It's the only time he gets any. And if I come back to find anyone has conveniently disappeared..."

"I have no idea what you're talking about." Isabella leans back in her chair and glares at Aaron, the girls cowering in the back room make her hate him more than before. *They have faces now.*

Aaron puckers his mouth and makes a kissy noise at her before leaving.

———

Isabella glances around the warehouse as she leans back from the desk and stretches her arms over her head. She checks her watch as she brings her hands down and drums them on the desktop. 23:52.

"You aren't thinking of going back in there tonight are you?" James sits and peers at Isabella over his monitor.

"Maybe?"

"Tom will have every single person in this warehouse for breakfast if you go back over there when you shouldn't."

She looks around the deserted floor and winces. "I know. I won't. But how can we just leave those girls there?"

"Greater good." James smiles. "We'll help them when the time is right. It's how this works." He puts his hand on Isabella's shoulder. "We'll get them out. This was only night one. And I have cameras watching every inch of that place."

"You've hacked his camera's?"

"Yeah…"

Isabella nods. "Let me make you a coffee." She walks to the kitchenette and fiddles with coffee filters as the back door opens. Tom walks in with Abbie behind him. Isabella looks him up and down. "Wow. Don't you look thunderous."

"Wasted day. We saw a postman, a woman walking five dogs at once, and a pamphlet drop."

Abbie leans against a desk and smiles. "Hi, Isabella."

"Hey Abbie. Nice to see you."

"And you."

The three of them stand and no one speaks for a moment.

Isabella sips her coffee and grins into her mug.

"Right well… this is awkward as shit. I'm going to brief Martha." Tom walks across the floor a little faster than he needs to and Isabella laughs, watching him barge straight into Martha's office without knocking.

"Awkward?" Abbie raises a brow at Isabella.

"For him maybe. Not me. And I hope, not you?"

Abbie visibly drops her shoulders and exhales. "Excellent."

"Coffee?" Isabella grabs a mug out of the cupboard without waiting for an answer.

"Thanks Isabella." The tone in Abbie's voice makes it clear she is thanking her for more than the coffee.

"Of course." Isabella pours the coffee. "It's hard starting over. I get it."

Abbie drops her eyes to the floor and sucks on her bottom lip. "I owe you an apology, actually."

"For?"

"Well, I knew Tom a long time ago. And I assumed he was the same. But… he isn't. I made a few comments I shouldn't have…" She winces as she looks up.

Isabella smiles at Abbie. "Don't worry about it. Knowing Tom he probably loved the attention."

"I honestly don't think he did."

"We're good. So how's the job going?" Isabella hands her the mug and they walk back to her desk.

"Apart from feeling like a fish out of water you mean?"

"Yeah, apart from that."

"It's fine. I feel completely lost but I'll get there."

Martha's office door opens and Tom stalks out. He heads to the changing rooms without looking at the girls and James.

Martha follows him out and watches as Tom disappears down the hall.

Isabella blows on her coffee while Abbie sits upright and clasps her hands in her lap. Martha turns and gives them a curt nod before disappearing back into her office.

"You know, it does seem strange," Abbie muses, staring across the office.

Isabella looks at Abbie. "What does?"

"Well, it's like Tom's taking this whole thing personally. But it's Martha that's being stalked. Not him."

"Hmmm." Isabella sips her coffee and makes no effort to say anything more on the subject.

"Hungry?"

Isabella jumps at Tom's voice and spins in her chair. "Do you have to sneak?" Hot coffee sloshes over the rim of her cup. She puts it down and shakes out her hand. "Ouch."

"I wasn't."

"Trying to eavesdrop and see if we're gossiping about you?" Abbie smirks.

"No."

They both peer at him and say nothing.

"Okay, maybe a tiny bit."

Isabella nods once. "Well rest assured, we have better things to talk about." She stands. "And yes, I'm hungry. Abbie?"

Abbie's eyes widen and she coughs. "Oh. No. Um. I think I'll hang out here and read through some... stuff."

Tom nods once. "Excellent plan."

Isabella slaps Tom on the arm. "Tom," she whispers.

Tom sighs heavily and rubs his eyes. "You have to eat, Abs."

"I don't want to... intrude."

"You aren't." Isabella grins and jerks her head towards the door. "We'll get some all night dodgy take out and eat here. Join us?"

"But I—"

"Oh Jesus. Just eat with us, Abs." Tom rubs the back of his neck.

"Okay. Let me go get my stuff."

"Great." Isabella smiles, watching her scurry to the locker rooms.

"Remember how I said you're too nice?" Tom says.

"She's our workmate. Not the weird neighbour."

"So you think he *is* weird now?"

"No. Well...yes. But I feel more sorry for him."

"And Abs? Do you feel sorry for her too? I swear you'd bring home a stray cat if you found one."

"I would actually."

"I know."

8

TOM

"It's just inconvenient is all." Edward's voice echoes through the hallway as Tom and Isabella reach the top of the stairs.

"Still sounds like a weasel even when he's yelling at someone."

Isabella pushes Tom in the back. "Stop."

Tom peers down the hall and watches Edward wrestling with the lock on his door while he grumbles into his phone. He looks up and his eyes meet Tom's. He drops the phone from his ear and shoves it in his pocket. "Evening."

"Yeah. Not happy, Ed?"

"Oh. No. Just… work stuff."

"Is that right?"

"Yeah. That's… right." He shoves his shoulder into his door and it opens. "Anyway… dead tired. G'night." He walks into his flat and shuts the door.

"Who stands in the hallway yelling on their phone at one am? Why is he always out and about at one am?" Tom unlocks their door and walks in with Isabella behind him.

"Don't get stuck into him because you're in a mood."

"I'm not in a mood."

Isabella snorts. "Okay."

Tom rubs at the back of his neck and flops into his armchair.

Isabella leans against the door. "Do you think Abbie was uncomfortable eating with us?"

"No doubt."

"She apologised to me today."

"For what?"

"She said she'd been inappropriate towards you."

"Oh. That." Tom scrubs a hand through his hair.

"I like her."

"She's a good person. And I think she's taken the hint."

"I trust you, Tom." Isabella walks across and sits on his lap. She drops her forehead against his. "I don't want you to worry about me. Focus on your job. You're going to need to."

Tom breathes her in and rests his head against her shoulder. He tightens his arms around her and tries to ignore the nagging at the back of his mind. *What if we both just move to the country and milk cows?*

"I figured it out though." Isabella sits back and runs her hands through his hair.

"Figured what out?"

"You've never had a problem with me being in dangerous situations before."

"I always have a problem with it, Iz."

"No, but I mean... Paris, Russia. Even Malcolm. It's been you and I. We're a seamless team."

"We are."

"But this time..."

Tom's gut plunges and he swallows. "It's not—"

"Please don't insult my intelligence, Tom." Isabella gets off his lap and stands in front of him. She folds her arms and waits.

"Go on, then." Tom clenches his teeth.

"You think you need to protect me."

"No. I don't."

"Yes Tom. You do."

Fine. Tom stands up and goes to the kitchen. He looks out the window. *This isn't going to end well.* "You trust too easily, Iz."

"Pardon?"

"You're too nice." He turns around to look into her eyes. "The world is shit. It's fucking shit."

"You don't think I know that?"

"I know you *think* you know that but—"

"You *think* I know that?" She drops her arms and stalks across the room, stopping directly in front of him. "Are you forgetting what I spent half my life doing?"

"Which is the exact reason *why* you shouldn't be so trusting."

"You don't understand, Tom."

"What? What don't I understand?"

"I spent too long around bad people. I was always looking over my shoulder. Always afraid I would be killed. Afraid that one day someone would get my knife out of my hand and stab me with it."

"Iz—"

"No." Isabella holds a hand up and it trembles. "You listen."

Tom bites down on his cheek.

"Now I'm free. It's all over. I can be who I was always supposed to be. I'm loved. For the first time…" She stops and takes a breath, her eyes brim with tears.

Tom's chest collapses and he moves forward.

She steps back. "No one has ever loved me before you, Tom. No one. Not like this. I'm happy and I want to trust people. I want to be nice to people." She swipes the tears off her cheeks and shakes her head. "I want to let people into my life. Laugh, be silly and just…live. I want to believe that not everyone wants to hurt me."

"But that's not how the world works, Iz."

"I know but, can't I try?"

"We aren't talking about the job now are we?"

"I want my life to be full of all the things they took from me. Things I never got to have before."

"I get that you want those things but—"

"But?"

"But… I can't lose… I can't do it again." *I'm being selfish.*

"I'm not Claire."

Tom's head snaps up and he clenches his fists. "What?"

"I'm not Claire."

Tom squeezes his eyes shut and takes a breath. "No. But you're the one…" *Fuck.*

A heavy silence falls through the ceiling and blankets them.

"Pardon?" Isabella whispers.

Tom opens his eyes and sees her standing in the middle of the lounge, her face rigid. "I didn't mean…"

"Yes you did. She's dead because of me. Why else would you say it?"

"I…" Tom bites his lip.

"You blame me? Knowing what I went through? Knowing that I had no choices?"

"I don't blame you."

"I never even knew her, Tom." Isabella marches across the room and stops in front of him. Her breaths are loud and heavy and her jaw is taut.

Tom digs his fingers into his arms to stop himself pulling her into his chest and holding her. "I know."

"What would I have done if I knew they threatened her? Tell me. What would I have done?" Isabella's voice rises with each word.

Tom swallows. "Gone back to them."

Isabella nods slowly, her eyes never leave Tom's face. "In a heartbeat."

"You'd have been executed."

"Yes. And she would still be here. With you." Isabella's voice cracks and she clears her throat.

But I wouldn't have you. Tom's heart writhes in his chest.

Isabella puts her face in her hands. "Maybe I was wrong to think I deserved any of this."

Tom's stomach lurches. "It wasn't your fault, Iz. I've never blamed you."

"But you must have, at one time."

Tom drops his head and runs his hands through his hair. He hears the front door open and looks up. "Where are you going?"

"I'm going to stay at Mischa's tonight."

"Iz, no. It's one in the morning, let's just go to sleep."

"I need to breathe." She walks out and closes the door behind her.

Tom crumples to the floor of the kitchen and leans against the cupboards. "Fuck." He kicks a leg out and slams his foot into the wall. "Fuck!"

The heavy silence envelopes him and he pushes a hand into his chest as his heart deflates.

A sharp knock at the door fills the flat and Tom's heart restarts. *She walked out without her keys.* He jumps up and pulls the door open.

"Iz..."

Edward stands in front of him.

"Oh. What do *you* want?"

"I heard shouting. Is everything alright?"

Tom's pulse heats up and he curls his lip. "It's fucking perfect, Ed. Thanks for the concern."

Edwards raises both eyebrows and grins. "Ah, lovely. Is Isabella here?"

Tom grinds his teeth. "No. She isn't. She's gone for a walk."

"At one am? That's an odd time for a walk."

"For once I agree with you, Ed. But right now maybe you could go home and stay there?"

"Don't feel embarrassed. All couples fight."

What would you know about being in a couple? "We weren't fighting." Tom starts to close the door.

Edward slaps his hand against the door and Tom glares at him.

"What do you think you're doing?"

"You seem stressed."

"Do I?" Tom steps forward and Edward rocks back but doesn't move. "Do I, Edward?"

"Yes." Edward grins. "I'm here if you need a chat."

"I'm eternally grateful for your ever imposing presence, Ed. Thanks so much. I'd be lost without you." Tom steps back and slams the door in Edward's face. "Git." *Why can't people mind their own fucking business?*

A light chuckle comes through the door and it sets Tom's skin on fire. He throws the door open and grabs the back of Edward's shirt as he walks away. He pushes Edward face first against the wall.

"You come near my flat or Isabella again, I swear to God I'll rip your fucking head off."

"Tom?"

He spins around.

Isabella is at the top of the stairs.

He loosens his grip on Edward's shirt and he slides away from Tom, along the wall.

Isabella squeezes the handrail, her knuckles turning white. "What are you doing?"

"I'm... he..." *Fuck.*

"I was checking on you guys. I heard shouting."

"I see. And Tom? You thought that warranted throwing him against a wall?"

"No. He was being a smart arse." *I sound like a schoolyard bully.*

"Is that right?"

Tom rubs at his jaw and holds an arm out towards their flat. "Are you coming in?"

"I was going to. But no. I think it's better I stick with my original plan."

"Probably best." Edward smiles at Isabella, completely ignoring Tom.

"What the fuck?" Tom's adrenaline surges and he can't stop himself. "Are you fucking kidding me right now?"

"Stop!" Isabella shouts, glaring at Tom. "Goodnight Edward. I need to go." She spins and stomps down the stairs. Seconds later, the front doors slam shut.

Tom stares down the staircase and chews on his tongue.

"Well, as long as everyone is in one piece." Edward walks to his door. "Good evening."

Tom squints at Edward as he disappears into his flat before whirling around and storming into his own. He picks his phone up and his thumb hovers over Isabella's number. *She won't answer.* He stares out the kitchen window at the street light hanging over his parked motorbike.

Thirst claws at his throat and it's the first time in a month that he's felt the unrelenting pain of needing a drink. He leans forward and grips the edge of the sink.

It'll help me sleep. Just one.

He shakes his head.

It wouldn't be just one.

He walks into the bedroom and drops onto the bed. The pain grips his throat like a vice.

"Fuck…"

————

Tom's alarm peels through the early morning silence and he grunts, rolling over and slapping the screen of his phone. He flops onto his back and blinks. *Did I even sleep?* He drops his head to the side and observes Isabella's empty side of the bed. *Shit.*

In the morning's stillness, the few hours earlier hit's him with full force. He rolls over and picks his phone up. No messages or missed calls. He winces. He tries her number and it goes straight to voicemail. He hangs up without leaving a message and sends a text. **Please call me back.**

He stumbles out of bed and to the kitchen. Opening the fridge, he stares into it before shutting it and opening the pantry. He stares into that a moment too before slamming it shut.

He spies a pen and scratch pad next to the kettle and he pulls it towards him.

He writes; **I'm sorry. I love you.**

He puts the note in the middle of the worktop, texts Abbie, **I'll be late**, and walks to the bathroom.

I can fix this.

An hour later, gripping an extra-large coffee as though it's a life raft, Tom reaches the top of the stairs in a small office complex. The smell of new paint and carpet swirls around him and he walks to suite 3B. The reception desk is empty but thuds sound from the consulting room beyond. Tom pushes open the door and Mike stands upright from a box he is sorting through.

"Tom."

"Yeah…" He pokes a thumb over his shoulder. "Sorry, there was no one at the reception desk."

"Well no, Lisa doesn't start until nine."

Tom nods and sips his coffee.

"So… are you going to tell me why you're here at…" He squints at his wristwatch. "Seven thirty, two weeks before your scheduled appointment or do I have to guess?" Mike grins and points to a chair for Tom to sit in.

"I was in the neighbourhood?" Tom makes no move towards the chair. "Forget it. I'm fine. I'll see you in—"

"Sit."

Tom gulps another mouthful of coffee and sits.

"Sorry about the mess, new office and unpacking all my bits and bobs."

Tom nods and puts his coffee cup on the desk. They sit in silence for a few moments with Tom looking everywhere but at Mike.

"So are we trying mental telepathy today? Or are you planning to speak at some point?"

"I'm thirsty."

Mike folds his hands on the desk. "And the coffee isn't cutting it?"

"No."

"Go on."

"I shouldn't be wasting your time." He stands up.

"Sit."

Tom peers at Mike.

"You came here. So… make it worthwhile. If you leave here now, what are you gonna do?"

"Work."

"Really?"

Tom sits again. "Isabella and I had a… disagreement."

"Okay. What about?"

Tom blows a breath out and scrubs his hands over his stubble. "I accidentally said I blamed her for my fiancé's murder. But… I don't."

"You don't what?"

"Blame her. It wasn't her fault."

"I see. So how does one *accidentally* tell someone it's their fault if one don't believe so?"

Tom walks to the window and glares down at the street below. "Like I said… we were having a disagreement and it just slipped out."

"How did she take it?"

"Not well. But… that's the thing. I don't blame her. She wasn't even there."

"But?"

"She's the reason it happened."

Mike swivels in his chair to face Tom. "What was this disagreement about?"

"She doesn't see danger like I do. Which is ridiculous because she's lived a life full of danger. She takes risks and acts on impulse…"

"Interesting."

"What is?"

"Well it's just… she sounds an awful lot like someone else in this room."

Tom bites his lip and turns lean against the windowsill. "It's not the same."

Mike grins. "Does she worry about you?"

"Probably. But I can handle myself."

"And you don't believe she can?"

"I know she can." Tom shakes his head. "That's not why I'm here. I'm thirsty, so give me sage advice to stop me drinking something I shouldn't and I'll be on my way."

"What's giving you a thirst?"

"She slept somewhere else last night and I haven't been able to contact her this morning."

"You're scared?"

"Scared?" Tom spits the word out like it's an offensive slur. "I'm not scared. I'm… concerned."

"Okay, I'll play along. What are you *concerned* about?"

I don't want to lose her. "She's on a dangerous job." He stops talking. *This is pointless.* "I'll be fine. I won't drink. Don't worry about it." He moves towards the door.

"Tom one last thing?"

Tom stops but doesn't turn around. "Yes?"

"Do you think maybe the conflict you feel at having lost your fiancé because of Isabella and now being in love with her is something you can't quite grasp?"

Tom squeezes his eyes shut but the image of Claire dying on the cream carpet of their bedroom remains. "That was a sly move, Mike."

"Are you going to answer the question?"

He turns and sits back in the chair. "It's something I've wrestled with at times. But… the thought of being without Iz…" He puts his face in his hands and leans over his knees. "What I said to her was out of line. But I need to know she's safe. And I can't get in contact with her and it's making me thirsty."

"Maybe you need to have faith in her. She slept at a friend's house. She wasn't out hunting down serial killers."

Tom smirks behind his hands, and slowly slides them off his face. "I wouldn't put it past her."

9

ISABELLA

Isabella bounces Sylvie on her knee while drinking breakfast tea as Mischa walks into the lounge, towel drying her hair.

Isabella hands Sylvie over. "She's had some milk and marmite toast fingers."

Mischa smiles at Sylvie and looks up at Isabella. "Now you tell me why you came last night?"

"I told you, I was working close by and too tired to go all the way home."

Mischa holds Sylvie against her chest and pats her back. "That is not truth."

Isabella sits again and rubs her face. "No. It's not." She looks up. "Can I ask you something?"

"Of course."

"Do you blame Tom and I?"

"Blame you? For what?"

"For Sascha?"

Mischa blinks and inhales. "No. I do not." She rubs Sylvie's back and stares across the room. "We made choices. They were dangerous. It was risk he took for us." She looks down at the top of Sylvie's head. "For her."

"Of course."

"Is that what you and Tom had argument about? Sascha?"

Isabella shakes her head. "No. I got angry at him for being so protective. I accused him of not understanding. And he…" Isabella takes a breath. "He's afraid. Though he won't ever admit that." She gives Mischa a half smile. "He's afraid of losing me the way he lost his fiancé."

"That is fair. No?"

"It is." *It really is.*

She stands. "Thanks for letting me stay. Though your sofa?"

"Yes?"

"I would *not* recommend."

Mischa smiles. "I will get fold up for next time."

"There won't be a next time." Isabella blows a kiss and walks to the door. "Thanks Mish."

"Isabella?"

"Yes?"

"You are his true love."

Isabella smiles. "Did he tell you that?"

"He did not have to."

———

Isabella walks down the hall and groans. *Keys. No damn keys.* She stands staring at their closed door, cursing herself for stalking out without them. *That'll teach me.*

A soft mew sounds from behind her and she looks two doors down to Edward's flat. Pebbles sits in the middle of the hall and licks her paw. She picks her up, giving the little cat a cuddle. "Fancy meeting you out here."

A shaky shriek before a lot of little thumps hitting the floor pulls Isabella's attention to the top of the stairs. Lorna is there with apples rolling around her feet. She starts to bend forward and Isabella leaps down the hall.

"Lorna stop. I'll get them for you." She puts Pebbles down and picks up the apples. She drops them into Lorna's string bag, taking it and her other heavy bag from her.

"Oh, Flossie. Thank you dear." She pulls her key out and hobbles to her door. Pebbles weaves around both their ankles.

"I'll bring this stuff in for you." Isabella walks into the flat and puts the bags on the worktop.

Lorna sits in her chair while Isabella puts her kettle on.

"I'm not quite as nimble as I used to be."

"You shouldn't go all the way to the supermarket on your own Lorna. Let me come with you next time."

"You would do that for me, Flossie? I forgot a few things and was going to go again tomorrow."

"Of course I would. I'll even mark it on your calendar. Tomorrow?" Isabella circles the day in red pen and writes her name so Lorna remembers.

"You aren't working?"

"Later in the day."

"I am so happy you came to live with Tom. I don't know what I did before you were here." She smiles as Isabella brings her a fresh cup of tea.

God if she knew I'd knifed over three hundred people. "I'm sure Tom looked out for you. Even if he did it in secret." She winks and sits across from Lorna.

"I must say, it's always nice running into him in the hallway." She gives Isabella a little wink. "I have a little soft spot for your fella." She giggles and sips her tea.

Isabella hides her grin. "I would never have guessed. Okay Lorna, well, I'll leave you be. But I'll come get you tomorrow around ten and take you shopping. Don't forget."

"Thank you, Floss." Lorna holds her bony hand out and Isabella gives her a squeeze.

Isabella wanders across to her front door and leans against it. *I should call him.*

———

Isabella decides to walk to the warehouse. It's a mild day and not too windy. She shoves a hand into her pocket and fiddles with her phone. Unrest bubbles in her belly and she wrestles with calling Tom. *I need to fix this.* She pulls the phone out and looks at her screen, where a photograph she tried to sneak of Tom, but he stuck his hand up is her wallpaper. The photo consists of his palm obscuring most of the camera lens but his mouth is visible and he is laughing. It's one of her favourites. As she stands in the middle of the pavement, being bustled by passers by, she shakes her head and puts her phone away. *Face to face.*

The closer she gets to the warehouse, the more she thinks about the girls, huddled together in a dark room in a seedy brothel. Guilt sits heavily on her shoulders. *I should have got them out.* As though being pulled by a stronger force she turns and walks away from the direction of the warehouse.

A short walk later and she stands across the road from the brothel, studying every inch of the front door, windows and side alley. *Should I be going to the warehouse and sorting things out with Tom? Yes. Will he kill me for coming here without backup? Definitely.*

Tingles spread over her skin from the base of her skull as she looks up at the filthy facade again. She walks across the road and peers down the side alley, looking from wall to wall realising it's wide enough for a truck to back down. A chill works its way down her spine.

She rounds the corner at the end of the building and finds herself in an open, deserted car park. The building extends further than she thought it did and she realises that the new, extended part of the building is where the cleaning room is. *Interesting.* Her eyes shift to the door in the back of the old part of the building. It's ajar but she can't see any movement inside. She creeps towards it as her heart leaps into her throat and the gravel crunching under her feet suddenly sounds five hundred times louder.

This is a bad ide—

Her phone vibrates in her pocket. She pulls it out, expecting to see Tom's number after the missed calls overnight, but **James** flashes instead.

"Hey James."

"What are you doing lurking around the back of Aaron's place?"

Isabella spins and looks around the empty car park before concealing herself behind a skip.

"Don't bother looking for the camera's I planted... I'm too good for them to be found and you know it."

"Don't go all Tom on me, James." Isabella grins to herself as she peeks around the bin at the ajar door. It almost closes before hanging ajar again in the wind.

"I'm not. But you shouldn't be there today. Get out."

"And why are you manning the cameras, may I ask?"

"There was movement there early this morning. A truck arrived and left within the space of half an hour. I got an alert. But I can't stick around, I've gotta... I've got shit to do."

A truck. Isabella's gut plummets. "What kind of truck, James?"

"I think you know. Your girls were moved. C'mon Iz. Get out of there. You can investigate tomorrow, when you're meant to be there. If Aaron finds you—"

"Moved?" Her stomach twists. "Moved where? And what other shit do you need to do?"

"Nothing. Personal stuff... C'mon Iz... get out. Now."

"Okay, okay keep your jocks on."

"Now who's going all Tom on who?"

Isabella creeps out from behind the bin and prickles erupt down the back of her neck. "Okay. I'm leaving. Stop watching me."

"Fine. Just get out."

Isabella glances around as she walks towards the street. The prickles don't let up. "Okay well... I'll catch you later." She hangs up before James has a chance to say anymore.

She doubles her pace as she walks out to the street. Looking behind her, an old lady rustles through her bag outside a corner store, and a kid on a bike rides down the street without holding the handlebars. Commuters pace past her, not noticing or caring that they nearly knock her over. She stops at the front of the brothel and tries to peer through the grimy front windows, but the dingy red curtains and dirt prevent her from seeing anything.

Shoving her hands into her pockets she grips her phone as the sensation of being watched grips her. She turns but doesn't see anyone taking a particular interest in her.

Calm down.

The wind picks up. *Four seasons in one day.* Rubbish nestling in the gutters dances across the road and a door slams somewhere nearby. Dust swirls around Isabella's face, making her screw her face up and shield her eyes. More people push past her. She starts to jog. She rounds the block and stops in a bus shelter to catch her breath, and looks up and down the street. People hiding their faces in scarves, or chattering on their phone. No one is looking at her and yet... something isn't right.

Concealing herself in the recess of a fire exit, she pulls the phone from her pocket and swipes through to Tom's name. Just as she presses call, her phone is plucked from her grasp and a forearm clamps around her neck from behind, pushing the pink pendant on her necklace into her throat. She grabs the arm against her throat and digs her nails in. *Shit.*

Warm breath coats her right ear. "Sshhhhh…" someone whispers as her airway constricts.

She tries to twist and kick but the forearm tightens and a sharp prick in her neck sends terror through her veins.

She slips into a fuzzy limbo before… nothing.

10

TOM

Abbie looks up from the laptop she's sitting in front of as Tom walks into the surveillance house.

She smiles. "Nice of you to join me."

"I walked slowly."

"I see." She closes the laptop. "You look tired."

"Didn't sleep well."

"Why?"

Tom peers at Abbie. "I ate cheese before bed."

"Sorry. None of my business. I forgot for a second." She smiles.

"Have I missed anything?"

"No. Martha hasn't left the house yet."

Tom's jaw clenches. "She's in there?"

"Yeah..."

Without another word Tom slams out the front door and stalks across the road. He bangs a fist on the door. "Open up,

Martha." He pulls the keys he has to her house out and goes to unlock the door as it swings open.

Martha gives him a tight smile. "I knew you'd turn up."

"What the hell are you doing here? You shouldn't be staying here. Remember?"

Martha studies Tom's face and says nothing. She fiddles with the hem of her jacket and clenches her jaw.

Tom notes her odd behaviour before leaning forward. "Well? I assume this is why you decided a night watch wasn't necessary?"

"Someone was in my house last night."

Tom's pulse hammers in his neck. "Say that again?"

"I must have been sleeping. They were very quiet. I'm quite a light sleeper as you kn—"

"Stop." He holds a hand up. "You're prattling."

"I most certainly am not."

"Except you are." Tom grinds his teeth and watches Martha straighten imaginary wrinkles from her trousers. "This is exactly why you shouldn't have come back here. What if he hurt you? Killed you? What if…" He slams his hands into the top of the door frame and taps his fingers. "Did this person take anything?"

"Hospital records."

"Hospital records?"

Martha waves her hand dismissively. "I had pneumonia when I was thirty."

Tom jerks a corner of his lip up and tilts his head. "Huh?"

"I was in hospital with pneumonia and maybe he's looking at my weaknesses."

"That's the most ridiculous thing I've ever heard."

Martha looks at Tom impassively and fiddles with her hair.

"Right. Well. If you're gonna keep lying to me. I'll be off then." He turns to leave.

"There was a note."

Tom stops and tries to work out why her voice is so weak. "Note?" A rustle of paper sounds behind him and he turns. Martha holds out a piece of paper, shielding her fingers from it in a handkerchief. Tom slides his own hands into his jacket sleeves and takes the paper from her. He reads the typed note. "It's been so long. Maybe next time we can have tea." He looks up at Martha. "What the hell?"

"I'm taking you off this job."

Tom's blood bubbles. "Excuse me?"

"I think it's best if you aren't on this job. It's too close to home. You can't be objective."

"You put me on it in the first place!"

"Yes. And now I'm taking you off it." She holds her hand out with the handkerchief for the note.

"Like *hell* you are."

"Tom—"

"I started this and I'll damn well finish it. Why the hell would you want to take me off this job?" He takes a breath. "What the *fuck* is going on?"

Martha's face is pale and the hand she holds out has a slight tremble.

Tom's chest softens and he sighs. "Martha, you need to stop lying to me and tell me what's going on." He hands her the note and leans against the wall.

"I'm not lying to you."

"Fine. Then you need to tell me everything."

"I have."

"Why would he take hospital records? It's weird." Tom marches down the hallway to the room that used to be his. The moment he opens the door a sense of comfort hits him, even though it's nothing more than a spare room these days.

The wardrobe door is ajar and boxes he remembers storing on the top shelves for Martha years before, are on the floor and open. "We should get those examined, along with the note."

"Yes. I'll organise that."

"You haven't already?"

"No, well..."

"This isn't something you would put off."

"I'm rattled."

"You don't get *rattled*." He turns to her. "You shoot traitors in the face. You arm wrestle men half your age. Even *I* do what you tell me. And I don't listen to anyone."

"It slipped my mind. I'll get right on it once I'm in the office."

He looks at Martha. "Something has shifted today. Don't think for one minute I haven't noticed."

Martha nods, while staring at the window. "I'm just tired. Being burgled will do that to you."

"Lie." He waits until her eyes meet his. "Go back to the warehouse. It's not safe here."

"Okay." She wanders down the hall, suddenly looking older than she has ever before.

"Martha?"

She turns and tilts her chin up. "Yes, Tom?"

"I'm not dropping this. So work out how to tell me whatever it is you aren't telling me."

"Okay," her voice crackles and she clears her throat.

"I'll call you later."

Martha nods and continues down the hallway.

———

Tom walks back across the road and finds Abbie in the bedroom with the laptop open on her knees.

"Abs. Have you reviewed footage from last night?"

"Doing it now."

"Someone broke in."

Abbie looks up. "What?"

"Am I speaking Italian?"

Abbie tilts her head and glares at Tom.

"Sorry. Someone broke in last night and stole some... stuff." He runs a hand through his hair.

"Okay well, maybe now Martha will put a night shift on this?"

"Now she will. She didn't want me to know she came back to the house. Something isn't adding up."

"Maybe she knew you'd hit the roof if she came back there after you told her not to."

"Yes. True. It's more than that though. It's bizarre." He shakes his head and looks over Abbie's shoulder at the screen. "Let me know if you find something. I need to make a phone call."

He walks into the living room, pulling his phone out. A missed call from Isabella. Relief washes over him and he pushes the screen to call her back. The call goes straight to voicemail and Tom restrains himself from hurling the phone across the room.

"Tom. Quick."

He runs to the bedroom. "Got him?"

She points to the screen. "Someone went down the side of the house and disappeared around one thirty this morning."

"What time did Martha get there?"

"She arrived home at twelve thirty. All the lights went out around one."

Tom nods and watches the footage of the unknown person walking down the side of the house. "Can you zoom in?"

"Yeah but it doesn't help. He's all in black and has his hood up."

"Maybe I'll put myself on the night shift."

"You're not going home?"

"I... I have a job to do."

Abbie raises both brows. "Having a squabble?"

"A disagreement."

Abbie snorts. "Okay."

———

Tom groans and rolls onto his back. Pain shoots down his spine and he stretches his arms above his head. His eyes focus on the pink wallpaper and velveteen sofa he's stretched out on. He sits up, cracks his neck and grabs his phone. *07:14.* No notifications on the screen. He sighs and leans back on the sofa, clunking his head against the wall. *I should have gone home. Shit.*

He presses Isabella's number and again it goes straight to voicemail.

"Third voicemail message in a row. C'mon Iz. Call me back. Please."

The front door rattles and Abbie calls out a moment later. "You decent?"

"Yeah." Tom slides back down to lie across the sofa again. "Did you bring breakfast?"

Abbie walks into the room and puts a coffee on the wide table near his head. "Coffee."

Tom takes a deep breath and absorbs the aroma of coffee, hoping it'll perk him up. It doesn't.

"Sleep well?" Abbie grins and takes the lid off her takeaway coffee.

"Nope. I drifted off about an hour and a half ago." He sits up and takes a gulp of his own coffee. "I'm gonna go home and sleep. You'll be right here?"

"Yeah I'll be fine."

Tom nods and stumbles out the front door.

———

After an hour and a half sitting in traffic, Tom walks toward his flat as Pebbles prowls down the hall. He sighs and scoops the cat up. He knocks softly on Lorna's door, leans his forehead against it and yawns. A chain rattles from the other side.

Lorna opens the door. "Oh good morning, Tom." She holds both hands out. "Are you coming shopping with me too?"

"Shopping?" Tom hands the cat over.

"Isabella is taking me to Tescos at nine."

"She is?"

"Well it's on my calendar."

Tom nods. "I'm sure she'll be out in a minute."

"No rush, Tom. Have some time together." She winks and retreats into her flat.

He slides the key in his lock and holds his breath. Angst riddles his veins as the door swings open. The flat is dark; the curtains drawn and everything as he left it the morning before.

He throws his keys on the kitchen worktop. Clicking the light on he sees the note he left her, still sitting in the middle of the worktop only now there's something on top of it.

What…

He picks up Isabella's silver necklace with the pink stone pendant and his vision tunnels. He peers at the pendant and grabs hold of the edge of the worktop. He slides the note he left her across and reads it again to make sure she hasn't added anything.

What the fuck does this mean?

He walks to his armchair and sits, pulling his phone out. He presses Isabella's number. It goes straight to voicemail. He waits for the tone and exhales slowly. "Hey. Um. Please call me back. I'm… confused." He winces and hangs up.

He drops the phone on the floor and leans over his lap, running both hands through his hair. The unsettled feeling hanging over him brings on a thirst in his throat and he claws a hand at his neck. He stumbles across to the sofa and lies on it. The thirst intensifies. He squeezes the bridge of his nose.

Shower.

He trudges to the bathroom. Turning the shower on he notices empty spaces in the shower caddy. He spins and opens the cupboard above the sink. Her toothbrush is gone.

His pulse races and he goes to the bedroom and flings open the wardrobe. Empty shelves and an empty hanging rack greet him. The walls of the bedroom close in and he stumbles backwards to sit on the end of the bed. He stares at the empty wardrobe and grips the comforter in both fists.

This isn't happening.

———

Tom slams into the warehouse still wearing his helmet. He can't work out why he came in, he should be at home, but that could lead to whisky and that's never going to end well. He takes his helmet off as Penny stands up.

"Hey Tom, how are yo…" She stops and bites her lip. "Oh, you look… tired."

"Thanks Pen. You're a real motivator." He pulls his phone out of his pocket as a text from Isabella flashes on the screen. His heart fights against his ribcage as he keys his pin in.

"I thought you did an all nighter?"

"Yeah well… what can I say I'm committed."

Penny is rambling, trying to apologise but he ignores her and walks onto the main floor as he opens Isabella's text.

It's better this way.

He stops walking and stares at the message. *What way? What does that even mean?* He jabs her number and slaps the phone to his ear as he makes his way to Martha's office. The phone rings and Tom inhales a sharp breath and waits. It rings out and goes to voicemail. *Fuck.* "It's me. Again. Please don't do this. I can't…" He slumps onto the nearest chair and rests his head in his hand. He sighs. "I need to talk to you." He drops the phone on the desk and rubs his face.

"Tom?" Martha's voice is behind him.

He slides his phone into his pocket and looks up at her. "Yeah, I'm coming in." He stands and gestures Martha into her office.

"You look terrible. Why are you in?"

"I… nothing. I didn't sleep well." He crumples onto the lumpy sofa and taps his foot. He swallows as the insatiable thirst climbs up his throat. *No.*

"Okay." Martha peers at Tom. "What's going on?"

Tom shrugs her off and stands. "Nothing. I'm fucking fine."

"You are not."

"Well, I guess that's two of us that don't want to tell the truth. Isn't it?" He glares at her before marching out of the office.

I'll pay for that later.

He walks into the changing room and stumbles against a locker as he finds his own. "Fuck!" He slams a palm into the locker, and leans his forehead against it. He slams his palm again, and again.

"Tom?" James walks out of the shower in a towel and runs a hand through his wet hair. "You alright?"

Tom drops onto the bench. "Yeah. I'm incredible."

"Right, ah… so the locker offended you?"

"No James. You offend me."

James tilts his head and stares at Tom.

"No, you don't. That was uncalled for." Tom grabs his jacket and puts it on. "You irritate me. But you don't offend me."

"Between you and Martha…"James walks to his own locker and opens it. "So, what's up your nose?"

"Nothing. I'm tired." *I'm tired of all of it. I need to go home.* Tom picks up his backpack and goes to leave. "James… what did you mean by between me and Martha?"

James keeps his head in his locker. "Nothing."

"Bullshit."

"It's just hard to keep up with both of you… that's all."

"You think you'd be used to it by now."

"I'm kept busy by you both, that's for sure."

"What does that mean?"

James pokes his head out of his locker and chews on his lip. "Nothing. It means nothing."

Tom waits a beat but decides not to push. "James?"

"Yeah?" His voice floats out from behind his locker.

"Forget it."

"Did you want something from me?"

"Yeah… can you…" Tom stops and bites his lip.

"Can I?"

"Um. Just… ask Iz to call me?"

James sticks his head out as he pulls a shirt on. "What?"

"I haven't… seen…" Tom huffs. "Forget it."

"Is everything okay, Tom?"

"No. Everything is *not* okay." He walks out as his throat dries.

He stalks through the desks and anyone in the office space keeps their head down. *Smart move.*

"Tom."

He stops in the middle of the floor and closes his eyes. "Martha."

"Come in here please."

He blows a slow breath out and walks into the office, straight past her and sits on a chair. "I'm going home. Don't panic."

"I was hoping you could explain this?" She holds her phone in front of his face and he blinks a couple of times to focus.

"I quit." He reads before looking at the name of the sender. Isabella. He goes cold and ringing hits his ears.

"What's going on? I tried to call her and it didn't go through."

He grabs the phone from Martha's hand and reads the text again. "When did she send this?"

"About ten minutes ago. Just after you stormed off."

He places the phone on Martha's desk, screen down and chews on his bottom lip.

"I don't think I need to tell you how disappointing it is to be hit with a text like that without any courtesy—"

"She left."

"Excuse me?"

"We had an argument. I said some stuff I shouldn't have and she went to stay at Mischa's. That's the last I saw her. I came home this morning and all her stuff is gone."

Martha lowers herself into her chair and folds her hands on the desk. "But to cut and leave? That really doesn't seem like her."

Tom rubs his eyes. "God, I'm so tired." He hunches over his lap and digs his fingers into his hair.

"Go home, Tom."

There is no fight left in him to argue. "Okay."

"I'll let you know when I find her."

He stands. "Yep."

"Tom?"

He turns. "I'll get to the bottom of this."

"I know."

11

ISABELLA

Isabella's mouth is dry, as though someone dumped a bag of sand into it while she was sleeping. Her eyes peel open as though her eyelids have been glued together. It's dark and she's lying on the floor. Her arms are stretched above her head.

The tick of a wall clock is the only sound in the room. Something pinches her left hand, and she rolls onto her side; the effort is akin to being chained to a boulder, trying to roll it with her. *What's happening?* Both arms remain stuck above her head.

She blinks a couple of times and tries to focus on her hands in the gloomy haze of the empty room she's found herself in. The effort of holding her head up proves too much. She flops back onto the floor and looks to the ceiling above her. A lone ceiling fan spins in lazy circles and something in her peripheral makes her look to her left again. A hook in the wall with a bag on it, full of liquid, hangs above her and she follows a tube down to her pinched left hand. Claws of ice dig into her chest as she realises whatever is in that bag is also inside her veins. She jerks her right hand, but it doesn't get any closer to the cannula and she realises both wrists are handcuffed to a bolt in the skirting board, far enough apart to be useless to one another.

She drops her head back to the carpet and stares at the ceiling again, this time tears slide down the sides of her face and into her hair. "Tom…" Her voice crackles. The effort of trying to move has exhausted her and she fights the urge to close her eyes as they droop and get heavier.

A door opens and she squints against the sudden onslaught of bright light. Someone --a man-- walks in, stands beside her and fiddles with the bag, replacing it with a new one.

"Who…" She swallows and tries again. "Who are you?"

The man ignores her, and Isabella can only make out he's dressed in a black hoodie and something covering his face.

She wants to kick and scream the place down but whatever he's feeding into her arm slows her movements and she can hardly keep her eyes open.

Her captor pats her on the shoulder as though she's a pet cat before leaving the room and plunging her into dingy darkness again.

The clock ticks as she drifts into an empty sleep.

12

TOM

Tom stands in front of his block of flats and stares up at the building. If he goes inside, it's empty. No Isabella. Nothing that belongs to her - except for the necklace he gave her. The only thing she left behind. The only thing she didn't want to take.

He crouches onto his heels and swallows, wishing he had a bottle of water to quench the thirst he knows won't go away no matter how much water he drinks.

Someone taps him on the shoulder and he glances up into Abbie's face.

"What are you doing here?"

"Martha asked me to come check on you. Gave me the day off. Said you and Isabella were having a drama?"

Tom sits on the small brick wall at the front of the property. "She um…" He takes a breath. "She left."

"She what?" She sits next to him; her mouth hangs open.

Tom shakes his head. "Forget it."

"She left you?" Abbie raises an eyebrow. "No. I think you might be overreacting."

"All her stuff is gone, Abs. I'm fairly sure I'm not overreacting."

"Did she say anything?"

I don't want to have this conversation. Tom rubs his face and says nothing.

"Grant?"

Tom opens his text messages and holds the one from Isabella up for Abbie to read.

Abbie covers her mouth with her hand. "Wow. I'm sorry. That's brutal."

Tom doesn't say anything.

Abbie stands. "What are you doing now?"

Tom shrugs. "No idea."

"Come for a bite? I'm meeting some of the old crew down at the pub for lunch and beers." She jerks her head towards the end of the street where the old pub with low doorways and stone walls is.

Tom winces. "You really know how to entice me."

"C'mon. They'll be stoked to see you."

"No, they won't."

"Come and eat some food, drink some water and then come back here and sulk."

"I think I'll just do the sulking."

"I'm sorry she left, Tom."

He watches her for a moment and stands. *They do a good steak and ale pie there.* His stomach grumbles, reminding him he needs more than coffee and chewing gum to survive. "Fine. I'll eat."

———

Around lunchtime they walk into the pub. Tom stands at the bar and drums his fingers on the bartop.

Abbie waves at someone across the bar. "I'll be back. We'll both have water. Understood?" Abbie grins and takes off.

"Alright?" The bartender raises an eyebrow.

Water. You want water. His throat aches with thirst and he swallows rough. "Ah, just…" He blows a breath out. His eyes drift to the spirit bottles behind the bar and he clears his throat. "Mineral water and…Glenmorangie. Neat. Please." Tom winces inwardly as the bartender nods and turns to the shelf. *One. Just one to take the edge off.* The drink is placed in front of him, and he hands over his card.

He wraps a hand around the glass and squeezes, but doesn't lift it. *Don't do it.* He lifts the glass and throws the whisky down. It warms his blood as it splashes down his throat and his shoulders relax.

"Another?" The bartender holds Tom's card up and raises a brow.

No. "Yeah. Thanks." *Fuck. Last one.* "Make it a double."

"What do you think you're doing?"

Tom takes his card from the bartender and turns to Abbie. "Relaxing."

Abbie purses her lips but her eyes smile.

"Don't bust my balls, Abs. Not today."

"Okay. I'll refrain." She turns to the bar and picks up her water while Tom takes his whisky. "But if Martha asks, I tried to stop you."

Tom walks to an empty table and slides onto the booth seat. He puts his glass on the table and leans forward, studying the contents like it might attack him. *It will.*

Abbie slides in across from him and holds her glass up. "Cheers Grant."

He clinks his glass with hers and drinks. His muscles relax a little more and he sighs. *Yep. Bad idea.* He gestures to Abbie and returns to the bar. "Two doubles. Neat. Thanks." He leans on the bartop and watches Abbie sip her water.

Why am I here?

He stares at the glasses as the barman puts them on the bar. *Fuck it.* He downs both doubles, one after the other and squeezes his eyes shut.

He walks to the booth. "I have to go."

Abbie glances up and raises a brow. "You alright?"

"Yep. But… I'm going."

Abbie finishes the last of her water and stands up. "I'll come with you."

"What about the boys?"

"They don't matter, Tom. It was a mistake to bring you here. Let's go."

————

Hours pass before Tom walks Abbie up the stairs to her flat and she has three tries at sliding her key in the lock. It's seven pm and Tom lost count of the whiskies four pubs ago.

Tom grabs her key. "Jesus, Abs." He bends down, squints at the lock and slides the key in.

Abbie giggles as she stumbles into her flat, Tom is behind her. Boxes are scattered around the flat and her clothes are in a messy pile on the floor next to the sofa.

"Sorry about the mess. I haven't bothered to unpack properly yet."

Tom collapses on the sofa and puts his feet up on an unopened box. "I'm here for the coffee, Abs. I don't care about the boxes."

"Yes. Coffee. Excellent idea." She fills the kettle. "So your two whiskies turned into how many?"

Tom sucks air through his teeth and frowns. "I'm seeing two coffee tables so…"

"Ugh, Grant, you idiot." She abandons the kettle and slumps onto the sofa next to him, putting her feet up on the same box. "Isabella would rip your head off."

"Yeah well." He drops his head back and she does the same, the sides of their heads touching. "She won't know about it." His stomach contorts as the words leave his lips.

"No, I guess she won't. Well, I won't tell." Abbie turns her head slightly so more of their faces are touching.

Tom closes his eyes. "You're a trooper, Abs."

Abbie lips brush against his. "Thanks, Grant."

Tom keeps his eyes closed and imagines Isabella's mouth is against his. "You're welcome."

Abbie presses her lips against his and kisses him.

Isabella's face is all he sees in his mind and his eyes snap open.

He slides away from Abbie and wipes the back of his hand over his mouth. "Fuck."

Abbie takes some deep breaths and slides into a sitting position. "I'm sorry."

"No..." Tom stands. "It's... fine. I need to... go." He blinks a couple of times and rests a hand on the nearest box to get his bearings.

"She left, Tom." Abbie stares up at him from the sofa.

He chews on his lip and sits next to her again. "Maybe," he whispers. "Maybe it's a mistake." *She took all her clothing.*

"Grant—"

"Maybe she just needs space." *She took her toothbrush.* He grips the edge of the sofa. *She left her necklace.*

Abbie slides her hand across the sofa cushion towards him. *No.*

He jumps to his feet. "I'm going home, Abs." He stares at her face a moment too long. He shakes his head and blinks. "Please lock the door behind me."

He walks out and leans against the wall taking a few deep breaths.

Bad idea.

———

Tom takes a deep breath through his nose and keeps his eyes jammed shut. The musty smell and scratchy blanket is unpleasant and he runs through the day before in his head. *I went to the pub and…*

He opens one eye and takes in the frilly bedroom with the sheer pink curtains and the single wardrobe with a rose motif on the door. *I'm at the surveillance house?* He slides his head under the pillow and groans into the mattress.

"Wakey wakey."

Tom groans louder and presses the pillow harder against his head.

"C'mon Grant… emerge from your cocoon of shame. I brought you coffee."

It's not a cocoon of shame. Is it? Ugh. This is bad…

Tom throws the pillow off the bed and pushes himself into a sitting position. He blinks a couple of times and focuses on Abbie, perched on the end of the bed sipping her own coffee. He grasps the duvet and slaps a hand to his chest. *I'm wearing a T-shirt and…* he peers under the duvet. *Jocks. Thank God.*

"Well, don't you look a treat."

"Don't." Tom reaches to the rickety bedside table and grabs the coffee. He takes the lid off and gulps.

"I must say Grant, the morning after doesn't suit you."

He gulps more coffee and ignores Abbie.

"Hey, I brought you breakfast *and* coffee. Don't be a dick."

Tom rubs his eyes and stretches. "I have no idea why I'm here."

"Where?"

"Here. Why the fuck did I sleep here?" *It's very pink.*

"Oh… Grant." Abbie shakes her head and sips coffee.

"What?" He takes a big sniff. "Can I smell bacon?"

"Yes. As I said, I brought you breakfast." She nods at the bedside table and Tom notices the cardboard takeaway container. "You're welcome."

"Thanks," he mumbles shoving bacon into his mouth.

"And to answer your earlier query. You slept here because you don't want to sleep at home."

Tom quirks a brow and swallows. "That makes no sense."

"'Course it does. At home you're in your bed… which is empty and you don't wanna feel that shit. And you wanted to drink without feeling like the flat was watching you I'd imagine."

Tom shoves more bacon in his mouth and says nothing.

"I know you better than you think I do, Grant."

"I'm not the same as before."

"Oh? Is that why you drank yourself into a coma?"

Tom chews. "Yep." Nausea smothers him and he stops chewing to take a cleansing breath.

Abbie rolls her eyes and stands up. "Go shower and get dressed. I'm not putting up with your shit all day."

"What the fuck?"

"She walked, Grant. Deal with it and stop wallowing. It's very unattractive. Plus… Martha is gonna cut your head off."

"No she won't." *Yes she will.* "Wait… did you tell her?"

"I didn't out you. But I'm pretty sure she knew anyway."

Tom's phone rings and Abbie disappears down the hallway. His heart double taps and he leans down to his trousers on the floor and yanks the phone out.

Judith.

He slaps the phone to his ear. "Don't start."

"Headache?"

"I feel fantastic, thanks for asking."

"I'm this close, Tom… this close to taking you off this job and putting you in a holding cell." He imagines her pinching her thumb and pointer fingers together.

"You won't."

"Do I need to?"

"Probably."

"I believe you had a social drink yesterday? How lovely for you."

"I was thirsty."

"Goodness sake, Tom."

Tom shuffles to the edge of the bed and stands up. His head swirls and the room contorts into a myriad of pink walls and powder blue carpet. He slaps a hand to his head and sits back down. "Okay listen, you sound like an angry parent. Stop that."

"Maybe it's what you need right now?"

"I don't."

"This is your M.O. Tom. Personal tragedy, get drunk."

"Wow. Harsh."

"But true."

Yes. Tom attempts standing again and holds his breath while his head adjusts to the movement.

"I'm putting you on leave for the next three days to sort yourself out."

"I'm fucking fine." He hangs up before she can say anything else. He stumbles into the bathroom and slams the door behind him.

Abbie looks up from the laptops ten minutes later as Tom

walks into the lounge scrubbing at his hair with a towel. "Look at you all fresh and awake."

"Fresh. Awake is a stretch." He slumps onto the sofa and closes his eyes. "I need more coffee."

"Well off you go."

He opens one eye and peers at Abbie. "I thought you were looking after me?"

"No. You rejected me. I'm not looking after you."

"Ouch."

"You didn't?"

"No. I did. But… rejection is harsh."

"You're telling me."

Tom rolls his eyes and sits up. "I'll go get the coffee myself."

"Are you sure you're up to it?" Abbie snickers and settles back on the sofa.

Pain akin to a dagger slits through his forehead and he jams his eyes shut. "Maybe I'll go home."

"I think you should. Go sleep. I'll call if something happens here."

Tom watches Abbie for a moment, chewing on his lip. "Thanks Abs."

Abbie clicks her tongue and winks. "Go."

————

Loud banging on the door pulls Tom out of a restless, foggy sleep. He rolls off his sofa onto the floor and squeezes his head.

"Tom?" Martha's voice comes through the door.

"Shit, what time is it?" He stumbles to his feet and grabs his phone. *18.16* and eleven missed calls from Martha light up. "How did I not hear…" He spies an empty bottle on the floor and groans. His head pounds and he rubs his face.

"Tom! Open the door or you know my next move."

"Okay. Calm down." He grabs the bottle, throws it under the sofa and unlocks the door. He pulls it open, shuffles back to the sofa and lies face first on it.

"What the *hell* is going on, Tom?" Martha storms in. She bends down and pulls the empty bottle from under the couch. "If you're going to hide this, make sure you push it all the way under." She slams the bottle onto the coffee table and the noise jabs a spear straight through Tom's brain. "Is this what you've been doing all day?"

"No. I slept too…"

Martha glares at him. "Three days. Get it together." She turns and marches out of the flat without another word.

His throat closes up and he slides a hand over his neck and glances up at the cupboard above the fridge. He pictures the two bottles he put in there only the day before.

"I need to find Iz," he whispers, trudging to the kitchen. *But I need to sleep.* He opens the cupboard and pulls out a new bottle. He looks at the label and saliva coats his tongue. He slumps onto the worktop and rests his forehead against the bottle. *You are a weak piece of…*

He cracks open the bottle and lies on the sofa. *Three days.* He flicks the TV on and takes a swig. The moment the liquid hits the back of his throat, the muscles in his shoulders and back melt into the sofa cushion and he drops his head back. *What the hell am I doing?* Swig.

He tries to focus on the television, and flicks through the channels. He comes to a replay of a World Cup Rugby game and shrugs. He drops the remote and takes another swig.

An hour passes and the flat remains silent and dark, although Tom's blood is warm and his eyelids droop. His phone rings and he grumbles while checking the screen. *Mischa.*

"Hey…" Tom drinks.

"Tom? Are you okay?"

"No. I'm… not. Umm… have you heard…" he shakes his head and tries to form the sentence he wants in his head. "Iz? Have you spoken to… her?"

"Are you drunk Tom?"

"Yes. A bit."

"It is only seven pm."

"Yes."

"Well, I must come see you."

Tom's heart lurches and he sits forward. "No. Mish. I'm fine… I just." He pauses and takes another gulp. "I don't need a visit. I just… I need Iz so… if you hear from her…"

"I will see you soon." Mischa hangs up and Tom sits back and looks at the ceiling.

"Shit." He lies down on the sofa and brings the bottle to his mouth. *Three more sips. Gulps. Who am I kidding?*

———

Soft knocking startles Tom as he thinks about opening another bottle. He sits up and blinks, his eyes dropping to the half empty bottle of whisky sitting on the coffee table. The room wobbles a little and he stands up, closing his eyes a moment to get some bearings.

"Tom?" Mischa's soft voice floats through the door.

Shit.

He stumbles to the door and rests his head against it. "Mischa. I'm fine."

"You are drunk. Open door."

"No. I'm not. I'm… I had a sleep and I'm… good." *Liar.*

"Open door. Now please."

Tom lets out a loud huff and opens the door. He peers through a tiny crack at Mischa and her eyes find his. There's no admonishment or anger in them. He slumps against the doorframe and opens the door. "Hey."

"Oh, Tom." She walks in, hugging Sylvie against her chest. She dumps the nappy bag on the armchair and sits Sylvie on the floor with some toys. Sylvie coos at Tom and holds both arms out to him.

He drops onto the floor and lies on his back next to her. "I don't think I should be picking you up right now."

Sylvie topples onto her hands and knees and climbs up on Tom's shoulder and swats him in the face.

He grins and holds her hand. She wraps her tiny hand around his finger and plops onto her backside.

"Tom?"

Tom squints up at Mischa, who has perched herself on the couch. She taps the half empty bottle with her index finger. "What is this?"

"Whisky."

Mischa tilts her head and gives him a frown.

Tom sighs and sits up. The room wobbles and he swallows, rubbing his head. "Don't judge me. I'm pathetic. I know." He speaks slowly to try and curb any slurring.

"You are not."

"But, I am."

"Have you eaten today?"

"Yes."

Mischa tilts her head again and stares at him.

"No."

"I will make you food." She stands and walks to the kitchen.

Tom sighs but doesn't bother arguing. *There would be no point.* He lies back down on the floor and lets Sylvie grab at him. She babbles in his face and grabs his nose. Tom screws his face up and laughs.

"Tom? You know you cannot be of any use to anyone like this, yes?"

He glances over at Mischa as she walks in and puts a mug on the coffee table. "Yes. But—"

"And you want to speak to Isabella, yes?"

"Yes, but—"

"Then you cannot be drinking this way. What would she say?" Mischa folds her arms over her chest and peers at him.

She would cut my head off. "She'd be angry."

Sylvie coos in his ear and gums his earlobe. He turns onto his side and leans up on his elbow. "You're ganging up on me too?"

Sylvie giggles and tries to climb on him again. Tom shuffles back and sits against the sofa, letting Sylvie pull herself up, holding his knees.

"No one is ganging up on you, Tom. I am concerned for you."

"Why?"

"Because you are my family and I love you as brother." She walks back to the kitchen and Tom watches as she clatters about the cupboards, avoiding his eyes.

"I'm sorry, Mish."

She stops and looks at the worktop a moment before nodding. "I know… but if she knew I left you like this. She would be angry."

"I'm a big boy. I can even dress and feed myself."

Mischa rolls her eyes. "Well, you cannot with no food in flat. What have you been eating?"

Tom shrugs and Mischa pulls her phone out. She presses the screen and waits. "Hello… I am fine thank you. Are you busy?"

Tom frowns and holds both palms up. Mischa holds one finger up and listens to her phone.

"Can you get some take away food and come to Tom's flat? After your meeting?"

Who the fuck?

"No. He is drunk and not eating."

Tom drops his head onto the sofa. "Are you kidding me…" Sylvie claws at his chest and he picks her up and sits her in his lap facing him. "I feel like you're the only one who gets me."

Sylvie giggles and squeals, slapping her hands into his chest.

"That is because you both act same age." Mischa is back and sits on the sofa next to Tom's shoulder.

Tom jerks his head and looks at her. "Who was that?"

"James."

Tom huffs and scowls at the ceiling. "What meeting?"

"He did not say."

"Did you have to call *him*, though?"

"Would you prefer I call Martha?"

Fair point. "No."

Mischa stands. "I am going to clean kitchen and work out what food you need."

He lies back onto the floor and cradles Sylvie against him. "I'm gonna just lie here and talk politics with Sylvie."

———

An hour and a half later Tom wakes to gentle shaking of his shoulder. He blinks a couple of times and looks down, seeing Sylvie sleeping in the crook of his elbow.

"Food is here. I will put Sylvie in cot." Mischa picks up Sylvie and wanders into Tom's bedroom.

Tom hauls himself into a sitting position and slaps a hand to his head. "Shit."

"Here. Eat." James' voice sounds from the kitchen and Tom grimaces as James arranges take away containers and bowls.

I am not in the mood for you. "Righto, Dad." Tom stands and shakes his head a couple of times. He plonks himself on a stool at the worktop and massages his temples.

Mischa sits on the stool next to Tom and he wraps an arm around her shoulder and pecks her temple. "How did you get the cot up?"

"James helped me."

Tom looks at James, who has pulled a stool around to the other side of the island worktop and is scooping rice into a bowl. He keeps his eyes on the rice and avoids Tom's stare.

"I see." Tom slides a bowl in front of himself and spears a dim sim with a lone chopstick. *I can't work two of them right now.* "What meeting were you at?"

James swallows some food and coughs. "Huh?"

"Mischa said to come here after your meeting on the phone earlier. What meeting was it?"

"Oh… Nothing. Just updating Martha."

"On what?"

"Everything." James' cheeks take on a pink hue.

"What aren't you telling me?"

"Nothing. Pass the soy?"

"Are you feeling better, Tom?" Mischa nibbles at a spring roll and gives James side eye, passing him the soy sauce.

"Not really." Tom sweeps his eyes around the kitchen and lounge room.

"I emptied rest of bottle down sink." Mischa chews on a mouthful of rice and waits.

"Why?"

James rolls his eyes. "Okay, I may be stupid but that's the dumbest question you've ever asked. Anyone. Ever." He snorts. "Why." James shakes his head.

Tom ignores James and keeps looking at Mischa. "Don't you trust me?" He blinks away the fog still hovering around his head.

"Yes. I trust you with my life. But I do not trust your thirst."

Tom swallows. *Well, fuck.* He flicks his eyes to the cupboard above the fridge.

"I got rid of that one, also." She scoops another mouthful of rice and avoids Tom's gaze.

Tom drops his chopstick into his bowl and lays both palms flat on the worktop. "What do I do now?" he whispers.

"Do?" Mischa swivels on her stool to face him front on.

"She's gone. I can't speak to her. I have this job I have to be focused on. And... I can't sleep without... I need..." Tom drops his face and rubs his eyes. Panic bubbles in his gut. "Fuck." *I'm a mess.*

"I'll get hold of her Tom."

Tom looks up at James, who is looking directly at him. His Adam's apple wobbles as he swallows under Tom's intense stare.

"How?"

"She hasn't evaporated into thin air," he says. "Go see Mike. Stop drinking. It's not helping you or her."

Tom gives James a double take. "Pardon?"

"It's true." James shrugs.

Just because it's true doesn't mean you have to say it. "I don't need to see Mike."

Both Mischa and James snort softly into their bowls.

"I don't."

Mischa puts her hand on Tom's arm. "Tom. I let Sylvie near you even though you were drunk. Because I trust you. You will never hurt her. Or me."

"What does that have to do with getting my head shrunk?"

"You are hurting yourself." Mischa bites her lip. "And I cannot allow this."

Tom huffs and shoves more dim sim into his mouth. "I just don't..." He swallows and looks at Mischa. "She knows my weakness. And she wouldn't want me drinking."

"Da."

"Jesus Christ." He jumps up from the stool. "She would have called." *She would have by now. Fuck.* "Even if she was angry. Because she knows me…"

Mischa's eyes widen. "What are you saying?"

Tom's gut plummets through the floor. "Something's happened to her. I can feel it."

Mischa and James say nothing.

"Tell me Mischa. The last thing she said to you. What was it?"

"She asked me if I blamed you and her for Sascha."

"And?"

"I said I did not. And she told me you were afraid of losing her the same you lost your first love."

Tom closes his eyes. *Yes.* He waits a beat to swallow the lump taking over his throat. "And then?"

"I told her I would get fold up for next time. And she said there would not be next time."

There wouldn't be a next time. "She was coming home?"

"Da. I told her she was your true love and she smiled."

Tom drops his face into his hand and rubs his eyes. "That doesn't sound like someone about to come home and take everything and leave. Does it?"

13

ISABELLA

Isabella opens her eyes. Everything is dark and blurry, but she makes out light coming under a door on the other side of the room. The clock still ticks away the time, but otherwise she hears nothing. She gently pulls her left hand towards her face and the pinch of a cannula tells her she's still hooked up to the drip. But she's awake. She gazes up at the bag and tries to focus on it through the gloom.

Empty.

She stills and listens again, but the clock ticking is still the only sound she hears. While her brain is half alert she rolls and squirms towards her left hand and bites at the tape over the cannula. She rips a piece off and spits it on the floor before going back to tear the rest off. Just as she has the tube in her mouth and is about to yank, the door opens and the same man from the day before runs in with his face obscured.

He swats her across the cheek and she recoils towards her

right shoulder as he tapes down the cannula again. Isabella flexes her right arm but she's still handcuffed to the bolt in the wall. She kicks her legs trying to move around enough to kick her captor but he slaps her again and wags a finger in her face.

"What am I doing here?" Her voice is raspy.

The man doesn't answer, instead pulls another bag of fluid from inside his hoodie and fastens it to the hook.

Her heart beats faster and she kicks out again before whatever he's giving her slows her movements again. "What are you giving me?"

He ignores her and inspects the drip.

"What the fuck is going on?" she screams, or at least tries to. The urgency in her tone is enough to make him stop what he's doing and crouch down next to her.

"Ssshhhhh…" He strokes her hair off her face and tilts his head. "Sshhhh."

Dizziness overcomes her and she drops her head back to the floor, unable to keep it up. "Why are you… doing this?" Her eyelids droop and she closes her eyes as the man in the hoodie leaves the room.

Kostya leaned over Irina and snapped the cuffs around her wrists. His sweaty body odour and foul breath blanketed her face.

"There's a good girl. Sleep time."

Irina flopped onto the pillow and turned her face away from him. He'd taken what he came for and now she wanted to be left alone. He ran a finger down her cheek and she grimaced.

"You have a big job tomorrow, Irina. You must sleep tight."

"Yes, Uncle Kostya," she whispered before burying her face into the pillow.

She waited until she heard the door close before turning onto her back and staring at the bunk above her.

"Irinia?" Kat's timid voice floated down from above.

"Yes?"

"Are you okay?"

"No."

Irina heard chains jangle as Kat moved above her. "We won't get chained up forever."

"I never want to be chained up again."

Isabella's senses come back to her as she wakes with sweat dotting her brow. The grogginess from before is still there, but her mind seems clearer. She blinks through the gloomy darkness and realises there's no light coming under the door.

She brings her mouth to her hand and tears the tape away with her teeth again. She stops and waits. No-one comes. She tears the other piece of tape away. Silence.

She positions her teeth on the plastic tubing attached to the cannula and squeezes her eyes shut. *This is gonna be messy.* She clamps her teeth down and rips the cannula from her hand. Warm blood oozes from the open needle site. The sting of the needle being yanked out subsides a little and she pushes her hand against the floor to stem the bleeding. She looks up at the bag with her blurry eyes, but it has no writing on it that she can see through the gloom, but it's empty.

She blinks again as more of her gross motor skills return. She heaves herself into a sitting position against the wall between both cuffed wrists and looks around the room. There's a window, with a blackout blind keeping her in darkness. It's hard to tell in the dark, but there's something familiar about the window. *Have I been here before?*

A door opens somewhere beyond her dark room and light suddenly streams under the door again.

Shit.

She looks up as the door opens and light engulfs the room. Her eyes close against the brightness and she can't see what lays beyond.

The door closes and darkness once again shrouds the room.

The man stalks towards her, tutting quietly. He grabs her bloodied hand and squeezes it. Adrenaline hits her veins and she uses every ounce of strength she has to thrust her hips and legs around, kicking her captor in the side of his thigh as he crouches besides her. It's not hard enough to floor him, but he lands on his backside and lets go of her wrist. She kicks out again with both feet, landing in his gut.

He falls against the wall and lets out a groan.

"Aaron?" Her underused voice comes out in a croaky rabble. She clears her throat as he gets to his knees and swings around, punching her in the left side of her jaw. Her head slams into the wall and stars explode behind her eyes.

Before she can gather herself, he runs from the room slamming the door behind him. She slides down the wall and onto the floor. The back of her hand stings and her neck and head throb.

Help me, Tom.

14

TOM

Tom spins the chair in front of Martha's desk and straddles it. He taps his thumbs on the top rung and glares at Martha as she reads her computer screen. He should be hungover and feeling sorry for himself but this time, the morning after has purpose. And all the ibuprofen and paracetamol he swallowed helps.

Finally she looks up. "You cleaned up."

He rubs at his chin. "It was itchy."

"Abbie and James will be here in a moment."

Tom pulls his phone out and presses Isabella's number. *Straight to voicemail.* His jaw tightens as the office door opens and James walks in with Abbie in tow.

"Still nothing?" James drags a chair across and sits beside Tom as Abbie leans against the edge of Martha's desk.

"Why do you think we're all here, James?" Tom shifts his glare from Martha to James.

"Don't be a dick, Grant." Abbie gives him a push to the knee with her foot.

Tom holds both palms up.

"Yes, stop being difficult Tom." Martha takes her glasses off and rubs her eyes. "James. Can you get inside Aaron's and sort out vision and sound? I believe they have some sort of jammer inside?"

"They do. But I've hacked his cameras"

Martha nods as Tom intertwines his hands and squeezes until his knuckles turn white. "We're wasting time sitting here."

"I understand that Tom, but we don't know that he has her or even if anyone has her. We have no grounds to go bursting in—"

Tom leaps up from his chair and it falls backwards. "I don't give a fuck about *grounds*, Martha." He leans on the desk, a growl sits in his throat but he swallows it away, remembering who he's talking to.

"Ah… If I may?" James says.

Tom turns his head but remains leaning on the desk. "What?"

"Well, when I saw her last it was…" James swallows. "It was outside Aaron's…"

"Excuse me?" Tom stands and turns to face James.

"I was monitoring the vision of the outside because there had been a truck… and I didn't think anything of it because it's Isabella and she's impulsive and—"

"Spit it the fuck out."

"She was creeping around out the back of Aaron's and I spotted her and told her to get out. And she did. But I lost vision when she walked around the corner of the block… I would have told you yesterday but you were—"

Tom lurches forward and grabs James' shirt at his throat.

"Tom!" Martha moves around the desk as Abbie jumps off it and grabs Tom's arm.

Tom tightens his grip and ignores Martha and Abbie. "Who else is in the vision?"

"No one. There was a kid on a pushbike riding like an idiot down the street and heaps of people going to work or whatever..."

"Aaron." Tom grinds his teeth.

"Well, I can't say I saw him. I mean—"

"Who the fuck else would it be, James?" Tom throws James back into his chair and without another word or look back, he stalks from the office.

———

"Tom!" Footsteps slap on the pavement behind Tom as he storms towards the brothel. "Tom! Don't be a dick. Stop."

He reaches the front door, ignoring Abbie and pounds his fist on it. She grabs hold of his forearm and yanks on it.

He whirls towards her. "What?"

"You can't just go storming in there. Are you mad?"

He turns back to the door and pounds on it again before stepping back a couple of steps. "Move back," he says to Abbie before raising his leg and slamming his foot into the door below the handle. It flies open and he grabs his gun from his waistband as he storms inside.

"For the love of..." Abbie mutters from behind Tom.

"C'mon," Tom says without looking at her. He peers at the

front desk and the closed door leading to the hallway of sleazy bedrooms. "Door number two…" He raises his leg again to bash it open.

"What if there's someone behind it?"

Tom shrugs. "They get hit."

"What if it's Isabella?"

Tom stops. "He's not gonna dump her in the hallway."

"You don't know that."

"Okay fine. Stay here. Don't let anyone in or out. I'll go 'round the back."

"But Tom, this isn't a good idea. You know it isn't—"

"*Like* I said… no one in or out." He stomps out the front door and moves down the side of the building before Abbie can talk any more sense. He stops halfway down the side alley. *Nothing.* He continues on, knowing James and Martha are no doubt watching.

Tom's mouth is dry and the sound of the road is white noise as he sidles towards the back door. He mirrors his kick from moments before and the back door opens with a loud crack. He finds himself in an anteroom with another steel plated door in front of him. *Of course.* He takes a breath and ignores the ache in his hip from the first entry. He kicks and the door moves but stays locked. "Fuck's sake." He kicks it again and it loosens but the lock is still in tact. "Fuck!" He takes a few steps back before running at the door and shoulder barging it. The door crashes open and he goes with it, landing face first on the floor.

He scrambles to his feet and looks around. He's at the end of the hallway, Aaron's office is to his right, and a white painted door is in the wall next to the door he just broke through. He puts his ear against it but hears nothing. He runs a hand over the surface of the door and puts his face against it again. "Iz?" He jiggles the handle but the door doesn't budge. "Iz?"

He moves to Aaron's door and tries the handle. It opens but the office is empty. He notices the Scrabble board still open, but moved to a shelf behind the desk. The word 'fucked' is still spelt out down one side by itself. *Weirdo.*

Loud pounding on the door at the end of the hall, leading to the reception area grabs his attention and he runs to open it.

Abbie has a man of about thirty with too much gel in his hair on the ground with his arm goosenecked behind his back. She looks up as Tom stands over them. "Hey Tom."

"Your girls play rough..." the man on the floor says.

Tom leans down and grabs his goosenecked wrist, yanking him off the floor. "Get the fuck out." He pushes him towards the front door.

"Wait a second... is that really any way to run a business?"

Fine. Let's play. "What's your name?"

"Dean."

"Well... Dean. I believe I asked you to leave."

"And I said—"

"You refused. Which gives me more grounds to throw you out, for being a pain in my arse. See, if I *was* running a business here I would want high class clientele... and not some skinny chav with yellow teeth and more hair gel then an Elvis convention."

Dean squares up and puffs his chest out. "What'd you say?"

Abbie giggles. "Oh Dean."

Tom pulls his gun out and lines it up between Dean's eyes. "Get the fuck out or your brains paint the front windows."

Dean puts both hands up; colour draining from his face, and stumbles backwards against the door. "Righto righto... all you had to do was ask."

Tom replaces his gun, lurches forward and grabs Dean by the throat. He yanks the front door open and throws him on the pavement outside. "Please leave us a review on Google at your earliest convenience." Tom slams the door shut and leans his back against it. "Fuck me."

"It's okay for you, he thought I worked here... like... *worked* here."

Tom shrugs. "You probably would have had time. Three second sticky mess I reckon."

Abbie raises both eyebrows. "Pardon?"

"C'mon." He pulls his gun out again. "We need to clear these rooms and get into that door at the end."

"The place seems empty."

"Never assume Abs. C'mon."

15

ISABELLA

A loud bang somewhere beyond the darkness rouses Isabella from her twilight dozing. A door slams and muttering from a male voice floats through the closed door. A new pressure is against her cheeks and mouth, and she tries to shout but can't get anything out but a muffled moan. *Bastard's gagged me.* Her head is still full of cotton wool but there is a familiarity about the cadence of the voice outside. She shifts to sit against the wall again and pulls against her cuffs. She attempts another scream but is thwarted by the gag pushed into her mouth and tied behind her head. She drops her head against the wall, and it makes a dull thud.

She does it again. And again.

There are still voices on the other side of the door somewhere. She brings her chin to her chest before throwing her head back and hitting the wall again. She stamps her feet on the floor, but the carpet absorbs most of the sound. She bangs her head again, knowing the headache it will cause, but not caring.

Somewhere beyond the door she hears the familiar voice get louder for a moment before another door slams shut. She bangs her head backwards again and tries to scream.

The door opens and hoodie-man runs to her, grabs her jaw, and holds a blade against her throat.

She glares into his masked face, biting down harder on the gag.

I'm not afraid of you.

Hoodie-man puts a finger to his lips. "Shhhh." He stands and turns towards the door.

"I... need the... loo." Isabella manages to push sounds that resemble words through the gag... muffled and gurgled .

He stops at the door and bows his head a moment. He turns and holds a finger up, as though asking her to wait, before disappearing out the door.

Isabella kicks out at the darkness. She pushes her frustration out through the gag in her mouth, over and over until her throat is raw.

16

TOM

Tom pulls a drawer from Aaron's desk and turns it upside down. Pens, papers and a stapler fall onto the desk. The stapler bounces once and hits Abbie in the side of the head as she kneels next to the chair, looking through a box.

"Ow! Calm down Grant or I'll—okay this is disgusting."

Tom peers down at her.

She holds up a pair of frilly red french knickers. "You don't like red?" Tom throws the drawer on the floor and pulls out the second one.

"I don't like crusty old knickers that have clearly been in this box for ages. Who knows who wore them."

Tom grabs a stack of papers from the drawer and sits on the chair to leaf through them. "I'm just gonna point out, you're still holding them." He snorts.

"Ugh." She drops them back into the box. "Thanks for the leadership."

"You're welcome." He throws the papers onto the desk. "Financials. James can deal with that."

"What are we looking for?"

"I want to know where Isabella is. I want addresses, phone numbers, P ornhub subscriptions… whatever leads me to where that piece of—"

The front door opening makes Tom's mouth slam shut. He stands and pulls out his gun. He creeps to the office door and leans against the wall. He holds a finger over his lips.

Abbie scrambles from the floor and tucks in beside him.

A floorboard creaks at the other end of the hallway.

"The fuck?" A voice whispers. A voice Tom knows.

Tom steps into the hallway and levels his gun at Aaron. "I could do with an extra pair of hands in here."

Aaron's eyebrows dip. "What's going on?"

"Where's Emily?"

"Excuse me?"

"Emily. Where is she?"

Aaron's face relaxes and a smile creeps along his lips. "Visiting a sick Aunt?" He takes a step backwards and his smile widens. "I do wish I could help."

Tom squeezes the grip of his pistol.

Aaron turns and runs.

Tom sprints down the hallway and reaches the front door just as Aaron slams it in his face. He shoves his gun back into his waistband and yanks the door open.

"Tom!" Abbie's voice is somewhere behind him but he doesn't stop. He bolts out the front door and spots Aaron getting into a black BMW. The pedestrians crowding his way remind him it's the start of rush hour as he takes off towards the car, dodging a woman with a pram, a businessman on his phone and kids trying to dribble a football between them along the pavement.

He reaches the car just as it takes off, with Aaron giving him the courtesy of raising his arm out the window and flipping the middle finger as he turns the corner.

"Fuck!" Tom punches the nearest lamp post. Pain spikes through his knuckles and he immediately regrets it.

"I bet that hurt." An elderly man with a zimmer frame hobbles past Tom grinning and shaking his head.

Tom ignores him and glares at his now red, cut knuckles. Before the urge to punch something else hits him, he turns and trudges back to the brothel.

Five minutes later, Abbie looks up from the box she is sealing as Tom leans against the doorframe. "Enjoy your morning jog?"

"He took off in a car. First part of the plate read L H two one." He walks in and sits on the edge of the desk. "He has her somewhere else."

"How do you know?"

"Because if she was here." He nods towards the locked room at the end of the hallway. "He would have been nervous and not just taken off for fear we would find her. Plus... It's Iz. Unless she's knocked out cold she would have found a way to make some kind of noise." His eyes travel over the office and land on the Scrabble board, still sitting on the shelf behind the desk. He squints and leans forward.

Abbie whips her head around to follow his line of sight. "What are you looking at?"

Tom reaches across and grabs the notepad from the inside of the Scrabble box. "Interesting."

"A Scrabble score sheet?"

"Yeah."

"I don't follow."

"Have you ever played Scrabble?"

"Yeah. Loads when we went to Cornwall for holidays."

"Did you ever rip off the old score sheets? Or did you simply fold the paper over and draw up a new score card?"

"Well, Dad used to score." Abbie chuckles. "It's funny cause Mum is a hopeless speller and he—"

"Abs!"

"Sorry, Ummm… no I think he used to write the next one on the back of the previous one."

"Right. So why are the old score sheets ripped off and sitting in that box?" Tom nods at the box. "And the fresh paper is just sat there, blank?"

"Maybe he had to write down a phone message?" Abbie shrugs.

"Exactly." Tom grabs the lead pencil from the box and lays the paper out flat on the desk. "Let's see what was so important he had to write it down and take it with him somewhere." Tom shades lightly over the paper as white squiggles and lines appear.

"Holy shit Grant. How did you think of that?"

"Voodoo magic bullshit."

"What?"

"Nothing. Write this down."

Abbie scrambles to grab a pen and scrap paper. "Go."

"Frith. Electric Blue. Second Friday. Two blonde, two brunette, one red." Tom's gut twists. "It's a fucking shopping list."

Abbie looks up from her note taking. "Girls?"

Tom grabs her wrist and yanks her off the floor. "Let's go."

"But, what about that locked room?"

Tom stops outside the locked door and pulls out his gun.

"Tom! You can't shoot the lock! What if she's in there and you're wrong?"

"She isn't in there. And shooting a lock won't do shit. You watch too many movies. I just want to blast apart the door jam. Stand back." He waits until Abbie retreats before pointing at the door jam and unloading half a magazine into the frame and around the catch. He takes half a pace back and kicks the door open. It flies open and bangs against the wall. He feels around, finds a light switch and flicks it on. Dust floats through the air on account of his dramatic entrance, but what Tom sees makes bile threaten at the back of his throat. "Jesus." He scans the tiny windowless room, no bigger than a jail cell.

"Are those... chains?" Abbie brushes past him into the room and stands in the middle of the floor.

Chains are fastened along the walls, enough to chain eight people at a time. Wrist cuffs are still attached. The floor is stained, but with what, Tom can't tell. He walks to the back wall and examines the five I.V. poles and a couple of gas tanks with face masks. "What the...?" He lifts some plastic tubing hanging from one of the poles with the muzzle of his gun and inspects it. "This hasn't been used in a while. The plastic has yellowed."

"That doesn't make it okay, Tom." Abbie's face twists. "He tethered those girls like animals."

He peers at Abbie. "I know that."

"God this is horrific. Can we get out of here?"

Tom drops the tube and nods. "Yes, we can. This makes me sick." He pulls his phone out and dials Martha. "But first…" He steps outside into the carpark.

Martha picks up after half a ring. "Tom."

"Can you get Aaron's place secured? We need to be able to go back through it."

"Fine. Get your backside in my office." She hangs up.

Tom stares at the phone for a moment. "I feel like I may be in her bad books."

Abbie snorts. "What's new?"

———

"This is exactly why I wanted you off my job and why we need to plan and organise where we go from here, Tom." Martha paces back and forward while Tom stands in the middle of her office, staring at the wall behind her with his arms folded. "You can't just go running off half cocked and tear apart venues of interest and chase away one of the only leads we have."

He bites harder on his mouth the louder her voice gets.

"You've been drinking, you're irritable—"

Tom opens his mouth to object.

She spins to face him. "*More* so than usual, and you're supposed to be overseeing Abigail with her first field job."

"The same job you want me off all of a sudden for reasons you won't divulge?" Tom raises his eyebrows.

"Isabella is now our priority. I'm sure you agree." Martha huffs. "Things will need to be reassigned and further planning—"

"Is he still harassing you?"

Martha stops pacing and stands with her back to Tom. "The electricity cut out in my house last night."

"And I'm assuming there was no legit power outage?" Tom moves to stand in front of her, keen to let his upper hand continue.

"No, my fuse box had been tampered with and…" She clears her throat. "Anyway—"

"Whoa, whoa, whoa. I don't think so. And what?"

"And a smiley face had been drawn on the inside of the box in one of those thick black texta pens."

"A smiley face?"

"And the words *not long now.*"

The top of Tom's head may as well have blasted into smithereens as his blood pressure shoots to extreme. "Are you *fucking* kidding me? You didn't think this was worth mentioning? That he came into your home and defaced it? You didn't think to replace me at the surveillance house last night? You didn't happen to *think* at all?" Tom glares at Martha and tries to even out his breathing, while she walks around and sits at her desk avoiding all eye contact.

"Umm… sorry am I interrupting something?" Abbie's voice comes from behind Tom.

"Yes," Tom says at the same time Martha says no. "She means *yes*." He turns to Abbie. "Can you give us a few minutes please?"

"No, Abigail." Martha stands. "That won't be necessary." She motions Abbie into the room. "Come in."

Tom drops into a chair and seethes as Martha rearranges pens on her desk.

Abbie sits next to Tom, and after shooting him a glance, addresses Martha. "James thinks he knows what Frith and Electric Blue means."

"Well don't keep us in suspense, Abs." Tom holds both hands out, palms to the ceiling.

Abbie tilts her head and smiles at Tom. "Are you being a petulant child again?"

"Yes Abigail. He is. Go on."

Abbie takes a breath. "It's a club in Soho."

Tom leans forward. "A club?"

"Yep. Whatever Aaron has planned… it has something to do with this nightclub. And we think *second Friday* means the second Friday of the month… which happens to be today."

"Excellent." Martha starts typing, peering over her glasses at Tom. "You and Abigail have a date tonight."

Tom grinds his teeth. "Fine. Abs?"

"Yeah?"

"Get James in here."

"Excuse me?" Abigail folds her arms and fixes Tom with a stare.

"Please."

Abigail nods once and stands up. "No problem." She walks out.

The air between Tom and Martha is thicker than fog on a winter's morning. Martha continues to type and Tom inspects his nails.

"Hey," James says from behind Tom.

"Come in James and shut the door... please." Tom stands up and folds his arms again.

"What's up? You want comms for tonight?"

"Yes. But before that... You are to escort Martha to her house." Martha looks up from the computer screen and narrows her eyes at Tom. "You will help her get clothing, toiletries, tea, biscuits, whatever the hell she needs to be comfortable and you will take her to my flat."

Martha huffs. "Tom—"

Tom holds a hand up without looking at her. "This is *not* a negotiation."

James looks between the pair of them and chews on his lip. "Okay... I can do that."

"Great." Tom turns to Martha and points his finger at her. "And you'll stay in my goddamned flat until I come and tell you it's safe to leave. Am I making myself clear?"

She looks at his finger and back up at his face. "Are you forgetting who—"

"*Clear?*" Tom doesn't flinch.

James lets out a low whistle.

"Yes, Tom. Clear."

17

ISABELLA

Isabella sits with her back pressed against the wall and pulls against her cuffs. Everything beyond the door is quiet and no light has come underneath in quite a long time. She figures it's been about an hour since it fell silent. She pulls against her restraints again. *It's not like there's anything else to do.* Her head throbs from her attempt at gaining attention earlier and she tries to ignore the need to use the bathroom.

Frustration peaks in her veins so she yanks harder against her cuffs and a noise like a crack or tear sounds. She stills and waits for someone to come in. Nothing. She pulls again but this time only with her left hand. No noise. She yanks her right hand a bit harder and the same noise lifts from the wall or floor... or skirting?

Her heart beats a little faster. She takes a deep breath and with everything she has left she jerks forward hard and fast pulling both wrists with her. The skirting board creaks and moves the slightest bit. She bites down on the gag in her mouth as tears spring into her eyes. Happy tears.

Something wells in her chest and she lets out a muffled chuckle, which builds and turns into laughter. She jerks the cuffs back and forth, enjoying the fact the skirting comes with her the tiniest bit.

A door slams beyond the darkness. She stops moving and sits back against the wall, relaxing her hands by her sides. Moments later the door opens and the same man as always walks in. He's holding a large tub and what looks like a roll of toilet paper is jammed between his chin and chest.

He drops the tub at Isabella's feet and it hits the floor with a heavy thud. She leans forward and peers inside. *Kitty litter?* She stares up at the faceless man standing just out of kicking distance.

"Are you kidding me?" She tries to shout through the gag, but the words come out nonsensical. "I'm not a fucking animal!" She kicks both feet out in a useless attempt to kick him.

He throws the toilet paper on the floor and without a word, leaves the room.

18

TOM

Tom steps out of his shower and grabs a towel to drag over his wet hair. "Fucking night clubs," he grumbles. He wraps his towel around his waist and leans closer to the mirror to inspect the dark circles under his eyes.

A thud in his lounge room snaps his face away from the mirror.

"For goodness sakes James, be careful with that. It's a very valuable piece of equipment."

What the hell?

Tom walks out of the bathroom and into the lounge. Martha has her back to him, directing James and two other men, dressed like the secret service, in arranging her office furniture in the tiny lounge.

"What on earth are you lot doing?"

Martha turns and looks Tom up and down. "You're all wet."

"Thanks for the newsflash." He walks further into the

lounge, which ends up being only a few steps on account of the huge desk and filing drawers hindering his way. "I don't suppose anyone would like to explain to me what the fuck is going on?"

James leans against the photocopier he wheeled in on a trolley and rubs his eyes. "Don't drag me into this."

Martha turns to the other helpers and waves them away. "Thank you lads. We can take it from here."

They both nod at Tom and James before leaving.

Tom's temple throbs and he pushes both palms into his eyes. "Martha," he struggles to keep his voice calm. "Why is your office in my lounge room?"

"You told me to bring whatever made me comfortable."

Tom drops his hands from his face and narrows his eyes at her. "I said tea and biscuits. And maybe a toothbrush. Not your whole fucking office."

"If you're going to have me holed up here like some sort of prisoner, I need to be able to work. And for the record, I did bring biscuits."

James leans across the copier and picks up a packet of custard creams from a box and waves them at Tom.

Tom flings his arm out towards the antique desk at the end of the room that now has his sofa and arm chair piled in front of it. "You couldn't set your PC up on that?"

"And what about everything else?" Martha sweeps her hand around the room. "I need to be able to work as per normal."

Tom scrubs both hands through his hair and shakes his head. "Whatever. I haven't got time for this."

"No. You haven't. Abigail will be here any minute and you

aren't dressed." Martha claps her hands as though corralling a child into the bath. "Off you go."

Tom grits his teeth. "You and I are gonna have words about this."

Martha smiles. "I look forward to it. I'll make tea. And we can have biscuits."

Tom stomps into his bedroom and slams the door behind him. The room only reminds him once more that Isabella isn't there and he shakes his shoulders out. *Game face.*

He grabs black trousers, a black shirt and shoes from the wardrobe and throws them on the bed. He runs his fingers through his hair and decides it's done before getting dressed.

Abbie's voice floats in from the lounge as he laces his shoes. "Oh wow. I bet Tom's loving this." She laughs and Tom rolls his eyes.

"Tom isn't amused." He announces as he walks out of the bedroom, concealing his gun in the back of his waistband under his shirt.

Martha is boiling the kettle in the kitchen and opening the biscuits.

Abbie turns and it gives the full effect of her barely there, silver sparkly dress.

"Jesus Abs. You look like a half dressed disco ball."

"Cheers Grant. What about you? You look like a cocaine dealer."

James laughs from where he is connecting Martha's computer cables. "Yeah Tom, when was the last time you went clubbing?"

"When I was young and stupid. Much the same as you are now, James."

James snorts. "Okay. I worked my magic and got you both on the list by the way. You're welcome."

"I don't know what I'd do without you." Tom gives Abbie's shoulder a tap. "Let's get out of here. I'm getting an eye twitch."

"Are you sure you wouldn't like a cup of tea before you go?" Martha smiles from the kitchen where she stirs her cup.

Tom glares at her. "Save me a biscuit."

———

Tom and Abbie walk through the crowded street towards Electric Blue.

"So tell me again why Martha's entire office is in your flat?"

"Because she's making a point. And I'm not biting."

Abbie laughs as they reach the royal blue velvet rope outside the club. "First time for everything I suppose."

Two women standing in front of them turn and look Tom up and down. One of them, dressed in leather hotpants and a patent black corset winks at him before stepping up to the bouncer.

"Still got it hey, Grant?" Abbie elbows him in the ribs.

James snorts through the earpiece in Tom's ear and Abbie giggles as it obviously sounds in her earpiece too.

Tom grunts as the bouncer looks at the pair of them with a raised brow. "Names?"

"Nathan Parker and Melissa Brown." Tom slides his hand around Abbie's waist and pulls her against him. She drops her head onto his shoulder.

The bouncer peers at them both before consulting his iPad.

He taps the screen a couple of times before unclipping the rope and jerking his head towards the door. "Enjoy your evening."

Tom grins at the bouncer. "I intend to."

Inside, the air thickens and the music sounds more like heavy booms and thuds with a little bit of synthesizer over the top. Tom grabs Abbie's hand and they wander into the sweaty throng.

"Can you guys still hear me?" James' voice fills Tom's ear.

"Yeah," Tom answers, his eyes sweeping the rest of the dancefloor and beyond as he pulls Abbie into a dark corner.

"Okay… muffled but okay."

"What do you expect, James?"

"Thanks James'" Abbie says. "Give us a few minutes."

Tom pulls Abbie against him and drops his forehead against hers. "There are what looks like some VIP booths at the back. He's gonna be in one of them."

"Okay. And stop being so crabby," Abbie tilts her mouth towards his to keep up the charade. "James is only trying to help."

"She's right you know." James pipes up. "By the way, I can see you through the surveillance. You look like you belong. In case you were wondering."

"I wasn't. What cameras have you got access to?" Tom slides his hands down Abbie's back and keeps her against him.

"Everything inside the main club. It seems they have some others but I can't crack them—"

"James! I'm not swanning around looking like a coke dealer for my own health."

"I was gonna finish with… yet. I haven't cracked them yet."

"Well if you could get on to that?"

"Grant. Crabby." Abbie's lips brush his as she speaks.

"I'm on it. Go mingle you two." James falls silent.

"Let's walk. I'm thirsty anyway." Tom pulls her out of the corner.

"Thirsty? Are you mad?"

"Water, Abs. I'll have water. Barmen know things. I need to make some friends."

"You shouldn't have a problem with that. With your winning social personality and all." Abbie grins at him as she walks backwards still holding his hand.

"Flattered."

"I'm going to go and flash my wares at the private booths." She winks and before Tom can say anything she disappears into the throng on the dancefloor.

Tom clenches his jaw. "Abbie… don't do anything stupid."

"I won't." Her voice replaces James' in his ear. "Make sure you don't either. You know what I'm talking about."

Tom looks up at the colourful bottles behind the bar and grunts. He pushes to the front and slaps both hands on the bar and drums his fingers.

"Whaddya want?" A barman asks.

"Mineral water."

"Mineral water?" The barman raises a brow. "That's it?"

Tom makes a show of taking a big sniff of air. "Yep."

The barman grins and clicks his tongue. "Right." He dashes off to the other end of the bar.

"And you?" A woman behind the bar shouts over the music to another person but her accent pricks Tom's ears. "Okay. You want top shelf?"

Russian.

He peers at her. She's wearing a tight leather skirt and a barely there sparkly bra. Her hair falls down her back in dark brown waves and her makeup looks as though it was put on with a trowel. But underneath it, Tom suspects she is only just of legal age.

She pours a drink into a measuring cup and stops to glance at Tom. "Take a picture?" She raises an eyebrow and gives him a well rehearsed, sly smile.

Tom blinks. "Sorry. You... remind me of someone."

She pushes the drink to her customer and moves to Tom, sliding a finger across the bar as she goes. "I have heard this before. You must try harder." She leans across the bar, pushing her face and chest closer to him.

He stays where he is and smiles. He's about to speak when the barman returns with his water. He slides it across to Tom before turning on the girl and berating her in Russian. Tom listens to every word and squeezes his glass.

"What's he saying, Tom?" James comes alive again.

Tom moves from the bar back to his isolated corner. "He told her to keep working or he would send her out with the others." He turns into the corner, so people don't notice him talking to himself.

"Holy shit."

"Have you got into those cameras yet?"

"Yeah, but they're currently dark. Must be in an amenities room and office or something. One of the rooms has light coming in under the door but I can't see anything else."

"Keep watching."

"Copy."

Tom is just about to turn around when a hand grabs and squeezes his backside. He glances out of the corner of his eye and finds a man, wearing a lime green shirt unbuttoned to the navel and blue jeans that look as though they're strangling him.

Tom turns slowly towards him and the man winks.

Tom huffs out a chuckle before leaning in to the man's ear. "I sincerely hope... you're trying to steal my wallet."

The smile fades from the man's face but he doesn't go anywhere. "You seemed lonely."

"I'm not. So maybe be on your merry way?"

The man pouts. "Shame." He walks backwards into the crowded dance floor and disappears.

Tom leans against the wall, remembering all the reasons why he hates places like this.

Abbie appears beside him. "Okay I found out some things."

"What do you know?"

"Well I started getting cozy with a fella in one of the VIP's, Luis he said his name was. He reckons he liked my dress." She does a spin and ends in a pose.

Tom glares at her. "And?"

"And he started talking about how he loves beautiful women blah blah. He nods at some bloke who checked in on our booth... next thing you know he brings out two girls and stands them in front of us."

"Girls?"

"Yeah like... seventeen tops. Luis points at one of them and the bloke pushes her towards us and the other one starts crying and pleading with him not to take her back there. She had some European accent. He dragged her away."

"To where?"

"Somewhere out the back maybe?"

"What did this bloke look like?"

"Completely outrageous. He was wearing a lime green shirt. Looked like something out of a Barry Manilow film clip. And the tightest jeans I have ever seen. Literally. I could see every single lump and curve if you know what I mean."

Tom stares onto the dance floor and flares his nostrils. *Fuck fuck fuck.*

"What is it, Tom? You look like you're about to murder someone."

"I had him. Right here. He grabbed my arse."

"Excuse me?"

Just as Tom is about to take off into the throng of bodies to find his admirer, James pipes up. "Oh my God."

"Have you found him, James?" Tom scans the dance floor but can't see any lime green.

"Shit Tom. You need to get out the back. Now."

"Why?" He grabs Abbies wrist and drags her through the dance floor.

"One of the rooms just lit up. Six men with laptops and there's a double sided mirror window thing in front of them."

"And?"

"One of them is Aaron."

Tom grips Abbie's wrist tighter and her cry of protest is drowned out by the music and bodies writhing on the dancefloor.

"Go right to the back of the club. There's a fire exit. Go through it into a hallway. You'll see another door opposite. That takes you into the part of the building they're in. I don't have any floor plan for it, sorry."

"Don't be sorry. You did good."

"Wow thanks, I mean I—"

"Shut up James." Tom reaches the door and goes through, pulling Abbie with him.

"Jesus Grant." She rotates her wrist. "You've got an iron grip on you." She leans against the concrete wall in the hallway while Tom inspects the door opposite them.

"Are you gonna try and kick it open again?"

"No."

"Good. You're too young for a hip replacement."

Tom ignores her and tries the handle. It clicks open and he blinks at it. "Well, fuck."

Abbie draws in a breath behind him. "It's open?"

He peeks through the crack in the door and finds a scarlet carpeted hallway, painted black from wall to ceiling. He widens the door a little more to see three doors, two on one wall and one on the other. There's a man in a black suit wearing earbuds, prodding his phone screen standing outside one of them. Tom pulls the door shut again and turns to Abbie.

"Time to put on a show, Abs."

19

TOM

Tom conceals himself against the wall beside the door and peeks through as Abbie stumbles into the hallway. She giggles and falls against the wall and the man with the phone looks up at her.

"Hey. You shouldn't be here." He goes to her and grabs her elbow.

"Oh umm..." Abbie peers at a name tag on his shirt. "Sorry Gary... is this the... ladies?" She looks around, frowning before giggling again. She falls against Gary, pressing her chest against him. "Ooopps. Sorry... I'm a little bit... drunk." She bends at the hips and laughs.

"Okay well... get out of here. This is private."

Abbie stumbles and falls on the floor. She giggles again and turns her body so Gary has his back to the door.

Tom squeezes the grip of his gun. *You play an annoying drunk frighteningly well.*

"Shhh. Be quiet you stupid tart." Gary bends down to take her arm again.

Tom slides through the doorway, grabs him around the neck, jamming his forearm against Gary's throat.

Abbie kicks her legs around and sweeps him off his feet.

Tom points his gun directly between Gary's eyes and puts a finger to his mouth in a shoosh action.

"Where's Aaron?" Tom asks, as Abbie scrambles from the floor and pulls her dress back into place.

Gary puts both hands up. "Who?"

"Aaron. The one who brought the girls."

"Oh him. It's his first time, sorry we aren't acquainted." Gary shrugs and gives Tom a satisfied grin.

"What?"

"But I will say his livestock are top shelf."

Tom pushes the gun hard into Gary's temple. "Where are they?"

"The livestock?"

"They're human. Girls. Not fucking livestock."

Abbie kicks him to the side of the head and knocks him out.

"Abs!"

"He made me angry. Sorry."

"You can't just—" A thud against one of the pair of doors to the left reminds Tom he's on a time limit. "Quick." He nods towards the single door opposite them and Abbie grabs Gary's ankles while Tom grabs under his arms. They slide him across and Abbie opens the door.

"They should really lock up their secrets a little better," Tom says as they get inside the dark room and shut the door. "Is there a light?"

A second later the room is filled with a dull orange glow from a single, filthy lightbulb hanging from the middle of the ceiling.

Tom spins to look for something to tie Gary up with and stops when his eyes adjust to the scene in front of him.

"Shit." James says in his ear. "It was more pleasant when it was dark."

Four girls lie on the floor with their hands cuffed to an iron bar attached to the wall. All four are attached to an IV drip on a pole next to them. A couple of them look up at the light with unfocused eyes. One has sick down her front, and none of them look any older than seventeen. The room smells musty and thick.

"Oh God," Abbie gasps and slaps her hand over her mouth. "Grant."

Tom drops Gary on the floor and slides to his knees in front of the girls. He takes the face of the first girl in his hand and looks into her eyes. She blinks a slow, sleepy blink and gives him a half smile.

"I'm... beeeng good," she slurs and drops the weight of her head into Tom's palm. He slides his hand away, leaving her head resting on her shoulder and looks at the other three girls, all in the same state.

None of them are Isabella.

Rattling behind him draws his attention and he turns as Abbie sets up one of the empty IV poles. "Quick, help me get him hooked up to this thing." Abbie nods at Gary, starting to squirm on the floor.

Tom stares at Gary and falls onto his backside. "Jesus," he whispers.

"Grant!"

He shakes his head. "Right. Yep." He scrambles to Gary, hauls him into a sitting position against the wall and trains his gun on him. *Focus.*

Abbie taps the top of his hand a few times before she jabs the cannula into Gary's vein and wraps a torn bandage around it a few times. "Who would have thought my corpsman training would come in so useful?"

Gary winces before opening his eyes and focusing on Tom, sitting in front of him with a gun pointed at his chest.

"Morning Sunshine."

Gary startles and tries to jerk his hand away from Abbie.

Tom moves the gun up to the middle of Gary's forehead, pushing his head against the wall. "This is the deal, you either have a nice little twilight nap. Or I shoot you between the eyes. What would you prefer?"

Gary stops squirming and his gaze follows the gun as Tom lowers it back to the middle of his chest.

Tom grins. "Excellent choice. Who doesn't love a catnap?"

"They'll kill you." Gary's voice crackles.

"No. They won't."

Abbie drops Gary's hand and stands. "I've got the girls."

Tom nods without taking his eyes off Gary. "Are they selling the girls? Is that what's happening across the hall?"

Gary glares at Tom and keeps his mouth shut. His eyes start to glaze.

Tom pushes the gun against Gary's forehead again. "I asked you a fucking question."

Gary's head droops. "Yeah…"

"Tom!" James' voice comes alive. "Aaron's coming. He's coming your way."

Tom stands and points his gun at the door. "Is he alone?"

"He has a girl with him. She looks drugged."

The door opens and Aaron freezes in the doorframe. He drops the girl beside him and she crumples to her knees. Aaron puts both hands up. "Stop. Stay quiet."

Tom frowns. "What?"

"I'm going to step inside and close the door."

Tom gives his head a shake. "Excuse me?"

"You might want to help her. She needs water." Aaron nods at the girl he brought in with him.

"What the hell?" Abbie says from behind Tom.

"We need to do this fast. If they discover the light's on…"

A prickles cascades down Tom's spine and he cracks his neck. "Where's Emily?"

Aaron tilts his head, pausing as though considering his answer. "I don't know."

"Liar."

"We don't have time for this," Aaron says.

Tom leaps across the floor and jams his gun under Aaron's chin. "Like fuck we don't."

"I told you." Aaron stares directly into Tom's eyes. "I don't know where Isabella is. Or is it Irina?"

Tom swallows. "What did you say?"

"If I don't get a girl out of here now and into that bullring they're all dead. And so are we. Do you understand?"

"How did you—"

"I'll explain later. This isn't the time. Tom."

Fuck. Tom grits his teeth and steps aside to let Aaron get the next girl. "Who are you?"

Aaron unclips the tubes from a cannula in the girl's hand and hauls her over his shoulder. "Go back inside the club. I'll find you."

"Are you insane? I'm not leaving these girls here, drugged and being sold like cattle."

"They aren't." Aaron opens the door. "I'm looking after them."

"You expect me to believe—"

Aaron sits the girl against the door and moves in front of Tom. "Indigo."

Tom's pulse quivers. "Pardon?"

"Indigo." Aaron raises his eyebrow a fraction.

"It's the sixth colour of the rainbow." *Well, fuck.*

Aaron nods. "Meet me in the club." He picks the girl up and walks out.

Abbie puts her hand on Tom's shoulder. "What was all that about?"

Tom pinches the bridge of his nose. "James?"

"Yeah… I'm researching."

"Call me old fashioned but shouldn't you have done this research… oh I don't know… before now?"

"I did. I found nothing. And we got no heads up."

"Grant?" Abbie stands in front of him. "What's going on?"

Tom clenches his jaw. "He's MI6."

"What?"

"Would have been nice to know." Tom grabs her elbow. "Let's go."

"We can't just leave—"

"They'll be fine."

"They will?"

"Yes. James however... I'm going to shoot."

———

Tom paces three steps one way and three steps the other in his dark corner of the club. Abbie leans against the wall staring onto the dancefloor, but her eyes appear stuck and glossy.

"Abs?" Tom leans against the wall next to her.

"How did MI6 have an operation going and we had no idea, Grant?"

"Happens all the time between agencies. Everyone wants to be the hero. I mean... we didn't exactly notify them. Did we?"

"No, but..." Her eyes widen and she moves closer to Tom.

Aaron pushes through the dance floor and beckons to Tom. "Come with me."

They walk through the humid, smoky club, Aaron leads the way towards a private room off to the side of the VIP booths. He opens the door and ushers them inside. Tom walks into a tiny, circular room enclosed in purple, crushed velvet curtains. There's a circular sofa in the same velvet in the middle of the floor around a table presenting a chilled bottle of Grey Goose and an ice bucket.

"You want to know why I didn't say anything when you nabbed me. Right?" Aaron leans against the closed door and folds his arms over his chest.

"Among other things." Tom sits on the back of the couch and mirrors Aaron's folded arms.

Abbie wanders the room, dragging her hand along the plush sofa cushions.

"Tonight's the night I've been working towards. I needed to see girls being physically sold. I needed to get that evidence. It's crucial."

"Where are the girls now?" Tom asks.

"They're in a van being taken to safety. Their buyers were my agents."

"Ask him about the two girls Isabella found the night she worked in the brothel." James whispers through Tom's earpiece.

"What about the other girls? The two Iz found inside the brothel?"

"I had them transported out the following morning. They're in a safe house."

"Explains the truck I saw," James says.

Tom glares at Aaron. "And Isabella?"

"I told you. I don't know. She never came back. I thought you'd pulled your op."

"But you attacked her in your office." Tom clenches his fists by his sides.

"I needed to stay under. I was trying to get her to leave before it got dangerous for her."

"Maybe if you'd told us what was going on the night we got you, we could have worked together on this. Instead... Isabella is god knows where, and I'm standing here in the middle of a shit fight that has nothing to do with me."

"I wanted to. I didn't have the authority. This whole operation was to find the head of this ring."

"And?"

"And tonight I was about to be given that… *privilege*."

"And what a privilege it is." A voice says. The purple curtains around the room part and the man with the lime green shirt and too tight jeans steps out. "Hello lads. And lady." He nods towards Abbie and holds his gun at Aaron. "I knew there was something odd about you." He looks at Tom and winks. "I'd still like to steal your wallet though."

"You?" Tom frowns. "You're running this?"

"There's a lot of money in pretty girls. And given they don't interest me I don't get distracted." He laughs at his own joke. "We haven't been properly acquainted." He gives a slight bow in Tom's direction. "Zane. And you are?"

"Pissed off."

"Yes. I must say I'm a tad perturbed." He inspects his fingernails before smiling at Aaron. "You cost us a truckload tonight."

"Us?" Abbie says.

Zane glares at Aaron. "Us." He squeezes the trigger and a gunshot blasts. Aaron slams against the door before crumpling to the ground. Zane swings his arm around and points the gun at Tom's face.

Fuck. "Aaron?" Tom's eyes never leave Zane's smirking face. "If you know something you need to tell me." Tom clenches his fists.

"I... don't know...where she is."

"Do you know who does?" Tom's eyes move from Zane to Aaron. Blood darkens his once crisp white shirt.

"No." He coughs and blood dribbles down the side of his face from his mouth.

"You must. It makes no sen—"

"Grant!"

Tom turns to find a middle aged woman with a gun to the back of Abbie's head. The woman has a sharp jaw and her dark grey hair is pulled into a bun on top of her head. Her flowing, peacock blue silk caftan belies the hardness in her face.

"No-one disrespects my boy." The woman glares at Aaron, now gasping and spluttering on the floor. "How dare you come into our house and mess it all up. Who do you think you are?"

A sudden movement in Tom's peripheral is accompanied with a laboured breath from Aaron before another gunshot blasts and Zane falls at Tom's feet.

"The Scrabble board..." Aaron's voice is hoarse.

"No!" The woman shrieks, pulls Abbie against her and fires at Aaron. Three shots slam into him and the gun he used to shoot Zane spins on the floor beside him. She wraps her forearm around Abbie's throat and presses her gun into the side of her face.

Tom swipes his hand across his back and grips his gun. He pulls it out and moves to Abbie and the woman. He presses the gun into her temple. "Drop it."

The woman stares at her dead son on the floor. "Zane? Baby?"

Tom pushes the muzzle harder against her head. "He can't

hear you now."

The woman's hand shakes and tears roll down her cheeks. "I should kill you both."

"You won't have time, old woman."

"Zaney?" The woman's breaths hasten and she adjusts her finger on the trigger.

Abbie closes her eyes. "Grant…"

The woman blinks and takes a loud sniffly breath in through her nose. She takes a step backwards, dragging Abbie with her. "I'm walking out of here with your slutty side piece."

"The fuck you are."

She smiles. "I think we both know you won't shoot me." She takes another step, Abbie stumbles but the woman keeps the gun against her face.

"Do we?"

"If you shoot me… everything your dead friend over there worked for is for nothing. Isn't that right?"

"The others have the girls." Tom tilts his head.

She laughs. "They know nothing of anything. I'm the one you all need. Or this goes on and on."

"She's right, Grant. Greater good."

Tom looks at Abbie and a glint in her eye along with an imperceptible nod gives him reassurance.

"Ah yes. The greater good." The woman throws another glance at Zane. "We all make sacrifices." She slips back through the curtain with Abbie, who gives Tom a wink before the purple velvet swallows her.

Tom shoves his gun into his waistband and runs to Aaron. He slides to his knees and grabs his lapels. "Aaron." His head drops as Tom lifts him from the floor. "Aaron..." Tom grips the shirt harder and clenches his jaw. "Where the fuck is she?" He shouts in Aaron's lifeless face. He drops his head against Aaron's shoulder and lets out a groan of anguish and pain but most of all anger. He lays Aaron back onto the floor and rifles through his pockets. He finds a balled up tissue and a single Scrabble tile. X.

"I doubt this is a time for playing board games, Grant." Abbie stands over Tom, her bottom lip swollen and bleeding.

Tom drops to his backside and leans against the wall. "Where's the old woman?" He plonks his head against the wall and closes his eyes.

"Who knows. I winded her and gave her a leg sweep out in the fire escape. She's pretty feisty for an old bat. She disappeared through some other door and I came back here." She presses two fingers to her bottom lip. "Though she got me a good one in the face."

Tom rotates the X in his fingers and stares at it. *The Scrabble board.* "James?" He taps his ear. "You with us?"

"Yeah. I'm here. Bloody hell, Tom. One day your gut's gonna betray you and you'll end up dead."

"Yeah one day. Listen... are there still people at the brothel?"

"Yep."

"I want the Scrabble board."

"Excuse me?"

"In Aaron's office there's a Scrabble board. I want it. The whole game. Get it to my flat."

"In the mood for a games night?" James chuckles.

"Just do it." Tom pulls the earpiece out and throws it across the room. "Idiot."

20

ISABELLA

Isabella leans forward, her neck strains as she pulls against the skirting behind her. A loud crack echoes through the dark room and both her hands pull free from the wall, though still bolted to what she assumes is a broken piece of the skirting. Her heart pumps as she falls to her backside and squirms to get her hands in front of her. There is no light under the door which means she has time. She bucks her hips and slides the piece of wood under and around her feet.

She slumps against the wall to take a breath, irritated at how much energy that simple action took from her. But, her belly rumbles and it reminds her she hasn't eaten in days. She holds her hands out in front of her and squints through the darkness. She's still cuffed and attached to the wood from the skirting, but it's quite a skinny shard…

She lays her hands flat on the floor, the wood between them

and stamps a foot on top of it. She grits her teeth and yanks both hands up, keeping her foot on the wood. It bends but doesn't break. She relaxes and catches her breath, just as a light goes on outside the room. With the little time she has to complete her goal dwindling, she yanks her hands up again and this time a satisfying crack sounds and her hands come apart, albeit with a shard of wood attached to each set of cuffs dangling from her wrists.

Shadows appear against the light coming under the door, and Isabella grabs two handfuls of kitty litter and presses her back against the wall alongside the door. The tell tale squeak of the door handle sounds and Isabella holds her breath.

She pushes herself harder against the wall as hoodie man moves into the room and stops in the middle. The sharp intake of breath from him brings a smile to Isabella's lips and as he turns back towards the door she throws the two handfuls of kitty litter at his eyes and lunges at him, punching the shards of wood into his gut.

He grasps at his face and a strangled yelp comes from his masked mouth as she drives him backwards into the wall. He slides to the floor and Isabella runs from the room, into the light. She blinks and squeezes her eyes open and shut a few times to get used to the onslaught of bright light, shielding her face with her hands.

She pulls the gag from around her face and takes it out of her mouth, coughing as she stumbles through the flat to the front door.

Wait a second.

She stops short of the door, blinks again and looks around the flat. Tom's flat. Her flat. *Their* flat.

Something heavy smashes into her head from behind, and her confusion is replaced with empty darkness.

21

TOM

Tom slams into his flat and scans the room, his eyes rest on James, sitting at the antique desk with a laptop open. "You!"

"Now, Tom." Martha steps in front of him. "There was nothing to suggest—"

"Don't." He glares at Martha before looking back at James. "At what point James, did you skim over the fact Aaron was an MI6 agent? Conducting an MI6 operation?" He moves across the flat as James stands, putting both hands up in surrender. "You were surveilling a *fucking* MI6 agent!" He grabs James by the shirt and twists it in his hands. "Who is now dead, by the way." Tom checks his watch. *07:00.* "And for the record I haven't slept in twenty four hours."

James wraps both hands around Tom's fist and pries his hand off his shirt. "He was obviously very good at his job."

Tom's neck prickles. "Unlike you, James. Although you have

been quite busy with your secret little meetings…" He glances at Martha who doesn't look at him.

James huffs. "Well… I…"

"Yes?"

Abbie puts a hand on Tom's arm. "We've got more important things to deal with, wouldn't you agree?"

"Abigail is right, Tom." Martha's voice has an edge to it Tom knows too well. "Maybe you should have a sleep while we work."

"I don't need a goddamn sleep. I need to find Isabella." He intertwines both hands behind his head and turns to stare out the window. "Do we have the Scrabble board?"

Martha sighs. "Yes." She hands the board to Abbie.

Tom pushes Martha's stack of papers and files off his armchair before sitting and swiping an arm across the coffee table, sending more papers and books cascading to the floor. "Give it."

"You know you're a real dickhead when you're angry." Abbie drops the Scrabble board on the coffee table and sits next to it with her hand flat on the lid. "So stop it."

"Abs, get your hand off the box."

"No."

"No?"

A knock at the door silences everyone, and Martha opens it. "Yes?"

No one answers her and Tom looks up to see Edward staring at Martha. *Just what I fucking need right now.* "What's up Ed?" Tom goes to the door and crosses his arms. "Well?"

"Ahh... well I was wondering if..." His voice trails off again and he looks back at Martha, who has returned to her desk.

"Her flat's being renovated so my... Aunt is staying with me."

"She's not your Aunt."

"Excuse me?" The hardness in Edward's voice stabs at Tom somewhere in the back of his neck. "An expert on my family tree are you?"

Edward meets Tom's eyes and gives him a strange, half smile. "No. Of course not. Sorry, you ... don't look anything alike."

"Did you want something?" Tom notices Edward's eyes are red and watery. "Have you been crying?"

Edward blinks. "What? No. No... allergies."

"Well, if you came here for antihistamine I don't have any. So... goodbye then." Tom closes the door in Edward's face and leans against it. "Fucking weirdo."

"Grant. Look." Abbie points at the Scrabble board. It's turned face down and a bunch of numbers are scrawled on the back of the board. "Do you think these numbers are what we're looking for?"

Tom looks over Abbie's shoulder at the numbers written in pen on the board next to what looks like a doodle of three peas in a pod.

842764

15522

1845

"James." Tom grabs the board and throws it to James. "Figure these numbers out. Start with map coordinates for London—"

"They don't look like coordina—"

Tom's temple pulses. "Well fuck, James! Maybe he wrote them in code. Maybe they're an address *and* coordinates. Maybe it's the phone number of the girl he screwed behind the bike sheds at school when he was fifteen. I don't know. Figure it out. And find out why he likes peas."

Abbie stands in front of Tom. "Hey…"

Tom pushes a thumb and forefinger into his eyes and lets out a breath. "I'm going for a walk."

He grabs a coat and glances at Martha. She purses her lips and says nothing.

She doesn't have to.

He walks out of the flat and slams the door behind him. Pointless, but it feels good to make noise. The door across the hall also opens. *Not now…*

"Ah, Tom. How lovely." Lorna squints at him. "My, you look tired, dear."

"I'm fresh as a daisy Lorna."

Lorna nods and looks up and down the hall.

"Has Pebbles got out again?"

"Dear?" Lorna raises her eyebrows.

"Have you lost the cat?"

"Oh, no no… I was expecting a delivery of kitty litter… it's too heavy for me to carry home so I have it delivered, but well… it doesn't seem to have arrived."

"Are you sure it was today?"

"Last night actually. By five they said." She clasps her hands in front of her. "I don't suppose…"

"Sure. Yes. I'll pick some up for you." *Why the hell not.*

"You really are a lifesaver, Tom."

Tom gives her a forced smile. "Don't be so sure." He nods at her and walks down the stairs. As he reaches the bottom his phone pings. He reads the name on his screen and rolls his eyes. *Martha.*

Mike is waiting for you. Get there by 7:30. Don't argue with me.

———

Tom walks into Mike's office at seven thirty five and sits on the sofa against the side wall. Mike drops the book he was reading and takes his glasses off.

"You're five minutes late."

Tom holds up his coffee. "There was a queue."

"I see."

"What are you reading?" Tom nods at the book in front of Mike.

"Harry Potter and the Order of the Phoenix."

Tom raises his eyebrows and sips his coffee. "Not the answer I was expecting."

"Escapism is good for the soul. Maybe you should try it sometime."

"You don't think I try?"

Mike leans back in his chair and steeples his forefingers under his chin. "When was the last time you slept?"

Tom shrugs. "Last time I was sleepy."

"You look exhausted."

"That's not sleepy."

"Have you been able to speak to Isabella?"

"She's still missing." Tom peels at the cup where the cardboard joins. "Or... left more likely."

"But didn't you say—"

"Yeah but I was wrong. She must have left. Nothing else makes sense now." The emptiness in his chest widens and coffee won't fill the void. He takes the last mouthful and tosses the cup into the bin.

"Now?"

"I thought she'd been taken. I was wrong."

"Maybe she needed some space."

Tom looks up. "Excuse me?"

"Well she's been controlled her whole life. Even when she escaped and came to the UK she had to pretend and hide. Right?"

"Yes."

"So maybe she wanted to figure out who she really is? Given she's been made to be other things for so many years."

"I never stop her being who she wants to be."

"I'm not saying you do. But independence for her would be hugely important I would imagine."

Tom leans over his knees and runs his hands through his hair. "Tell me this Mike. Would she do all that without saying goodbye? Without telling me what she needed? Leaving behind her necklace? A necklace I gave to her? Does that make sense to you?"

Mike taps his fingers on the hardcover of Harry Potter. "That does seem unusual."

"Turn her phone off? Not respond to text messages? Not turn up to work?" The more Tom throws out, the more his stomach twists in a knot. "But she wasn't taken so...I should go. This is pointless."

"Wait a minute." Mike scribbles on a pad. "Here. Take two of these." He rips a prescription off the pad and holds it out to Tom. "And sleep. And come back in a day or two. You need more than this brief conversation. But knowing you, doing so now is pointless."

Tom takes the prescription. "What's this?"

"Sleeping pills. One way or another you need sleep, Tom."

22

ISABELLA

The clatter of a cup and saucer prompts Isabella to open her eyes. She blinks through the fog of her brain and sits upright on a dining chair, placed in the middle of the lounge. Her head pounds and nausea swells in her gut. Her mouth is gagged again, and her hands are tied behind the back of the chair. Her eyes focus in the brightly lit room, and rest on a figure sat in the armchair sipping from a teacup.

"Edward?" she mumbles through the gag, the name coming out as a garbled murmur. She jerks her hands, but they don't give.

He ignores her, continuing to sip his tea and read from a newspaper balanced on his knee. She looks around the lounge, a perfect replica of her and Tom's lounge, exactly the same but still different. Tom's mother's desk is the only thing completely wrong. *What on Earth?*

"Edward!" she forces the words through her gag, still muffled but louder and clearer than before.

"Wouldn't mind some cake," he mumbles, standing and walking into the kitchen.

Isabella's blood thunders through her ears and she jerks her knee back and kicks the coffee table, splashing Edward's tea everywhere.

Edward sighs from the kitchen and walks to the table with a dishcloth. "Honestly," he whispers to himself as he wipes up the spilled tea.

She musters every ounce of strength, screams through the gag and kicks the table again, this time it bashes into Edward's knees.

He stands upright and throws the dishcloth onto the table. "That hurt!"

Isabella pushes herself forward, but gets nowhere due to being tied to the chair.

Edward walks to her and slaps her hard across the face. "Stop it. You're acting like an animal. I didn't tie your feet to the chair, but maybe I should?"

Isabella stares at him as the prickly sting of his slap travels down her face. She stops wriggling. *Fine. I'll play.*

"Now," he says. "I can ungag you and let you have some tea. But if you scream or yell I'll have no choice but to silence you. Deal?" Edward and raises both eyebrows. "Do we have a deal, Isabella?"

She nods.

Edward claps his hands together once. "Splendid. Your tea should still be nice and hot." He reaches behind her head and unties the gag, taking it away from her mouth.

The moment her mouth is free she takes in a deep breath and screams. She shouts for Tom, police, the postman— whoever might hear her.

Edward turns from where he started pouring tea from a pot and slaps her across the same cheek. "Shut your fucking mouth."

Isabella presses her lips closed and squints as the familiar sting lasts longer this time. As is subsides she clears her throat. "Why don't you just gag me again?"

"I'm trying to show you I'll trust you… if you behave. Now, if you scream again I *will* drug you and gag you. Understood?"

"Where's Tom?"

He leans in to her. "Who cares?" he whispers. He grabs the tea he half poured and pushes the cup against her closed mouth and tips. "Drink the damn tea, Isabella." She keeps her lips closed. "For goodness sakes. Now it's all down your front." He drops the teacup onto its saucer with a clatter and stalks back to his armchair. He takes a deep breath and closes his eyes for a moment. When he opens them again, he smiles and appears calm.

"What's in it?" Isabella's voice is dry and strained. She ignores the burning tea seeping through her clothing onto her skin.

"In it?"

"The tea. Is it spiked?"

Edward laughs his familiar laugh that Isabella always thought was strange but friendly. *Not anymore.*

"No Isabella. It isn't spiked."

"Where am I?"

"You're at home of course."

She looks around the room. "That's not Tom's desk."

"Ah yes. That was particularly hard to find. I had to make do unfortunately. Antiques can be difficult."

"This is your flat?"

"*Our* flat Isabella."

Isabella's stomach squeezes. "I want Tom."

"He does seem to be the number one choice doesn't he?"

Isabella frowns. "Pardon?" Her head is still woozy and she can't quite trust that this isn't some whacky dream.

"It'll all become clear soon enough."

"Does Tom know where I am?"

Edward snorts. "Do you think I'm insane?"

"Is that a trick question?"

Edward frowns. "Let's get one thing clear. I am *not insane!*" His face turns almost purple and spittle gathers at the sides of his mouth. "Understood?" He grips the arms of his chair and his fingertips pale.

Isabella stares into his eyes and keeps her face neutral. "Whatever you say."

"Lovely." He grins and picks up his tea again. "But no. I haven't informed Tom of your whereabouts." He giggles a weird, high pitched giggle. "Imagine his reaction. No, no. I'm not prepared for that quite yet."

"And if I scream again?"

"I shoot the old lady down the hall, snap her cat's neck and then shoot Tom while he sleeps."

"I see."

"So, I wouldn't scream if I were you. It could get messy." He giggles again.

"Why am I here?"

"Because it's where you're meant to be."

"How do you figure that?"

"Like I said… everything will become clear soon enough." He smiles again and flaps his newspaper before turning his attention back to it.

"You expect me to just sit here quietly?"

"Ah, of course." He springs from his chair and grabs the gag.

Isabella lets him tie it around her head. *I need thinking time.*

"There." He pulls it tighter than before, but Isabella doesn't flinch.

Fuck you.

23

TOM

Tom knocks on Lorna's door and leans his head against the doorframe. His eyes are scratchy and exhaustion washes over him.

The door opens. "Ah. That was speedy."

Tom holds up the plastic bag with the kitty litter inside. "Where can I put this for you?"

Lorna leads the way into her flat to the kitchen. "Just here is fine, dear." She pats the worktop and Tom plonks it down for her. "Thank you, Tom. My old arms can't carry it anymore." She notices the other, black plastic bag Tom is carrying. "What else did you get yourself?"

Anesthetic. "Oh.." He peers at the bag in his other hand.

"Sorry dear. It's none of my business. I forget how nosey I can be." She chuckles.

He smiles. "It's apples." He turns to leave.

"Would you like tea?"

He rubs his eyes with his thumb and index finger. "Thanks Lorna, but I need to go home."

"Of course, yes. It's just…"

Tom reaches the front door and stops. He swallows his irritation and turns back to her. "Just?"

"Well, something seems amiss."

"How so?"

"Well, I was in the hall a few moments ago chasing after Pebbles. Well I say chasing but hobbling more like." She stops to laugh. "Anyway… I could have sworn I heard a woman scream."

"Scream?"

"Yes, you know… like in those horror films?"

"As in… maybe someone was watching a horror film with the volume up?" Tom raises his eyebrows.

"Well… yes I suppose they could have been… It sounded like it came from Edward's flat."

He would *watch horror films at eight in the morning.*

"I'm sure it's nothing." Tom rubs the back of his neck.

"But—"

"I'm so sorry to run Lorna, but I really need to sleep." The second bag he carries knocks against his leg to highlight his lie.

"Of course. Thank you dear. Oh and keep an eye out for Pebbles? She's gone wandering again."

"I will."

"Do come in for tea another time. And bring Isabella too."

A shovel full of sand drops into Tom's gut. "I'm sure she'd love to come."

Lorna gives him a wave with her gnarled fingers and closes the door.

He steps towards his flat before stopping and glancing towards Edward's door. He trudges down the hall and raises a hand to knock. *Horror film.* He drops his hand.

———

"That didn't take long," James remarks as Tom walks into his flat.

"Timing me were you?" He heads towards his room. "Where're Abbie and Martha?"

"Oh they had to… a meeting."

Tom stops and turns. "A meeting?"

"Yep." James concentrates on the computer screen in front of him.

"Loads of meetings going on without my involvement. Wouldn't you say?"

James keeps typing and says nothing.

"James?"

"Martha wanted to go and check the surveillance op on her house. I think she wants to go home."

Tom grinds his teeth until his molars hurt. "I see."

"And she asked me about activity since she's been here and well… there hasn't been any. So I figured…"

"You figured."

"Abbie is with her."

A pang of resentment and irritation stabs Tom through the gut. "You know what? Fine. I'm done caring. I'm done with all of it."

James looks at him impassively. "What's in the bag?"

Tom looks down at the bag that, until this point, he hasn't realised he's holding in a sweaty palm. "Soap." He walks into the bathroom and slams the door shut behind him. As he leans over the vanity and blinks at himself in the mirror, voices float in from the lounge.

No sooner does he sit on the floor and pull the bottle of whisky from the plastic bag, Martha's voice comes through the closed bathroom door.

"Tom?"

Tom plonks his head back against the wall and closes his eyes. "Yep?"

"What are you doing?"

"Is that common etiquette when someone's in the bathroom?"

"The shower isn't on."

"I'm..." He glances at the whisky bottle, his mouth filling with saliva. "Busy."

"Did Mike give you something to help you sleep?"

Tom stands and yanks the bathroom door open. "Did you ask him to?"

"Of course not. One look at you would have given him all the cause he needed."

He bites his tongue.

Martha leans on the wall across from him. "I'm concerned."

"You have a funny way of showing it."

"Excuse me?"

"Did you or did you not go back to your house?"

"I didn't." She holds up a takeaway coffee.

Tom widens his eyes and waits.

"But I will be."

Tom flings his hand out. "And there it is."

"Nothing has happened there for over twenty four hours."

"Well *yippee*. Maybe your stalker got sick of it after three months? Or maybe he has a sniffle and plans to come back bigger and better tonight? Or maybe he realised you weren't there and is waiting for you to return?"

"You're obviously stressed with your space being invaded and I—"

"I have no issue with you being here. You know that."

"And yet here you are, not sleeping, snapping at everyone and hiding in the bathroom."

"I needed the facilities."

"The toilet seat is closed."

"For fuck's sake." Tom steps back and slams the door. "Do whatever you want. I don't care anymore." As he says the words to the closed door, they twist in his chest.

Silence meets him from the other side and he sighs.

After a few moments to ground himself, he walks into the lounge and finds Abbie sitting alone watching the TV with the sound down.

"Where are they?" Tom folds his arms.

"They're out," she says. "Martha walked out, pointed at James and the door said *now* and they both left."

"So, James is with her?'

"Yep."

Tom nods. *Better than nothing.*

Abbie flicks the TV off with the remote and turns to Tom. "So what's the deal with you two?"

"James and me?"

"No. Martha and you."

Tom stills. "She's the boss."

Abbie snorts. "Please. The way you two interact. It's more than that."

Tom sits on the edge of Martha's desk. "We're family."

"What? No you aren't. You were a foster…"

Tom looks up from the floor, straight into Abbie's eyes.

Abbie sucks in a breath. "Noooo.."

"I trust you can keep that in the vault?"

Abbie rolls her eyes. "There may still be a speck of room in there."

Tom stands. "I'm going to shower and sleep."

"We won't let anything happen to her, Grant."

He stops but doesn't turn around. "I know." He walks into the bathroom and turns the shower on. He doesn't get in, resuming his original position on the floor next to the vanity he picks up the whisky bottle. He grabs his phone and presses Isabella's number. The voicemail message plays, and he waits for the beep. "Tell me you're okay. That's all I want." He ends the call and drops the phone on the floor next to him.

24

ISABELLA

Isabella chews on the gag as Edward sighs, turns her phone off and drops it on the coffee table.

He puts both hands over his heart and smiles at her. "He's fretting. Bless."

She bites harder on the gag and flares her nostrils.

Edward tilts his head. "You seem to want to chat."

She nods slowly, glaring at him.

He crouches in front of her and cups her chin in his hand. "Pretty Kitten. Are you missing your big Tom cat?" he whispers, his stale breath all over her face.

She leans away from him and twists her face out of his hand.

He grabs the knot at the back of the gag and pushes her head down while he unties it.

The gag slips from her mouth and she resists the urge to scream. *I need to know what this is all about.* "How did you get into my phone?"

"I watched you punch your code in before I took you. You know, I would have thought you'd be more aware. Being a beautiful woman in a big city." He shrugs. "I guess having Tom around to look after you all the time makes you complacent."

A surge builds in Isabella's chest at the mention of being looked after. *I can look after myself.* "What did Tom say?"

"He wants to know you're okay."

She closes her eyes but the image of him drinking straight from a whisky bottle make her open them again. "When will this end?"

"Soon."

"Are you going to kill me?"

Edward's head snaps around and he peers at her. "Why would I kill you?"

Isabella jerks a brow. "You've tied me up, drugged me, gagged me, won't let me leave... need I go on?"

Edward stands, walks to the window, and stares out.

"So I'll ask again. When will this end?"

Edward keeps his back to her. "My life should have been very different."

The change of subject stumps Isabella for a moment. *Okay...* "What happened?"

He turns. "You don't care."

She watches him and says nothing.

"My father hated me."

"I'm sorry."

"No you aren't."

"Why did he hate you?"

He shrugs and wanders around the lounge. "I wasn't his.

Mum couldn't have kids... she convinced him to adopt a baby with her." He stops and puts his hand up as though answering a question at school.

"I'm sure he didn't hate you."

"He broke my arm in three places. He used to make me sit in a freezing cold bath if my room was untidy. He knocked me out once because I asked for a glass of water." He watches Isabella for a moment. *"Need I go on?"*

"What about your mother?"

"That weak, insipid excuse for a parent." He shakes his head. "It's her fault I ended up in prison."

"You went to prison?"

"Momentarily." He spins and walks to the kitchen. "Tea?"

"How do you go to prison momentarily?"

"I'll put a straw in it so I don't have to feed it to you. Would that be alright, Kitten?"

"Edward?"

He looks up at her as he fiddles with the teabags. "Yes?"

"Maybe you let me go home and I never tell anyone about this."

Edward laughs, a high pitched, almost maniacal giggle. "Ahhh you're just the cutest thing. No... you aren't going anywhere. I need you here."

"Why?"

Edward opens the fridge. "No milk." He slams it shut. "I'll need to get some. This really is quite inconvenient..."

"There's some in our flat."

"Our flat?"

"Tom and—"

"This is your flat." Edward's face is red, a vein bulges across his forehead. "Do you understand? You belong here." He slaps the kitchen worktop with his palm.

"Of course. My mistake."

Edward's face lights up and he smiles. "No bother." He walks to Isabella and picks up the gag.

"I won't scream."

"I need to get milk and I just don't trust you." He jams the gag into her mouth and ties it. "But I won't be long. Maybe if you're a good girl while I'm out I'll untie you."

Isabella rolls her eyes.

"You know, when I was a lad I drained all the blood out of a fox."

Isabella swallows her repulsion and stares past him at the window.

"Just some fun trivia for you. If we're going to make this work we need to get to know one another." He leans down and pecks a kiss on her forehead before grabbing a glass from the kitchen and leaving.

Isabella stares at the closed door. *Literally insane.*

———

Isabella wakes with a start. Her neck aches from being lolled on her shoulder. She looks around the lounge, stopping on Edward, standing beside the antique desk with a creepy grin.

"Hello Kitten."

She glares at him and bites down on her gag.

"So," Edward says, pushing himself off the desk and walking

towards her. He carries a shoebox. "I thought you needed some convincing to do as you're told." He drops the shoebox on the coffee table. "Shall I open it?"

Isabella's heart speeds up, and she stares at the box.

Edward sits on the sofa and looks at the box as though it's a long-lost friend. "I figured I took the litter so..." He shrugs and flips the lid off the box.

A lifeless, grey furry little body lays inside the box. The little cat's head is bent at an unnatural angle.

Isabella squeezes her eyes shut as tears burn the edges and her throat aches. She lets out a moan through the gag.

Edward lifts Pebbles from the box by the scruff of her broken neck. "Take it as a warning, Kitten." He drops her back into the box and puts the lid back on.

Isabella sobs. Her nose blocks, and she draws in big breaths through the congestion.

"Calm down, you'll pass out from lack of oxygen." He claps his hands once. "Now, we still need that milk."

She narrows her eyes at him.

He goes to the kitchen, slides the box into the cupboard above the fridge and picks up a glass. "That cat will come in handy, no doubt."

25

TOM

"Grant!"

Loud banging rouses Tom from sleep and he opens his eyes to be confronted with thick steam.

The banging on the bathroom door continues. "I swear to God, Grant. I'll kick the damn thing down. Answer me!"

Tom shakes his head and scrambles to the shower. "Abs, calm down. I'm fine." He turns the water off and sits on the edge of the bath. He focuses on the unopened bottle of whisky on the floor next to where he fell asleep.

"Open the door so I can see you."

Tom opens the door and leans against the doorframe. "I'm fine."

Abbie looks him up and down. "You were in the shower for an hour and a half in your clothes?"

"Actually... I was asleep on the floor for an hour and a half."

"You what?"

"So if you'll excuse me… I still need a shower." He closes the door and leans against it.

"You'll be the death of me, Grant."

"Or me," he whispers. He picks up the whisky and takes the lid off. The urge to bring the bottle to his mouth almost wins. He squeezes the neck of it and swallows the saliva pooling on the back of his tongue. "Fuck." He lays the bottle in the sink and leans on the vanity as the whisky empties into the drain. "Get it together."

He pulls his clothes off and turns the shower back on.

Minutes later, he walks into the lounge. Martha looks up from her computer screen. "You look slightly more human."

James waves but says nothing, concentrating on the computer screen in front of him.

"Had a sauna." He sits on the edge of his armchair.

"Did you sleep?"

"Got an hour in."

"On the bathroom floor," Abbie says as she rifles through papers on the coffee table.

"Thanks for the input, Abs."

Martha walks to Tom, stopping directly in front of him. "Are you alright?"

"Yep."

A knock at the door comes as a relief and Martha claps her hands together once. "I'll get that. Why don't you make yourself a coffee."

He goes to the kitchen as she opens the door.

"Hello!"

Tom squeezes his eyes shut at the sound of Edward's voice.

"Yes hello. Can we help you?" Martha puts her phone voice on and it makes Tom smile despite wanting to sit in a cupboard until everyone leaves him alone.

"I do hope so. I seem to have run out of milk."

Tom looks over to see Edward holding up a glass, grinning at Martha.

"I'm sure we can oblige." Martha blocks the doorway.

Edward smiles at Tom. "Tom."

"Ed."

"My, it's crowded in there isn't it?" He nods at the inside of the flat.

"My Aunt likes to work from home. What do you need milk for? Baking a cake?"

Edward's eyes harden for a fleeting moment, but it's enough to prickle Tom's skin. *Creep.*

"A cake? No… just making some tea."

Martha clears her throat. "What did you say your name was?"

Edward sticks a hand out. "How rude of me. Edward. Morgan. And… you are?" Something like a smirk crosses his face.

Tom clenches his jaw.

"Martha." She doesn't offer her surname.

"I must say it's absolutely delightful to meet you properly."

"We haven't met before?" Martha pulls her hand back from Edward.

The smile disappears from Edward's face. "No. Why do you ask?" He stares at her.

"You were busy when he was here the other day. That's

where you know him." Tom says, stepping forward. *Give me a reason to punch your lights out.*

"Yes. That must be it." Martha holds a hand out for the glass Edward brought. "You wanted milk?"

"Yes. Lovely." He hands the glass over and moves his stare to Tom. "You look very tired, Tom. Is everything alright with you and Isabella?"

"Is that your business?"

"I'm merely being neighbourly." He steps closer to Tom. "I would like it if we could be friends."

Tom stays where he is and squares his shoulders. "I'll keep that in mind."

Martha reappears with the glass of milk. "Here you go."

Edwards takes the glass. "Thank you ever so much. Really wonderful of you."

"Bye neighbour," Tom smiles as though they're best friends.

"Tata!" Edward closes the door behind him.

"I really hate that guy."

Martha grabs a folder full of papers from her desk and gives them to James. "Maybe you could do that other task, James?"

James takes the papers and shoots a glance at Tom before peering back at Martha. "Now?"

"No James, I was thinking next week."

Tom folds his arms. "What other task?"

"No worries. I just… yeah sure… going now. Wanna come for a drive Abbie?"

"Why not." She winks at Tom before grabbing her coat and following James out the door.

Tom lets the silence linger for a moment before turning to Martha. "Care to explain?"

"I must say, your neighbour is rather odd."

"No shit. Nice sidestep too by the way."

"Watch your attitude."

Tom holds his hands up in surrender. "Keep your petticoat on. What's with you?"

"Sorry. That was uncalled for. I'm feeling a bit caged in. I'd like to go home."

 Tom drops into his armchair and exhaustion blankets him. He closes his eyes to stop them stinging. "That's not it but I'm tired of asking."

"You should really get more sleep, Tom."

Tom nods. "Now, what do we know about Zane and his mother?"

"Ah, yes. James came up with the goods. I really can't fault the lad on his techy skills." She holds a folder out to Tom.

"Let's not praise him too highly. He'll buy himself a cape." He takes the folder.

Martha sits behind her desk. "Zane's mother's name is Benita. And she was married to a Russian. Pieter."

Tom looks up. "A Russian."

"Yes. Interesting, wouldn't you say?"

"They aren't married anymore?"

"He disappeared not long after the fall in ninety one."

Tom widens his eyes and his jaw clenches of its own accord.

"Relax Tom. We can't find any connection to Isabella or her father. It seems he was an oligarch of sorts. Benita now lives the lavish lifestyle as a result. But it explains his disappearance after the fall... depending which side of politics he sat on."

"Are we sure that—"

"Positive. Isabella's father and Pieter had nothing to do with one another."

"That doesn't discount anyone still being after Iz."

Martha chews on her bottom lip. "No... I suppose that's true."

Tom's stomach drops. "She could be anywhere by now."

"She isn't."

"How do you know? Martha?"

A silence descends as they eye each other. Martha finally bows her head. "I don't."

"You don't." Tom leans over his knees and claws at his hair.

"You're jumping to conclusions."

Tom springs out of his chair. "Well maybe someone has to. She's been missing for days. I can accept the fact she might have left me..." He swallows. "But she would have at least answered a call or text. And she wouldn't have just walked out on her job."

"Agreed."

"So we need to find the old woman." He rips a page from the folder. "You stay here. I haven't forgotten you're in danger either. The safest place for you is in this apartment block." He draws a square in the air with his finger.

Martha sighs.

Tom narrows his eyes until she sits at her desk.

He nods once, grabs his gun from the hall cupboard and leaves.

26

TOM

The aroma of freshly cooked street food dances around Tom's nostrils as he stands on the edge of the Portobello Road market. A kid walks past with a balloon in one hand and a sugary treat on a stick in the other. His mother laughs and chats with another woman pushing a pram. Tom moves away from the dangerously close lollypop and bumps into an older man inspecting an antique toast rack.

The man glares up at Tom.

"So sorry," Tom says and weaves through the market stalls, his senses being assaulted by shrieking laughter, crying children and people enjoying their Saturday morning.

Nice for some.

He reaches the far end of the market and steps into a stall to let a woman pass.

"Can I assist you?"

Tom turns to see a middle-aged woman with her grey

streaked, black hair chopped into a very square, severe bob smiling at him through much too red lipstick. She's wearing a kaftan in magenta and yellow. "Ah, no. Thanks. I was just..." He looks around and realises the entire stall is fitted out with an array of kaftans and scarves. He pulls the paper he tore from the notepad and reads the location. *Frequents Portobello Road.*

"Shopping for your wife? Girlfriend?" The woman sidles up next to Tom and brushes against his hip.

He shoves the paper into his pocket and steps away from the woman. "No. No... I was looking for my aunt actually."

The woman's smile brightens. "Unattached?"

Yes. No. Who the fuck knows? He smiles at the woman and drapes an arm over a nearby rack, leaning casually against it. "Maybe. But I was wondering if you could help me?"

The woman's eyes smile and she pouts her lips. "Absolutely Darling."

"Great. Do you know Benita?"

She taps her overfull red lips with a forefinger. "Kaftan Nita? Yes..." Her eyes widen. "She's your aunt?"

Why not? "Yes. And I've been away for a long time and want to surprise her... I don't suppose you know where she—"

"Bottle green door, three houses from the corner. Cambridge Gardens." She juts her hand forward and left to show Tom the way. "I make deliveries for her when she's busy and can't pick her own things. She's a lovely woman. I do wonder..." She steps closer to Tom, pushing her chest against him. "If that loveliness runs in the family?"

"Obviously." He grins and moves away from her, her chest

falling back to its original position. "Maybe I'll pass by after I have some tea with her?" He winks.

"My Daaaarling… I'll be here."

"*Fantastic.*" He walks backwards out of the stall. "Thanks again."

She kisses two fingers and blows the kiss towards him.

He lets the flap of the stall drop and darts away before she can follow.

His phone rings as he walks further down the road away from the bustle. He slaps it against his ear. "Yep?"

" What's the situation?" Martha clips her word.

"It's a lovely Saturday in Portobello Road. You should come and buy some antiques."

"I'm not laughing."

"Have you ever seen that show Ab Fab? Because I just met a woman who could play a role in a remake."

"You know I likened myself to Patsy back in the day."

Tom stops walking and grimaces. "And now *I'm* not laughing." Tom walks again, reaching the corner of Portobello Road and Cambridge Gardens. "Who *are* you?"

"I believe I asked you for the situation?"

"*That's* the Martha I know and tolerate. I'm about to visit a long-lost relative for tea."

"Where?"

"Cambridge Gardens. Behind a green door. I'll be fine."

"You know you always say that just before you *aren't* fine?"

Tom peers at the houses in front of him and finds a bottle green door, attached to a large terrace house. "All the answers will be in this terrace house. I'm—"

The phone is snatched from his hand and he goes to turn but a blow to the left side of his face makes him stumble sideways. Pain spikes through his cheek and jaw. "Fuck." He pushes a hand against his jawbone as a huge figure appears before him, charges and tackles him to the ground. He's flipped onto his front and eats a facefull of dirt and grit as a knee is pushed into his back.

"Looking for your aunt you say?" A forearm slides around Tom's throat as he squirms and kicks under the weight on top of him. A number of startled onlookers carry on, some shaking their heads. "S'alright, it's me brother. Haven't seen him in months." The man yanks Tom from the ground and slaps him on the back, before sliding the firearm from his waistband. "Maybe I'll hold on to this."

Tom squints through the dirt in his eyes and realises his new sibling is the same man he and Abbie hooked up to a drip at Electric Blue. "Gary."

"Why are you 'ere?"

"Antique shopping." Tom massages his throat.

Gary opens his jacket and shows Tom his pistol before nodding to the house with the green door. "After you."

Tom takes a step, but he's tackled again from behind. He hits the ground and huffs as all the air leaves his lungs. Tom jerks his head back and the satisfying crunch of a nose confirms he found his target. He rolls onto his back as his attacker presses both hands to his bloody nose, and wraps his legs around the attacker's waist. He lands an uppercut to the bloodstained face, before Gary shoves a gun under his chin.

Tom drops his legs and holds both hands up. "Fine. Fine."

Gary crouches in front of Tom and grins. "You didn't think I was all alone did you?"

Tom rolls onto his knees and stands up, dusting off his clothes. "Pushy, you pair."

"C'mon then, bigshot. You wanna see your aunt... she's waiting for you." Gary gestures Tom towards the house and he follows the bloke whose nose he crunched to the front door. His shoulders are huge and the jacket he's wearing is stretched to its limit.

Big shoulders opens the front door and Gary pushes Tom through into a darkened foyer. The door closes and a light switches on.

Tom massages his jaw as he takes in the scene before him. A crystal chandelier hangs over an ornate staircase. The floor appears to be marble and an antique hall stand is to his left.

"Lets go," Gary says.

Tom takes a step towards the stairs, but Gary grabs him by the back of the shirt and shoves him towards a steel door.

"Not up the stairs. We're taking the lift. I don't care if it's just one floor. Fuck that."

The three of them squish into the lift. Big Shoulders turns his back on Tom and faces the closing door.

Tom juts a thumb towards Big Shoulders. "Does he speak?"

"Russian," Gary says.

"*Mne nravyatsya tvoi sapogi,*" Tom says.

"*Poshel na khuy,*" Big Shoulders replies.

Tom snorts. "Charming."

"You speak Russian?" Gary raises his eyebrows.

"It's one of my talents."

"What did he say to you?"

"Well... I was being quite polite and told him I liked his boots. And he basically said, fuck you. Which frankly, I thought was uncalled for."

Gary sniffs and pops a piece ofgum in his mouth. "So you just wanted him to know you could speak Russian."

Tom raises an eyebrow and says nothing.

The lift dings and Big Shoulders steps out and to the side. Gary pushes Tom forward and he finds himself in an exquisitely furnished lounge. His shoes sink into the plush cream carpet. Leather sofas are adorned with velvet cushions and cashmere throws. The scent of cherry blossom wafts from an atomiser on the coffee table. Floor to ceiling windows at the front of the room are draped in sheer curtains. To his right is a corridor leading to more rooms.

"Welcome," a voice says behind him. "I must say your display down on the street was rather impressive."

Tom turns to find Benita standing by one of the sofas with a martini in one hand. She's wearing a bright yellow kaftan with blue flowers on it. Gary and Big Shoulders retreat to either side of the lift doors.

"You were expecting me?" Tom looks her up and down.

"Not until my friend at the market called me to say how handsome my *nephew* is." She juts her chin towards the windows. "Why don't you sit down." She sweeps a hand towards the opulent sofa, before she sits on the opposite one. "You look a little ruffled."

"Roughed up maybe. I don't get... ruffled." Tom sits.

"Unlike some..." Benita glares at Big Shoulders, whose nose

is still dripping down his front. "Leave us!" Benita says turning back to Tom.

Gary takes a step forward. "Ah do you think that's wise…"

Tom grins at Gary while Benita slowly turns her head to peer at him over her glasses. "You have his firearm, do you not?"

"Yes Ma'am."

"Wonderful. Leave us." She looks back at Tom. "You won't hurt me, will you, Darling?"

"Wouldn't dream of it."

"There you have it. He wouldn't dream of it. Out!" She flicks her wrist and turns back to Tom. "They're unwieldy but necessary." The lift doors close and they're alone. "You'll get your firearm and phone back when you leave. I have no use for them."

"Nice flat you have here." Tom looks at the gilt trimmings on the architraves.

Benita cackles. "Flat? No my dear boy… house."

"Most of these old places have been broken into flats."

"Yes. Not this one… it *was* of course, but I had it converted. I don't live in… *flats*." She says flats as though it offends her.

Tom stares at her and says nothing.

"I assume you didn't come here to talk about architecture?"

"You seem quite relaxed for someone whose son was shot in front of her and who, no doubt, MI6 are looking for."

Benita smiles and picks up a little bell from the side table and rings it. A few seconds later a woman dressed in an immaculate black and white maid uniform appears. "Ma'am?"

"We have much to discuss. Can you bring us some sparkling water and sandwiches?"

The woman gives a slight nod and scurries from the room.

Tom jerks an eyebrow. "Sandwiches?"

"With the crusts cut off, of course." Benita sips her martini. "Now… you want to know about Zane and MI6?"

"We can start there."

"He wasn't my son. He owned the club. I wanted to use said club. Therefore… I pretended I was his mother whenever I was there, so as to not… rouse suspicion." She picks up the toothpick and slides the olive off with her front teeth.

"And MI6?"

"They know nothing about me. They think it was all Zane. The first Aaron saw of me was when he was dying on the floor."

"How do you know Aaron's name?"

"Zane was an idiot. He told me everything thinking it would buy him points. I planned to kill him myself when I didn't need him anymore." She shrugs.

"So everything is on Zane and you get to walk out unscathed?"

The maid appears wheeling a trolley with sparkling water, two martinis, a small bowl of olives and a plate of rectangle cut sandwiches, sans crust. She parks the trolley at the end of the coffee table and leaves.

Benita picks up a fresh martini and holds it out to Tom.

"I'll stick with water."

"Interesting." She puts the martini glass down and hands him a bottle of water. "Now. What do you want?"

"I could ask you the same question." He cracks the lid and takes a mouthful.

Benita sticks two olives with a toothpick and drops them in her drink. "Oh?'"

"You just offered up a hell of a lot of information and you don't even know me."

"Maybe I think you're useful to me. I wouldn't mind your legs wrapped around my waist."

"Shucks."

"Who do you work for?"

"No one."

"MI6?"

Tom snorts. "Hardly."

"Why are you here?"

"I want Emily."

Benita sips her drink and watches Tom.

He stares straight back at her unmoved.

She puts her glass down. "You miss her?"

"Where is she?"

"Why don't we make an... arrangement?"

"You have her?" Tom's heart thuds faster.

Benita glares at Tom. "I want the girl."

"What girl?"

"Aaron was supposed to deliver her to Zane, who was then going to bring her to me. Although now I realise he was probably going to intercept her and put her into hiding. They're dead. You aren't. So now you deliver me the girl."

"You didn't answer my question."

"You'll get Emily when I get the girl. See? *Arrangement*."

"Where do I find this girl?"

"No idea."

Tom's stomach somersaults. "Pardon?"

"Aaron told me he would deliver her. He knew where to find her. All I know is that he called her Sweetpea."

"And why do you want Sweetpea?"

"Look at you… asking all the questions you have no business knowing answers to."

"You aren't giving me much to go on."

"You look like an enterprising lad. I'm sure you'll figure it out."

"Let me see Emily."

Benita throws her head back and cackles. "Darling boy. That's not how this works. I make the rules. And you'll follow them if you want to see Emily. Alive. Understood?"

Tom swallows.

"Good boy."

27

ISABELLA

Isabella rotates her wrists, but they won't budge. The gaffer tape and cable ties binding them together make it impossible to get free of the chair. She kicks the coffee table again and bites harder on the gag. A cup of tea she's been staring at for the past twenty minutes slops a little over the edge and onto the saucer.

How did I end up here?

She kicks at the table over and over, not caring about being silent. She eventually tips it on its side. The teacup breaks and tea spreads across the floor.

"Goodness me, Kitten." Edward's arm wraps around her shoulders from behind and he pulls her backwards, away from the coffee table. She keeps kicking at the air as her chair back hits the floor and it jars through her whole body. The curve of the backrest keeps her wrists from being jammed and she continues to try and free them.

Edward's face appears upside down, looking over her. "It

appears someone doesn't deserve any tea. What a waste of time it was to fetch the milk. Though it was lovely to see Tom. He did seem tired however. I also ran into that stupid old bat... looking for her cat she was." Edward giggles.

Isabella writhes, kicks and tries to scream. The strain in her throat aches but she doesn't stop, continuing to try and scream against the gag.

Edward stands over her watching and saying nothing.

Her body protests the movement while being bound to the chair by spiking pain through her back and sides. Her legs tire and her feet drop to the floor. She blinks to keep tears blurring her vision.

"Oh Kitten." Edward kneels at her feet and pulls out his roll of gaffer tape. "I didn't want to have to do this but you leave me no choice." He grabs her ankle and wraps tape around it, securing it to the chair leg. "Not going to protest me?"

Isabella stares at the ceiling. *I'm giving you nothing.*

He moves to the other ankle and does the same. Seconds later he rights the chair and takes Isabella's gag from her mouth. "Sweet girl. Are you okay?"

Isabella twitches her mouth to bring feeling back to her lips and tongue.

"I asked if you were okay? It's only polite to answer."

Isabella brings her eyes to meet his, and blinks. This time a tear tips out and rolls down her cheek. "Where is this going, Edward? When is it over?" Her voice is raspy.

Edward cups her face in his hand and swipes a thumb across her cheek, wiping away the lone tear. "Don't cry. None of this is your fault."

"No. It's yours."

He grins. "No. It isn't."

"Then who?"

"They know who they are. They just fail to acknowledge it. Even when I tried to make them."

"They?"

"Her, him. Them." He shrugs. "It doesn't matter anymore. It's almost over and I'll get what was always rightfully mine."

"When? When is it over?"

"Taken from me... without any consideration."

"You didn't answer my question."

Edward shakes his head. "Soon." He picks up the now broken tea cup. "You didn't drink your tea."

"I'm bound and gagged, Edward." She has no fight left in her voice. "How was I supposed to drink it?"

Edward stares at her, a slight frown appearing on his brow for a moment before disappearing. He smiles. "Of course. What was I thinking? I'll make you another one. And get you a straw. That's the kind of gentleman I am."

I don't want any fucking tea.

As he stands, Isabella's face heats up and all the hatred sitting in the pit of her belly won't stay put. "Let. Me. Go." She thrusts against her restraints and the chair jumps a little, she does it again.

A giggle comes from the kitchen behind her. "You adorable pain in the arse."

She thrusts again. *I'm dead either way.* She opens her mouth and screams. She thrusts again trying to make the chair thump on the wooden floor. "Help! Tom! *Tom! I'm down the—*"

28

TOM

Tom reaches the top step to his floor and finds Martha standing in the middle of the hallway, frowning. "Martha?"

She holds a finger up. "Shhh…" She's peering down the hallway, her eyes darting between the doors.

Tom creeps over and stands beside her. He looks around the deserted hallway. "What are we doing?" he whispers.

"Waiting."

"For?"

"I heard something."

Tom folds his arms across his chest. "Was it voices in your head?"

Martha turns slowly and glares at him.

Tom holds his hands up in surrender. "Just asking."

"It was shouting. Or screaming."

"Shouting?"

"It was just for a second or two. But I swear I heard something…"

"I have a question."

"Yes, Tom?"

"Why are you outside the flat?"

Martha rolls her eyes. "Because I heard screaming. Are you listening to me?"

"Someone around here likes to watch movies too loud."

"Movies?"

"Yes Martha, the talkies… I know it's been a while but movies have sound now."

Martha puts her hands on her hips. "Thanks for your input."

"And colour too. Sound *and* colour." He spins towards his flat. "I need James. Is he inside?"

"No, he's still out."

"Doing?"

"He's busy."

"Doing?" Tom follows Martha into the flat, closes the door and leans against it.

"A job for me. Now… What happened in Notting Hill? You have a bruised face and your phone was taken from you, was it not?"

Tom grinds his teeth. "Yep. I need James. Now. Can you get him back here, please?"

"Did you find out where Isabella is?"

"Not exactly. But Benita has her."

"You know this?"

"She said I get her back when I do a job for her. That's all you're getting from me. You have your little secrets… and now it seems I do too. Get James." He pushes himself off the door with one foot and stalks to his room, slamming the door behind him. "Shit."

He sits on the bed and scrubs his hands through his hair.

"Tom?" Martha's voice is muffled through the door.

"What?"

"I'm concerned."

"What's new?"

"Open the door."

"No. I'm naked."

"James should be here soon. He's already on his way back."

Tom sighs and goes to the door. He opens it enough to see Martha. "Why are you concerned?"

"You can't do a job for Benita."

"I know that."

"So?"

"So... I'll be doing a job for Benita."

"Tom—"

"I have no *choice*."

"What's the job?"

He lets the door fall open all the way, walks back to his bed, and sits. "Honestly? I really don't know. I have to find *the girl*."

Martha walks in and sits next to him on the bed. "What girl?"

Tom shrugs. "Sweetpea."

"Excuse me?"

He shrugs again and stares at the open wardrobe on Isabella's side. Empty. "But... all her stuff's gone."

"The girl's?"

"No." He holds his hand out towards the wardrobe. "Isabella's."

"Yes. That does seem odd if Benita has her. But... not out of the question."

Tom flops back onto the bed and stares at the ceiling. "Nothing makes sense."

"Hello?" James' voice interrupts Tom's thoughts.

"In the vault?" Tom looks at Martha.

"For now."

Tom nods and walks into the lounge. "Where's Abbie?"

"Martha's house. The place hasn't been disturbed in a few days now. Maybe he lost interest?"

Martha pushes past Tom and sits at her desk. "Thank you, James."

"That was your secret task? To check on Martha's place?"

"Well—"

"Yes." Martha raises a brow at James before turning back to Tom. "I want to go home."

"Right." Tom points a finger at Martha. "You stay put until I say so." He turns to James. "You. What do those numbers mean?"

James plops into his chair and taps his mouse. "I don't know."

"Work it out."

Tom's phone rings in his pocket. "Yes?"

"Aaron's place. Come alone. It is imperative." A thick Russian accent comes down the phone line.

Before Tom can answer, the call ends. Martha and James watch him. "Sure. Yes... I'll bring it in now." He shoves his phone into his pocket and grabs his helmet. "I forgot I booked the bike in for a service."

"What?" James holds both hands out. "You're leaving? I thought you wanted me to work out those numbers?"

"You suddenly need me here to hold your hand?"

Martha tilts her head. "Off you go then." Her eyes narrow. "*Do* ride carefully."

"Always."

———

Tom parks the bike at the back of Aaron's place. He sits and taps his fingers on the handlebars. *Go in? Wait outside?* He looks around the deserted rear yard and Martha's face appears in his mind's eye. *You will wait outside. Understood?* He gets off the bike and jogs to the back door. It's unlocked, and he goes inside.

The corridor is dark, and Tom flicks the light switch, but nothing happens.

"The power has been cut off." The same deep Russian voice from the phone call comes from the shadows.

Tom grabs his pistol as Big Shoulders walks out from a side room with his hands up.

"Please. I am not armed."

"You'll excuse me if I don't believe you."

"Understood."

"Who are you?"

"My name is Aleksandr. I will not hurt you."

"Again... I may need some convincing."

"And again, I understand." He gestures to Aaron's office. "Please come in."

Tom follows Aleksandr, keeping his gun trained on the back of his head. "I thought you only spoke Russian?"

"As far as they know, I do." He sits behind Aaron's desk and crosses an ankle over his knee.

"I'm still pointing a gun at you." Tom sits on the edge of an old two draw filing cabinet.

"I am Interpol."

"And I'm The Flash."

Aleksandr grins. "You certainly have speed when it comes to the fighting."

"How's your nose?"

"I will survive."

"Look, I don't have a lot of time. So if we could move this along?"

"I am very honoured to be in the company of one Tom Grant. And I need your help."

Tom doesn't need a mirror to know the colour is draining from his face at an alarming rate. "What?"

"Also, I want to help you find Emily. Or should I say… Isabella Wirth. Or perhaps… Irina Petrov."

Tom's jaw tightens. "Who the fuck are you?"

"Interpol. Did I not just tell you this?"

"Words don't hold much weight."

"Aleksandr Balabanov. I will wait." He gestures to Tom to call someone. "But I will say… that to know about Irina and yourself, I must have some status. Yes? To know of your top secret, nonidentifiable agency. Yes? To know that you are the only one who can help me now?"

"Phones don't work in this part of the building."

"They do now."

Tom slaps his phone to his ear.

James picks up halfway through the first ring. "Hey. Those numbers are gibberish. Honestly I haven't—"

"Aleksandr Balabanov. Search him."

"Is he your bike mechanic?"

"Interpol. Allegedly." Tom hangs up.

"Allegedly?" Aleksandr leans forward, resting his elbows on the desk. "I am who I say."

"If you're Interpol, he'll find you."

"What shall we do while we wait?"

"Well… there used to be a Scrabble board here. Or maybe you tell me who this girl is that Benita is so desperate to have. And why you need me? I'm kinda busy with a thousand other jobs at the minute."

Aleksandr bows his head. "Very well. Sweetpea was one of Benita's girls. She was trafficked off to a very rich man on a yacht when she was sixteen years old, just off the coast of Aruba."

"How old is she now?"

"She is twenty four. She escaped and is now a key witness in the case building against Benita and her organisation. The most important witness. So important that even I do not know her real name. Only her story and codename."

Tom's phone rings and he answers, not taking his eyes from Aleksandr. "Yep?"

"Legit. Interpol. Former MMA fighter. He's bloody huge—"

"Thanks." Tom drops the phone and gun on the desk between him and Aleksandr. "Sorry about your nose."

Aleksandr smiles. "I am sorry I told you to fuck off."

"That's fine, I was lying about your boots."

Aleksandr puts his hands together as though in prayer and rests his mouth against them. "So… now we must find Sweetpea together. Benita must not find her first."

"Agreed. But you forgot to mention we're also finding Isabella."

"I do not know if Benita has her. If she does, I did not see her, but that does not mean much. I will help you, but you must help me. It is life or death for Sweetpea."

Tom's mind flashes back to the empty wardrobe. "But…" He shakes his head. "How can I contact you?"

"I will contact you." Aleksandr stands up. "I know Sweetpea is meant to be coming into country in next few days or may already be here. But I do not know her name to check manifests. But that is not to say she is not traveling on fake papers. Aaron knew. He was the only one, but he is now dead."

"Did he know who you were?"

"He did not. I am only telling you now because Benita has pulled you in. I must work with you. Not against you. If Benita gets to her, she is dead, and our case falls apart. "

"Why am I involved in another shitfight?" Tom says, more to himself than to Aleksandr.

"Because you are Tom Grant. I know you cannot leave this be. And nor would Irina."

Tom rolls his eyes. "Well, fuck."

"Fuck indeed."

———

"Well?" Martha accosts Tom as soon as he walks into the flat. "What happened? Why were you speaking to Balabanov?"

"Can I get some water?" Tom raises an eyebrow and continues to the kitchen. "He's infiltrated Benita's fucked up little world."

"And? Does he know where she's keeping Isabella?" Abbie's voice pipes up from the hallway as she enters the lounge.

"No. But he reckons there's lots he doesn't know. He's basically being used as a heavy."

"Shit." She sits on the sofa.

"Articulate Abs."

Martha huffs. "I've spoken to one of my contacts at Interpol. Balabanov has been working on trafficking cases for years. He wants Benita on toast."

"She'd be a sour spread." Tom collapses onto the sofa next to Abbie with his bottle of water. "What about those numbers, James?"

James looks up from the screen of his computer. "Well, I was thinking… what if they stand in for letters?"

Tom gulps some water and gestures for James to go on.

"So I found the corresponding numbers for each letter in the sequences…"

"And?"

"And… H D B G F D and under that A E E B B and then A H D E." James grins at Tom.

"The triumph in your face doesn't match with the rabble of letters you just read out to me. What do they mean?"

"Well, I haven't got that far yet."

Tom holds his hand out. "Give me the scrabble board."

James frisbees the board across the room to Tom before looking back at his random letters.

Tom scans the board, his eyes resting briefly on the three peas in the pod. *Sweetpea.* "These numbers aren't here by accident."

James snorts. "No shit."

"Shut up, James."

Abbie giggles and shakes her head.

Tom holds the board up in front of his face and stares at the numbers.

842764

15522

1845

He glances between the first 8 and 4 to the other 8 and 4 written on the bottom set of numbers. *They're different.*

He jumps up from the sofa and goes to James. He slaps the board down in front of him and points at the first 8 and 4 on the top line. "They're different. Look… the side of the eight is straighter than the other one and the four… its cross line is on a weird angle compared to the others he's written."

James picks the board up as Martha and Abbie join them. They all peer at the board.

Something niggles at the back of Tom's mind, but he can't work out why. He paces around the coffee table, thinking back over the conversation with Aleksandr. *She was trafficked in Aruba… no one knows her real name… so checking manifests is point* — "Manifest." He leaps back to the desk and yanks the board out of James' hand. He squints at the first 8 and 4 again. "It's a B and an A." He grabs a scrap of paper and writes the numbers again in the same sequence, but putting a B and A where the first 8 and 4 are.

BA2764

15522

1845

Tom's heart throws itself against his ribcage as it all starts to make sense. "Fuck me. It's a British airways flight... arriving on the fifteenth of this month at six forty five in the evening. It's a goddamn plane. Shit." He drops the pen and looks at Martha. "What's the date?"

"It's the seventeenth, Tom."

"Fuck!"

James taps at his keyboard. "It's fine. Let's get some CCTV up for that date."

Tom's phone rings and it's an unknown number. "Grant."

"It is me. I have gone over the house. There are a number of rooms I cannot get to. She could be in any one of them. So it is not out of the question she is here."

"Alive?"

"Yes. Benita would not keep a dead body in her home."

At the mention of a dead body, a cold spike hits Tom in the heart. "She's not dead. She's not."

"No. I do not believe she would be. Not yet."

"You really have a way with words."

"I am sorry."

"Don't worry about it. Listen, I have something too. When can we—"

"I must go." The call goes dead.

Tom throws his phone onto Martha's desk. "Where are we at, James?"

"Almost there."

Abbie puts her hand on Tom's arm. "News on Isabella?"

"Not really. He basically said it's possible she's there, but he doesn't really know anything."

"Well, if she is, at least now you know there's someone there looking out for her."

"Yeah. That doesn't make me feel any better."

"I know but—"

"Tom!" James waves him over. "Here we go."

They all crowd around the monitor as James presses play.

29

ISABELLA

I sabella lolls her heavy head to the left, resting it on her shoulder. Her eyes peel open and adjust to the gloomy, empty bedroom. She slurps saliva as it trickles down the side of her face. *Not gagged…*

"Hello Kitten.

Isabella gasps in a breath as Edward's voice is right next to her ear. "Jesus."

"No, no." He grins at her, inches from her face. "Just me."

His breath brushes her cheek and she recoils. "What the hell are you doing?" Her mouth moves slower than her words.

"Watching you sleep. So peaceful. So serene."

"So psychotic."

Edward smoothes hair away from her forehead. "Shhh."

Isabella tries to move away, realising her arms and hands are completely restricted. She looks down at her body. "A strait jacket? You've put me in a *fucking strait jacket?"* Her words continue to slur and she gives her head a shake.

"The drug will wear off soon. You've been sleeping for some time."

"How long?"

"Fourteen hours."

"My God."

He continues to stroke her hair and face. "It's for your own safety, Kitten. I need you."

"Well I don't need you." Her voice raises but she doesn't care. "Do you hear me you *fucking freak?* I don't need *you."*

"Oh you misunderstand." He grabs her shoulders with both hands, shifts her into a sitting position and drags her over to the wall. "I don't *want* you. But I *need* you." He slaps a palm into the wall above her head. "Capice?"

She leans her face into Edward's so her nose touches his. "Why am I *here*?"

"You no listen?" He pulls away and waggles a finger in front of her face. "Rude, Kitten. Like I said… I need you. None of this happens without your involvement."

She grits her teeth and pushes harder against his nose. "None of what happens?"

"My plan." He stands up. "You're collateral damage at this point. When I don't need you anymore I'll dispose of you accordingly."

"You're gonna kill me?"

He falls to the floor on his knees and strokes her face. "It *would* be a pity." A softness grazes his eyes for a moment before he drops his hand from her face. "Look at me getting all sentimental."

His sudden but fleeting change in demeanour sparks something inside Isabella's chest. She casts her eyes to the floor. "I don't deserve this," she whispers.

"Excuse me?"

She looks up at him. "I said, I don't deserve this. I was always kind to you. I was your friend."

"Was?"

"We're no longer friends, Edward." She tries to shrug but the pressure of the jacket renders her unable to move.

He grins but there's a sneer attached to it. "You think *you* don't deserve this?" He grabs her hair at the back of her neck and winds it around his fist. He yanks, pulling her head back, pain shoots through every hair he has in his grip. "I *deserve* what's coming at the end of this. I *deserve* to be happy. Loved. And with a life I *deserve*."

"What does that life look like?" She winces against the pain in her scalp and keeps her voice as even as she can.

He loosens his hold on her hair, slides his hand down her neck and strokes her throat with his thumb. "The life I was born into was taken from me. I was cast off like a piece of rubbish. I was replaced with someone *better*." He puts the word better in quote marks with his free hand. "You have no idea what I've endured."

"Tell me." *I don't care.*

"Why? So you can laugh at me? So you can try and *understand* me?" He spits out a bitter huff. "People have been trying to understand me for years, Kitten. No one has come close."

"Try me."

"Tell me. Do you know your family?"

"They're dead." Her father's face rests in a warm corner of her brain and she takes comfort in him for a moment.

"But you knew them."

"Yes."

"How nice for you." Edward stands and folds his arms, staring into space.

"You don't know yours?"

He stays silent for a moment, his jaw twitches. "Within hours of being born my mother signed me away. She'd already decided I wasn't good enough for her."

"You were given up?"

"I like to think of it as disposed of."

"But—"

"That's enough heart to heart for one day." He pulls a syringe from his pocket and takes the cap off.

Isabella's heart slams against her ribs. "No. Please no more." She tries to move but can't.

He kneels beside her again and rests the syringe against her neck. "Like I said, Kitten. Collateral damage. It's best if you sleep so I can get everything ready in peace."

She squirms as best she can but he pushes her to the floor and rests a knee on her chest. "Shhh this is down to your recent behaviour. I can't trust you. Maybe when you wake up this will all be over." He pushes the needle into her neck and she squeals. "There's a good girl."

Anger spikes through her blood as he walks away from her. "Tom *will* find me." Her head is already woozy.

Edward stops at the door and turns to smile at her. "I do hope so."

30

TOM

"Honestly Tom, can you stop with the jittering?" Abbie slaps her hand on Tom's knee. "You're distracting me from watching the planes take off."

Tom picks Abbie's hand up and drops it in her lap. "I'm fine. I've had lots of coffee." *And my blood pressure is about to kill me.*

"Whatever you say." She twists in her seat and looks around the gate lounge. "I still can't believe you bought two tickets to Sydney just to sit here."

"Correction. *Martha* bought two tickets to Sydney, and also two tickets to L.A because she... I... can."

Abbie rolls her eyes. "I've always wanted to cuddle a koala."

"Why?"

Abbie huffs. "Because they're cute Tom. And cuddly. Unlike you right now."

"Well plan it another time, we aren't going anywhere today."

"Thanks for the heads up." She flops back against the seatback. "So how long do we have to wait?"

Tom unfolds the photograph James printed out for him and glares at the male flight attendant talking to the young girl with her back to the camera. "He's off the flight disembarking from this gate. James checked his roster."

Abbie plucks the photo from Tom and peers at it. "He looks more like a Jorge than a Faruq."

Tom snatches the photo back. "I don't care if he's name's Elton John. We aren't leaving here until we find him and ask him about her."

"He might know nothing."

"He spoke to her for a good ten minutes. And he kept looking around like he was about to be sprung the whole time."

"Yeah cause he probably wanted into her knickers, Tom. You remember being like that don't you?"

Tom raises a brow and glares at her.

"Still like that, maybe?" She waggles her eyebrows and stands up. "I'm gonna grab a muffin. You want something?"

"Faruq."

"I'll keep an eye out." She winks and disappears through the throng of people moving in every direction.

Tom's phone buzzes and he slides it out of his pocket. "James."

"Any sign?"

"Nope. What gate is he coming through?"

"What gate are you at?"

"James! I swear I'll rip your throat out."

"Okay, okay calm down. B sixteen."

"Terminal five?"

"Yes. His flight has already landed. He'll be walking into the gate lounge any minute. He'll probably have one of those rolly suitcase things."

"Great help. A rolly suitcase. What would I do without you?"

"I'm going now. Call me if you need more." James hangs up.

Can't blame him for that. Tom stands and wanders the lounge, trying to block out the shrieks and chatter of excited travellers. He pulls another photo from his pocket, this time of the girl standing at the cab rank with Faruq. Her long dark hair frames her face as she stands with nothing more than carry on luggage. *Travelling light.*

"God, she really is just a baby isn't she?" Abbie leans her chin on his shoulder.

Tom shoves the photo back into his pocket. "She's twenty four."

"She looks about fifteen."

Tom scans the lounge as the boarding door opens and a man with black hair, a perfectly manicured black beard and a cabin bag on wheels comes through. He checks his photograph again. "Hello Faruq."

"Are we gonna go speak to him?"

"Yep. But we'll have to wait til he stops yapping to his colleagues. If we go stalking over there now we'll freak everyone out and probably get arrested."

"Look at you, thinking before acting. I'm proud of you."

Tom sits and glares across the gate lounge at Faruq, who's looking at his friend's phone and laughing at whatever is on the screen.

Abbie plops into the seat next to him. "Want some muffin?"

Tom shakes his head, his eyes glued to Faruq standing next to the door as people file past him. *This is gonna be difficult.* Faruq finally bumps fists with his friend and walks away from the gate, wheeling his cabin bag behind him.

"Here we go," Tom says, standing up.

"We're on?" Abbie screws up the last of her muffin in its paper bag and tosses it into a bin.

"C'mon." Tom slides through the throng of people, his eyes glued to Faruq's back. He doesn't need to turn around to know Abbie is right there with him.

A minute later Faruq walks into the closest men's room and Tom stops.

Abbie stops next to him. "I guess you're on your own for this one."

"Looks like it."

Tom walks into the mens room as Faruq stands at a urinal. *Well this is awkward.* Tom turns a tap on and washes his hands, watching Faruq's back in the mirror. A quick glance around the men's room reveals an empty disabled cubicle.

Faruq moves to the tap next to Tom and places his hands under the water. Tom takes the opportunity to lean closer to him. "Dry your hands and walk straight into the end, disabled cubicle. Do you understand me?"

Faruq stops rotating his hands under the water and stills. "I beg your pardon?"

"Disabled cubicle. Or I break your neck."

"Is this about the girl?"

A lump of ice drops into Tom's gut. "What?"

"I will go with you to the cubicle. There is no need for threats." Faruq grabs a paper towel, dries his hands and walks to the cubicle with his cabin bag.

Tom follows him and watches as Faruq lowers the toilet seat and sits on it.

Tom scans the men's room and closes the door. "How did you know why I'm here?"

"She told me."

Tom blinks and stares at Faruq, calmly sitting on the closed toilet waiting for Tom's next question. "She told you?"

"She seemed upset on the entire flight from Croatia. Always on edge. Gripping the armrest whenever I offered her water. Strange."

"She came in from Croatia?"

"Yes that's right."

"What happened when you got here?"

"She got really upset at the baggage claim. I had bought myself a nice painting so I was also at the carousel. It was as though she couldn't find someone, always looking around and becoming more anxious very quickly. I was concerned because she reminded me of my little sister. I asked her if she needed assistance. She said she was supposed to meet a man. I asked her what man? She didn't want to answer but she became upset. I asked if I could call someone for her and she said no. She needed to leave immediately."

"Immediately?"

"Yes, she said that she must leave because it hadn't gone to plan."

"What hadn't gone to plan?"

Faruq shrugs. "She would not elaborate. I did ask but she started to almost hyperventilate. So I escorted her to the taxi rank and waited while she calmed down and felt better. Before I left her she looked around and I think she saw one of the surveillance cameras because she stared off over my shoulder for sometime and faced me towards the same camera. She says to me, there will be a man asking for me. Tell him I have gone to location B."

"Shit."

"This was two days ago. I thought you would never come or that she was crazy."

"It wasn't supposed to be me. It was..." Tom shakes his head. "It doesn't matter. Did she give you any indication of where she was going?"

"No. She would not even tell me her name."

Tom nods.

"I am sorry but I need to get home. My mother is making a huge dinner and if I don't turn up I'll never hear the end of it." Faruq stands.

"There's nothing else you can tell me about her? Nothing at all?"

"I am sorry no. She seemed scared to speak to me. She had a foreign accent, Eastern European."

Tom pulls out the photo showing the girl's face and holds it up. "Which cab did she get into?"

Faruq laughs. "I am good, but not that good. Although... that picture looks like it was taken as she told me a man would seek her."

"And?"

Faruq takes the photo and studies it. "I do remember a woman pushed past us into the cab that is currently parked." He points at the black cab behind the girl. "I remember because there was a long line and people started swearing at her and complaining. But she was carrying Gucci bags… need I say more."

"Then what happened?"

"The next cab… that is the one the girl got into. I helped her because she was so timid and I was concerned."

Tom's neck prickles. "So the next cab?"

Faruq nods. "Yes… yes definitely. The next cab. Yes."

———

Tom nods at Justin, the driver, as he and Abbie get into the back of the agency car waiting for them. He pushes James' number for the fifth time as they start moving through the airport traffic, bound for central London.

"Hey." James answers on the third ring.

"About time. Where were you?"

"Busy."

"Martha's secret job busy?"

"Bathroom busy. Would you like a play by play?"

"Don't get smart."

"Did you find Faruq?"

"Yeah. Listen I need you to look at that footage again of the pair at the cab rank. I want the number plate of the cab she gets into."

"I kept watching after you took off and already have it for

you… well most of it."

"Most of it?"

"I can't make out the last letter. It's obscured."

Tom sighs and knocks the side of his head against the window. "Well can't you clean it up?"

"I'm not on CSI Miami, Tom. This isn't the wonderful world of television."

"What did I just say about getting smart with me?"

"I'll try every letter of the alphabet. I'm assuming you wanna know where it went?"

"That would be helpful."

"I'll call you back." He hangs up.

"So, I have a question." Abbie turns her body to face Tom.

"Yes?"

"Why didn't we just get that number plate and go straight there? Instead of wasting time at the airport?"

"Because we didn't know if Faruq was someone of interest. We didn't know if he knew more. And… I went off half cocked before James finished looking at the footage and we spent the night sitting at the airport."

Abbie clicks her fingers. "See? You can't think straight when it's personal."

"Cheers."

Abbie shrugs and sits back in her seat. "Well, you can't. Are you actually doing this job for the wellbeing of the girl or because of Isabella?"

Tom purses his mouth and looks out the window.

"Exactly." Abbie claps her hands once. "I'm not saying you

shouldn't do everything you can to find Isabella. Not at all. But you get sloppy when your mind is elsewhere."

"Okay, I get it. I agree. Can we stop this now?"

"Of course we can. I'm just saying—"

"Got it."

Abbie shakes her head. "And maybe lay off James? You can be a real bastard to him sometimes."

"I'm a bastard to most people, Abs."

"Well, he's on our side. Best remember that."

Tom drops his head back against the seat. "I know."

Abbie slaps his knee and squeezes. "Good chat." She leans forward and addresses Justin. "Tell me... do you know everything about everyone driving these cars?"

Justin shoots Tom a look in the rearview with smiling eyes. "Sometimes more than I need to, Abigail."

She settles back into the seat. "Poor bugger."

Tom's phone rings. "James."

"It was an R. I made some enquiries and she was dropped off at Piccadilly Circus. I'm trying to get footage now."

"Just at Piccadilly Circus?"

"Yep. Driver remembered her because she was constantly looking out the window at the people in cars around them and concealing herself below the window line. He thought it was weird."

"But then she gets out of the car in the middle of Piccadilly Circus?"

"Seems so. Like I said, I'm still trying to find footage to check for her. But head there for now."

"Right. James?"

"Yeah?"

"Good job."

"Umm. Thanks."

Tom ends the call and ignores Abbie even though he can feel her eyes on him.

"You really are all squishy inside aren't you, Grant?"

"Give it a rest, Abs."

She chuckles as Tom closes his eyes as the car shoots along the M4.

31

TOM

"Well this is fucking useless." Tom stands in the middle of Piccadilly Circus next to the giant electronic coca cola screen and scans the masses of people moving in every direction. He pulls his phone out and checks the screen. No calls.

"Do you think she went into an office? Or the back of some little Tescos?"

Tom kicks at a plastic cup rolling past him on the pavement. "Fuck knows, Abs. Look around. There are a million places she could have gone. This is pointless."

"Agreed. We have nothing to go on."

"Well, we might if James could hurry the fuck up."

Abbie puts her hands on her hips. "What did I say about being a bastard?"

Tom rolls his eyes as his phone rings. "Where did she go?"

"Not even a hello or barking my name at me?"

"James... I'm really not in the mood."

"Okay... she got out of the cab in front of the tube entrance and disappeared into the station. And I lost her."

"You *lost* her?"

"Well crap, Tom. Sorry I can't control surveillance all over London. Sorry I can't direct you straight to the nameless ghost of a woman's doorstep. Do you know how many people ride the tube everyday? Do you think this girl may have been trained in disappearing?"

Tom says nothing as the weight of having no leads, and no information on Isabella sits squarely on his already heavily laden shoulders.

James grunts. "Sorry. I'm just... I've got Martha on my back, and you needing me and Isabella's still missing, and Mischa is devastated, I'm just..."

"It's okay, James. Thanks for trying. Go see Mish."

"Are you serious?"

"As a heart attack."

"But—"

"Jesus, James. Go have some time with Mish. I want my flat to be empty when I get there. I'm sick of everyone in my face. Got it?"

"Yes, well Martha will be here."

"No doubt." Tom hangs up and shoves the phone into his pocket.

"You're giving up?" Abbie leans against a shopfront and folds her arms.

"No." His phone rings again and he pulls it out. "Grant."

"She is gone." Aleksandr's voice makes his blood freeze.

"Excuse me?" Tom's voice is strained against the angst sitting in his throat.

"Benita. The house is stripped of everything."

Relief calms Tom's writhing gut. "Fuck's sake Alek. You can't start a conversation with that."

"I am sorry. I understand what you must have thought."

"So where has she gone?"

"I do not know. Both myself and Gary have been left without any information. It is as though she simply vanished."

"She knows something."

"Agreed. Sweetpea. It must be."

Tom squeezes his phone, torn between throwing it under an oncoming double decker bus and continuing the conversation to find out as much as he can. "So she took Iz with her?"

"If she was here. I can only assume Benita took her wherever she went."

"*If* she was there?"

"Remember I never sighted her."

Tom closes his eyes against the bustle of Piccadilly Circus and for a moment he's falling backwards down a dark tunnel, with no sound and no Isabella.

"I will be in touch." The phone goes dead.

He slides the phone from his ear and down his neck.

"Tom?" Abbie puts a hand on his arm.

Tom swallows and takes a long breath through his nose. "I am *fucking* done." He frisbees his phone onto the road and it slides perfectly under the front wheel of another oncoming bus.

Abbie and Tom watch the phone crunch under the wheels.

"Tell me, Grant... how many phones have you gone through in the past six months alone?"

"I lost count. C'mon." He starts down the steps to the Underground.

"Where are we going?"

"Notting Hill."

———

The front door to Benita's townhouse hangs open and Tom climbs the steps with Abbie close behind. He pushes the door open all the way. "Hello?" His voice echoes in the decadent foyer.

"This is a bad idea," Abbie whispers. "Neither of us have weapons. Let's go back and get prepared."

"Let's not." Tom moves further into the foyer, pulling Abbie by the sleeve.

"I knew you would come." Aleksandr's voice startles Tom and he spins around to find Aleksandr coming through a painted black door next to the foot of the staircase.

"Geez, Alek. Maybe a little less cloak and dagger, yeah?"

"I apologise. I thought you were Gary. He disappeared and I now seem to be here alone."

"He was here?"

"Yes. And now he is not." Aleksandr cranes his neck to look past Tom and Abbie out the front door. "He left the car."

Tom's eyes narrow. "Where does that door behind you lead?"

"A utility room. I had never been inside before."

"Is there any—"

"No. There is no evidence Isabella was held inside. Though I have not checked entire house." He nods at Abbie. "And who is this?"

"Abbie, Alek. Alek, Abbie. No time for tea and biscuits. Let's go." He bounds up the stairs two at a time while Abbie and Aleksandr exchange hello's and handshakes. "Turn this house upside down, Abs." He stops and leans over the bannister. "You understand?"

She waves him up the stairs. "I'm right behind you. Calm down."

"I will do first two levels. You take top two." Aleksandr walks towards the lift.

Tom hangs over the bannister again. "No offence Alek but I'm doing the entire house. If she was here. She left me a clue."

"Tom, you don't know that." Abbie leans against the wall and sighs.

"Yes Abbie. I do."

Abbie rolls her eyes and pushes past him up the stairs. "Fine. Let's start at the top and work down."

An hour and a half later Tom sits on the floor where the fancy sofa had been. He can still see Benita drinking her martini while smirking in his face. He pinches the bridge of his nose. Moments later Abbie and Aleksandr join him in the lounge room.

"This place is incredible." Abbie twists her neck to take in the gigantic chandelier hanging above them.

"You should have seen it when she had all her stuff here." Tom squeezes his nose harder to quell the ache forming in his head.

"I bet."

Aleksandr stands at the floor to ceiling window and stares down at the street below. "I have been called back. My involvement here is done."

Tom shakes his head. "Wait. What?"

"Oh boy." Abbie walks down the hallway towards the adjoining kitchenette. "I'll leave you gals alone to gossip."

Tom ignores Abbie and gestures for Aleksandr to go on.

"She will be on her yacht, she is no longer in United Kingdom. She moors in Monaco, though she would have sailed it from there by now. The question is why she left so suddenly."

Tom looks away from where Abbie disappeared and stands. "So that's it?"

"Months and months of work. And I have nothing. I was sent away by her last night to transport some girls." He holds a finger up. "I took them to safety, of course."

"She had this planned. Leaving without a trace."

"Yes. This chapter is over."

"Over?"

Aleksandr gives a slight shrug. "Over for now. Until we can locate Benita. But I will not stop. There is a girl out there in grave danger. I will find her."

"Two girls, Alex."

Aleksandr bows his head. "Yes. Of course. I am sorry."

Tom looks around the vast, practically empty lounge room. "She was never here, Alek."

"How do you know?"

"Like I said, she would have left me something. The house is clean, no marks on walls, no strategically punched holes in plaster. She wasn't in this house. We're done here." He turns towards the kitchen. "Abs!"

Outside the townhouse, Tom stops on the steps and holds a hand out. "Keep me posted?"

Aleksandr smiles and shakes Tom's hand. "I will."

"Thank you."

Aleksandr steps backwards down the last step and smiles at Abbie. "Good luck working with this one." He nods at Tom.

"Ha. Thanks." Abbie gives him a wave.

Tom looks up and down the street as Aleksandr walks across the road towards his car. "Wait. What about Gary?"

Alexsandr leans against the side of the car and jiggles the keys. "He will not be back. He knows it is over. She did not take him with her. That says everything." He opens the door and gets into the driver's seat.

Tom watches Aleksandr put his belt over his shoulder as though it's in slow motion. "Fuck." Tom grabs Abbie's arm and pushes her back towards the front door.

"What's going on?" She yanks her arm free as the car starts.

Tom turns back as a deafening boom fills the air and he is thrown off his feet.

32

ISABELLA

"Tom!" Isabella's eyes pop open and she gasps in a breath. Her heart beats as though she's run a marathon. She instinctively goes to rub her eyes and finds her wrists bound together by tape and fixed above her head. Attached to a bed headboard . *What the hell?* She yanks against the restraints, but Edward hasn't taken any chances in her getting free this time. He's used what looks like an entire roll of gaffer tape around both her wrists and the railing along the wrought iron bedhead. A drip hangs from a pole out of her reach with a tube attached to the back of her left hand. She runs her tongue along her top lip. *Not gagged.*

She tries to move her legs and finds them taped together at the ankles with the same amount, if not more tape. *You've made your point.* She looks around the rest of the room. It's been furnished with bedside tables, a mirror and her clothes are hanging and folded in the wardrobe, with the doors hanging open.

The bedroom door opens, and Edward sticks his head in, smiling. "Ah there you are. How was your nap?"

"Something's happened." Isabella squirms on the bed, trying to sit up but can't co-ordinate her body. The fog of whatever drug Edward keeps giving her slows her brain.

Edward sits on the edge of the bed and pats her leg. "You are such a perceptive little kitten. A few things have happened... I furnished in here for you. I thought you might be more comfortable." He flaps his hand around. "And I'm doing some baking in preparation for some guests for afternoon tea."

"Guests?" She shakes her head, trying to clear the fog. "No... but not that. Something's happened. Something bad."

"You like your new decor?" He leans across and strokes her face. "You're getting used to things. That's lovely."

She tries to pull away but has no energy. "Stop... stop touching me."

"Oh, Kitten." He continues to stroke her face and neck.

"What's *happened?*" Panic erupts in her chest and she thrashes and tries to pull away from the bedhead. "What have you done?"

"Kitten. Shhhhh..." He grabs her jaw and squeezes until she calms. "There we go. That's better. Now... what makes you think I did something?"

She glares at his smiling, insipid face. "Because you're insane. And I can feel it."

He widens his eyes and snorts. "You can feel it? I've taken you out of the jacket, you clearly disliked so much. And I gave you a lovely bedroom with a pink quilt and all. So… I suppose I did do *that* something."

The panic in her body quivers below the surface, and she takes a breath. "Is Tom alright?"

Edward's face darkens. "How the hell would I know?" He stands and paces at the foot of the bed. "More to the point… why would I care?"

Isabella stares at the ceiling. "I guess you wouldn't," she whispers.

"Bingo!" He leans over her and connects a new bag to the drip attached to her hand. "And as much as I'd love to take credit for doing something to Tom… I haven't. Yet." He winks and walks to the door. "Get some rest… we have guests later."

33

TOM

"Grant. Hey…" A warm hand pats his cheek. "Grant, open your eyes."

Pain shoots through his head and he grasps his left temple. "God…" Intense heat smothers his senses, and he opens his eyes to a wall of fire a few feet from him. Leaves and dust dance in the air.

"Grant… c'mon we need to get inside away from this fire. It might keep exploding."

The jiggling of keys rings in Tom's ears and Alek smiling at him as they shake hands sits in his mind's eye. "He's dead." His voice is gravelly and his throat hurts.

Abbie hooks her hand under one arm and pulls him towards the front door of Benita's house. "Jesus you're heavy. Get up Grant…"

He blinks a couple of times before stumbling to his feet and pushing Abbie into the house, closing the door behind them. His body wants to go one way and his brain another. He leans against the door and pushes both hands over his face. "Fuck." His skin is gritty and rough.

Abbie grabs one of his hands and pulls him towards the lift. "C'mon. We need to clean up."

Inside the lift, Tom grabs Abbie's face and looks at it. "You're okay?"

"You practically threw me inside the house as it went off. I was shielded by the door."

He inspects her eyes and turns her head to check her ears. "Are your ears ringing?"

Abbie rolls her eyes and places his hands back against his chest. "Yes Grant. A bomb just went off. They're ringing. It'd be weird if they weren't."

"Are you bleeding?" He steps back as the lift doors open.

"No. But you are. C'mon." She grabs the crook of his elbow and steers him into the empty top floor lounge. "Lie down. I'm getting some water for you."

Tom plonks onto the floor and massages his head, resting his elbows on his bent knees. "Fuck…" He looks at his hands and the fresh blood on his fingertips. "Shit." He dabs at the side of his head again and rubs a hand down his face.

"Are you trying to look like some kind of Halloween decoration, Grant?" She drops to her knees next to him and cups his face in one hand and pushes a cloth against his temple with the other. "You've copped some shrapnel to the side of your face, not to mention the gash where your head hit the front steps."

Her warm hand against his face brings him momentary comfort. "I'll live." He takes the cloth from her and pulls away.

"Thanks." He pushes it against the same spot and takes the cup of water she holds out to him. "Benita left the essentials, then?"

"This was in the bathroom cupboard. I washed it, don't panic."

Sirens scream into the street downstairs. Abbie moves to the window and peers down at the street while concealing herself behind the curtain. "Fire truck. People everywhere…"

A phone rings and Tom looks around the room. His eyes rest on an old-fashioned phone attached to the wall next to the lift. He stands up and takes a second as the room spins and pain washes through his head. "Not ideal." He stumbles across the room and picks up the phone. "Hello?" He leans his head against the wall as it throbs.

"You have blood running down the side of your impeccable face." Benita's voice has the touches of a smirk around the edges.

Tom looks up at the ceiling and follows line of it to the right corner. A white camera nestled above the ornate plaster cornice flashes its red light at him as though winking.

"Hello Darling. Tell me. How's the house?"

"Standing. You didn't have to kill Aleksandr." He glares into the camera.

Benita laughs. "Oh, Darling… you're exceptionally handsome but not too bright. Of course I had to kill him."

"You're admitting it?"

"Why deny it? He was a traitor and deserved it."

"Traitor?"

"Working for Interpol. Honestly… I do wonder what his countrymen would think."

"What do you want?" Tom squeezes his eyes shut as the

throbbing intensifies. "I'm feeling a little under the weather, so if we could hurry this up?"

"I'd apologise for your getting hurt but... I don't care."

"Clearly."

"Emily sends her regards."

Tom's gut plummets and he remembers why he's there in the first place. "She wasn't here Benita. You lied."

"I never said she was in my house."

No. You didn't. "Put her on the phone."

"Give me the girl."

"I *don't know where she fucking is.*" He slaps a hand to his temple and squeezes his eyes shut. "You're asking me to do the impossible."

"Nothing's impossible, Darling. I knew Aleksandr was Interpol did I not?"

"How did you know?"

"Nothing is watertight if you pay enough. You have forty-eight hours." The phone goes dead.

Tom turns to the wall and rests his forehead against it. "I don't know where she *fucking is.*" He bashes the phone receiver against the wall, and then again. And again. The receiver splinters into shards of plastic and he throws what remains as hard as he can, and it swings while bouncing on its spiral cord. "Fuck!" He kicks the wall before punching it with a right hook and following it up with another, ignoring the pain shooting through his knuckles.

"Grant." Abbie wraps her arms around him from behind and binds his arms down. "Stop. Calm down."

He doesn't bother to fight her. The pain in his head continues to intensify, his knuckles hurt and everything is fuzzy. He stumbles backwards against her, and they both fall to the floor.

Tom stays on his back, staring at the ceiling while Abbie stands and brushes her clothes down. "I called Martha while you were on the phone. She's sending a car to meet us in Portobello Road. We'll go out the rear door and through some back gardens. C'mon."

"I… I don't want to anymore, Abs."

"What?" She squats next to him and peers into his face. "What are you talking about?"

He sits up and pushes both thumbs into his eyes and rubs them. "I'm tired. I'm hungry and my head hurts."

"Isabella's still out there somewhere, Grant. She needs you."

"I'm out of ideas, Abs. For the first time in a long time, I really have no idea what to do."

Abbie grabs both his arms and stands in front of him, waiting for him to look at her. Tom eventually obliges, resting his eyes on hers. "Let's go home. We can work it out when you feel better."

Tom steps towards the lift and presses the button. The door opens. "You'll be waiting a while. This hangover's a big one."

"I've waited you out before, Grant."

———

Tom walks into his flat with Abbie close behind. Martha stops speaking to the man with his back to them and stands up. "You look frightful."

"Cheers," Tom nods towards the man. "Guest?"

The man turns and smiles at Tom. "You do look rather frightful."

Tom rolls his eyes. "Mike. What are you doing here?"

"I heard you needed some patching."

"I'm fine."

"Which means you aren't fine." He picks up his black case and nods towards the bedroom. "Shall we?"

"And if I say no?"

"I'll bench you." Martha folds her arms, narrowing her eyes at Tom.

Tom spins and stalks to his room without another word. He sits on the end of the bed and crosses his arms over his chest.

Mike walks in and shuts the door. "If I didn't know any better, I'd assume you were a petulant twelve-year-old."

"Just do the doctor thing." Tom flaps his hand around next to his temple.

Mike flicks on a small torch and shines it in Tom's eyes. "Even pupils… though you do seem to have got quite a bump on the noggin."

Tom huffs. "I fell backwards and hit my head. I've been knocked out worse on the rugby field."

"You play?"

"Not since I was fourteen."

"Ah." Mike grabs gauze and squirts saline on it before dabbing it against Tom's temple. "Doesn't look like you need stitches."

"I could have told you that."

"I'm sure. Heard from Isabella?"

Tom jerks his head away from Mike and grinds his teeth. "No."

Mike smiles and leans against the wall. "When was the last time you slept, Tom?"

"Can we not do this right now?"

"Then when?"

Tom pushes the heels of his palms into his eyes and falls backwards onto the bed. "Maybe I'll have a nap now."

"Sorry Tom. I can't let you do that."

Tom peeks out from under one palm. "What?"

"You've been concussed. You need to stay awake. Are your ears ringing?"

"Yes. There was a big boom, Mike. What do you expect?"

"You really are quite grouchy when you're tired."

"Who isn't?"

"Martha's worried about you."

"She usually is. But I'm fine. I have shit to do actually, so if we're done?" Tom stands up and goes to his wardrobe. He pulls out a clean hoodie.

"And what shit do you have to do, exactly?"

"Find Iz. Find Sweetpea. Make sure Martha's house isn't vandalised again. Make sure she isn't stalked anymore. And I need a filling at the dentist." He stops and frowns for a moment. "I think that's everything."

"Who's Sweetpea?"

Tom clicks his fingers and points at Mike. "Exactly." He pushes past Mike into the lounge to find Martha at the door, speaking to Edward. *Just what I need.*

"You know what, Edward? That sounds nice. I could do with

a little break from work." Martha turns to Tom. "Would you like to come for a cup of tea?"

"No. I would not."

Edward sighs out a loud breath. "C'mon Tom. You look like you could also do with a break and good brew."

"Shut up, Ed." Tom plonks into his armchair. "By all means, have tea Martha. I could do with the peace. Where's Abbie?"

"She's gone home for some sleep."

"Well, isn't that nice. Apparently, I have to stay awake."

Mike moves to the door. "I'll check in on you in the morning, Tom."

"Can't wait."

"I got you a phone, Tom. Maybe try and keep this one for at least a month?" Martha nods at her desk where the new phone sits.

Tom grunts. "Same SIM?"

"Of course."

"Thanks."

Edward crooks his arm and smiles at Martha. "Well... shall we?"

"Wonderful." She saunters past Edward without taking his arm.

Tom watches her leave and raises a brow at Mike. "She's only going to spite me."

Mike smiles. "Seems about right. Remember, no sleeping for the next four hours. See you in the morning."

Tom waits to hear the door click and drops his head back and closes his eyes. The feeling of drifting off is almost instantaneous. He forces himself to sit up and gives his head a shake. Resting his eyes on the stack of folders on James' desk, he stands, grabs the new phone, and dials James.

"I did what you asked."

"I know, James. I'm at the flat. But I need you to come back."

"Are you serious? You practically order me out and now you're—"

"I know. Okay? But I need to find this invisible girl and I need your help to do it."

James says nothing.

"James?"

"I'll help. Give me an hour." He hangs up.

Tom grabs the folders of papers, climbs over the clutter of desks and computers to lie on the sofa.

34

ISABELLA

"No, no… Liked the look of… homely. You know?" Edward's voice floats in and out of Isabella's ears as she wakes in a foggier state than she had before. "…maybe strange but… never comes to visit. Sugar?"

"No, just… dash… milk, please."

Martha? Isabella's heart wakes up, but her body and mind don't co-operate. She tries to shout out, but finds a gag restricting her again. *What the hell are you doing here?* Isabella pulls against her taped hands and wriggles on the bed, attempting to kick out at something— anything, but her legs won't respond to what her brain tells them to do. She peers down, expecting them to be tied to something but they aren't. He's given her enough of whatever is in the drip to keep her out of his way.

For now.

"And tell me… do you…" Edward's voice drips in syrup.

Isabella's urgency increases, though her body doesn't. *Get out. He will hurt you.* She glances up at the drip. *Empty.* But her mind stays foggy and dull. She strains to listen to what's happening on the other side of the door. *Is Tom here?*

"Working hard, just data analysis." Martha's voice is louder as she obviously comes closer to the hallway.

"How very interesting," Edward says. "And Does Tom work with you?

"You could say that." Martha's voice fades again as she moves, Isabella assumes, back into the lounge.

The exact replica of Tom's lounge... C'mon Martha! Isabella screams against the gag, but it's not loud enough. She tries to thrust her hips and thrash on the bed, but her body still doesn't want to assist her and she flops and moves in the opposite direction to what she wants, at a quarter of the intensity she is hoping for.

A loud bang like a door slamming stills her and she waits.

"Excuse me?" Martha's voice is higher now, loud and authoritative.

Isabella holds her breath.

"No. I've had enough, thank you. Open the door."

She strains to hear Edward's response, but he must be doing the creepy whisper thing. *Shit.* She tries again to make noise, but nothing works. Her body tires and she lifts her chin, staring at the ceiling.

Don't kill her...

35

TOM

A warm hand swipes across Tom's forehead. He frowns against the throbbing pain above his brows and takes a breath.

"Tom?"

He opens his eyes to Mischa, crouching beside the sofa with her hand now resting on his shoulder. "Hey…" He grasps her hand and squeezes it as he moves into a sitting position.

"You fell asleep." She folds her arms and purses her lips.

"Yes."

"You could have fallen into coma, Tom."

He squeezes his eyes shut. "Don't start on me, Mish." He opens them again, and her big brown truth extractors are still staring at him. "How did you know what happened?"

"James spoke to Abbie."

"Can't a bloke have some privacy?"

"Yes. But when this bloke will not look after himself and listen to reason… not so much."

Tom grins at her.

"What is funny about that?"

"The way you say bloke. It's hilarious."

Mischa rolls her eyes.

Tom picks up the papers that had fallen off his chest while he slept and sifts through them. "Where's Sylvie?"

"She fell asleep on trip over here. James is putting her down on your bed."

Tom nods as James walks into the lounge. "Out like a light. Good to see you aren't, Tom. Not smart, huh?" He drops another folder on the coffee table in front of Tom.

Tom slowly brings his eyes up from the plane manifest he's reading and glares at James. "I have one Martha in my life. I don't need two." He reaches across and opens the new folder.

James grabs another stack of papers and sits on the armchair. "Correct. You need about five. What are we looking for?"

Tom frowns and holds up a sheet of paper. "What's this? A prison escort?"

James leaps across and snatches it from Tom's hand. "Wrong folder." He thrusts the papers in his hands at Tom. "Look through this."

"No, no." He nods at the prison escort file in James' hand. "What's that?"

"It's nothing. Another job I was working on."

Tom peers at James.

Mischa stands. "I will make food." She scurries to the kitchen.

"What job?" Tom asks.

"One you don't need to worry about. Now… we wanna find this Sweetpea person, do we not?"

"Is it the secret job Martha's had you running around for?"

"No."

"James?"

"Okay, yes. But I didn't tell you that. She'll skin me alive." He looks around the room. "Where is she, anyway?"

Tom shrugs and the movement wakes up the ache sitting in his back. "Afternoon tea with my idiot neighbour. He probably made her watch some geeky movie like Ghostbusters with him. Weirdo. Meanwhile, I feel like I've been hit by a bus."

"Afternoon? It's pushing six."

"Which you would know if you had not gone to sleep, Tom." Mischa points a knife at him from the kitchen.

Tom's ears ring. "So where is she?"

"I don't know. Still watching Ghostbusters? I was about to have an enjoyable meal out with Mish and Sylvie when you called and ordered me back here, so—"

Tom doesn't wait for anymore from James. He storms out of the flat and down the hall, stopping in front of Edward's door. He pounds on it with his fist. "Ed! Open up."

The door opens a sliver and Edward peeks out. "Good evening, neighbour." The door opens a little more, and he jams his body between it and the doorframe, obscuring any view into the flat.

"Where's Martha?"

Edward's eyes widen. "Couldn't tell you. She left hours ago."

"Did she tell you where she was going?"

"Hmmm…" Edward taps his bottom lip and looks around the hallway. "No. I don't know that she did. Why do you ask?"

"I can't find her. And last I knew, she was with you… two and two and all that." Tom squints at Edward. Something about the way he's jammed in the doorway unsettles him. "So, did she say where she was going after your afternoon tea?"

"No."

"That's it?"

"Well." Edward gives a shaky chuckle. "You've caught me in the middle of… something. And I wasn't expecting company, so… I'm a little off guard."

"Middle of what?" Tom's neck prickles and he slaps a hand against the door, giving it a push. The door doesn't budge.

"Well, I'm… baking."

"Baking?"

"Yes… Martha enjoyed my tea and scones so much, she convinced me to make more for next time."

"Next time?"

"Yes. Well… It's been a long day. Thanks for stopping by." Edward goes to shut the door.

Tom jams his foot in the door frame. "What the fuck are you playing at?"

"Nothing. I'm tired. I don't want my scones to burn. So if you don't *mind*?" Edward pushes the door against Tom's foot until he moves it and the door closes in his face.

Tom glares at the door. He raises his fist to pound on the door again, but stops himself. *Weirdo.*

A moment later, he walks back into his flat and corners James against his desk. "What's the secret job?"

James sighs. "It's not secret, it just doesn't involve you. Right?"

"Snippy."

"You aren't the only one who's tired."

Tom pauses. *He's right.* "Okay." Tom steps back, freeing James from the desk. "So we need to comb everything we have and find something to tell us who Sweetpea is and where she may be. We have her face now... can you run it?" He sits on the sofa again and pulls the paperwork onto his lap.

James gives him a tight-lipped smile. "Yep." He climbs over the furniture to his desk and taps his keyboard.

"James?"

"Yeah?"

"Thanks."

James nods and keeps typing.

Mischa sits next to Tom. "You did not know what she looked like?"

"No. No-one did." James says, still staring at his monitor. "She was a code-name on a piece of paper. She was going to meet someone at the airport holding a card with her codename on it. But obviously... that never happened."

"So you gave Mish top secret clearance, did you?"

"Annika Novik," James blurts out.

Tom climbs over to James and stares at his computer screen. "Holy shit."

"Reported missing while on a cruise with her family. The boat docked in the Antilles. She went to bed and disappeared."

Tom can't take his eyes off the school photograph on the screen. "She looks about twelve."

"It says here she was fourteen when she disappeared."

"How does one disappear from their bed? On a boat? There would have been an investigation, go to the—"

"Tom!" James spins in his chair and stands up. "Here's an idea... leave me to do the computer stuff and go look through the rest of the info in those folders, maybe?"

Tom straightens up and peers at James, taking a step forward so they're practically nose to nose.

A crash in the kitchen draws both their attention and they turn to Mischa.

"You two give me heart attack." Mischa says, picking up the bowl and spoon she dropped. "Stop arguing about who is in charge and fix problem. You are like two brothers fighting over football."

"Brother is a bit strong," Tom says and walks back to the sofa.

"So it says here her parents never stopped looking for her. Maybe we need to contact them?"

"And tell them what, James? Sorry your daughter went missing eight years ago. By the way, they trafficked her into sexual slavery and she's now on the run from the very people who kidnapped her because they want to put a bullet in her brain. Oh, and she's now an informant, so there's a price on her head, no doubt. Any idea where she might be?"

"Maybe not in those exact words..."

"We can't contact her parents until we find her and she's safe. It's not fair to them." Tom flicks through a page. "Not to mention I need to make Benita believe I'm going to hand her over if I want Isabella back."

"You know she has Isabella?" Mischa clasps her hands under her chin. "Is she safe? Did you speak with her?"

"No, Mish. No. I haven't. I don't know that she has her. But it's the only thing I have to go on right now."

She drops her hands to the worktop and her fingers claw the laminate. "Okay. I am sorry." A tear rolls down her cheek.

Tom jumps up from the sofa and goes to her. "Don't cry." He holds her against him. "I'll find her."

Mischa nods against his chest as Sylvie cries from the bedroom. "I know you will," she whispers before going into the bedroom and closing the door.

Tom stands, staring at the closed door, willing the pain in his chest to go away.

"She's worried sick." James stands next to Tom. "She keeps telling me she knows Isabella didn't leave you."

Tom nods. "Yeah, well..." He clears his throat as his voice croaks.

"Listen sorry. I was a dick. I—"

"Can we do this later?" Tom nods at James' desk. "What have you found?"

"Right." James leaps across the room and sits. "Her last known location was Croatia."

"I know."

"Will you let me finish?"

Tom flaps his hand around for James to continue.

"So I might have done something slightly illegal."

Tom pinches the bridge of his nose. "What have you done?"

"I may have hacked into Interpol."

Tom's eyes widen and he inhales slowly before doing the same on the exhale. "You did what?"

"Well, my setup at the warehouse has been hacking in all morning and it's just gone through. I'm accessing it remotely here."

"Are you fucking insane?"

"Only for a minute... I'm in now. I'm using a VPN. It won't trace to your flat."

"They have a leak. So if there's a hack, they're gonna be on it."

"Like I said... it won't trace to your flat. I've got it pinging all over the place. But... leak?"

"Benita found out about Alek and blew him up, James. They have a leak."

"Maybe Benita's just smart."

"She all but told me she's bribing someone there. So... if you could hustle and stop asking questions you don't need to?"

James spins back to his monitor. "Gimme seven minutes."

"Seven?"

"It's more than five, but not as long as ten."

Tom jerks a brow and watches James. "You're an odd duck, James."

James nods; his eyes glued to his monitor.

"Who is this Sylvie?" Mischa says behind Tom.

He turns and his insides melt a little at the sight of the chubby cheeks and big blue eyes smiling at him. "My favourite girl." He holds his arms out and takes Sylvie from Mischa. She babbles nonsense in his ear and it's the most calming, beautiful sound he's heard all day. "You speak more sense than James." He rests his forehead against hers and lets her grab at his hair.

"Yes!" James whoops and jabs a finger at the monitor. "We have liftoff."

Tom hands Sylvie to Mischa and goes to the computer. "What?"

"Okay... now don't panic, I logged out, but not before I copied this." He sweeps his hands out at the screen with a smile on his face as though he's won Olympic Gold. "Every hotel *and* pseudonym she's used in the past year. She's moved around a lot, but look... what do you notice?"

Tom reads the list of hotels and names. *Alice Smith, Ariel Plunkett, Jasmine Blackett, Merida Green.* He looks up at James. "Disney princesses."

"Exactly. And I'm impressed you know that."

Tom grins at Sylvie playing on the floor. "I may have watched a couple with Sylvie."

"Did you notice what else, though?"

Tom looks back at the screen. "Hotels?" He counts the list. "Fourteen of them in the past year."

"Yes, but..." James points at the screen again. "They're all owned and operated by the same company. See?"

Tom scans the screen. "Accor."

"So..."

"We find the Accor hotel currently housing a Disney princess."

"Yep." James grins. "You're *fucking* welcome."

Mischa tutts and puts her hands over Sylvie's ears. "James. Language."

"Shit, sorry."

She raises her eyebrows.

"I mean… yeah, my mistake." He sits back down and starts typing. "I'll find every Accor and start searching."

Tom claps his hands together once, as his fourth wind hits him. "Great idea. I'm calling Martha. I swear if she's gone back to her house, I'll throttle her."

"Warehouse?" James' fingers fly over the keyboard.

"Just as throttle worthy." Tom dials and walks out to the hall. Martha's voice greets him, but not with a hello. "Voicemail," Tom mutters to himself. He dials again. *Voicemail.* "It's me. Where the hell are you? We've found something. Get yourself back here. I'm not amused." He ends the call and is about to walk back into the flat when he glances down the hall. Something draws him back in front of Edward's flat. He puts an ear against the door and listens.

Whistling. A faint whistle comes from inside, a cheerful whistle. Tom doesn't know why, but it makes his blood slow to a crawl through his veins and before he registers what he's doing, he pounds his fist against the door again.

"Yes?" Ed's voice comes from the other side of the closed door.

"Open the door."

"Tom. Again. One must really think you have strange obsession with me." He giggles his annoying giggle and even though it's muffled against the door it still reminds Tom of nails down a chalk board.

"Open up, Ed or I'm kicking the door in."

The chain jiggles, and the door opens enough for Edward to

slither into the hallway. He pulls the door shut behind him. "What's wrong Tom? Is my existence in your way?" He gives Tom a smirk, as though he's won a race just ahead of him.

Smarmy git. "What? No. I mean... your existence annoys the living shit out of me. But it's not *in my way.*"

"Hmm... interesting." He leans against his closed door. "What can I help you with now?"

"Martha must have mentioned something about where she was going?"

Edward scratches his forehead and sighs. "Look, I don't know where she is at the minute, but I *did* invite her over for a lovely roast dinner tomorrow evening. Maybe you'd like to join us?"

Tom stares at Edward a moment and gives his head a little shake. "She's coming to your flat for dinner?"

"Yes. Would you like me to set you a place?"

"But... that makes no sense."

"Why ever not?"

"Because Martha doesn't just *come over for a roast.*"

"Well, maybe Tom, she decided she liked my company? That I was worth being around? And I had value in... existing?" Edward's face turns a deeper shade of ruddy and a tremble seems filter through his body.

"What the actual fuck—"

"Tom!" James' voice bounces off the hall walls. "You need to come see this."

By the time Tom turns towards his flat, James has disappeared back inside.

"Well. Seems you have to go home. I'll set you a place anyway... just in case, eh?"

"I'm not coming to your flat for a roast. Thanks, but no thanks." *You'll probably poison the gravy.*

Edward fiddles with the door handle behind his back, opening the door and sliding through to his flat. "Tata then."

He walks back to his own flat and opens the door to a flurry of movement as James picks Sylvie up and spins her around. Her giggles fill the lounge.

"Maybe she'll vomit on you. That'd be worth watching."

James brings Sylvie down and holds her on his hip. "So... I ran a search of the Accor hotels in London for names associated with Disney Princesses. I expected there to be a few, but there wasn't. There was one. Just one. A Miss Aurora Fletcher is staying at the Hotel Ibis, Earls Court."

Tom's heart doubles pace. "Now?"

"Yep. Checked in a few days ago... hasn't checked out." He hands Sylvie to Mischa.

Tom grabs his gun from the top of the hallway cupboard, shoves it into his belt, and points at James. "You coming with me?"

James grins and vaults over the armchair.

36

ISABELLA

The bedroom door opens and Edward slides in, not leaving himself much room between the door and the jam. "You're awake, Kitten."

Isabella pulls against the gaffer tape holding her arms above her head and glares at Edward. Her heart beats faster, and she's breathless, straining to breathe through her nose hard enough while the tape restricts her mouth.

Edward leans across and rips the tape from her mouth. The sting ripples through her cheeks and lips. "God..." She presses her lips together to try to quell the raw pain prickling her skin.

"I knew I'd be otherwise engaged for a while, Kitten. I didn't want you waking up and doing something silly like shouting out. We can't have that now can we?"

" I heard a struggle. Where's Martha?" Isabella's voice is a rough whisper. "Is she okay?"

"Ah, you heard our little tea party?"

"I asked if she was okay."

"She's..." Edward glances around the room as though pondering. "She's having a rest." He sits on the edge of the bed, too close to Isabella for her liking but she can't do anything about it. "She's rather firey for an older lady. Isn't she?"

"You have no idea what she's capable of."

Edward grins.

She pulls against her restraints again, ignoring the pain in her arms and wrists from being tied up for so long.

Edward leans close to Isabella and puts a hand on her shoulder. "I know her. Much better than you think." He winks and sits upright again.

Isabella stops squirming against the tape and frowns at Edward. "Did she lock you up once?"

He laughs as though Isabella told him the funniest joke he's ever heard. "Locked me up?" Edward wipes an imaginary laughter tear from his eye. "No Kitten... goodness me no. Quite the opposite."

"Excuse me?"

"She freed me in a sense. Let me go... flung me out into the world without another thought. Free to be the very man I am today. It's all because of her."

"What? You're making no sense. I want to see her."

"I'm sure you do but..." He strokes his chin and pauses, looking out the ajar door. "You know what? I'm not an unreasonable man. I'll let you see her."

Isabella's heart races. "You will?"

Edward stands and pulls another bag of liquid for the drip from his pocket.

"No. Please. Enough Edward." She pulls away but gets nowhere.

Edward ignores her, attaches the bag and checks her cannula. "Lovely." He strokes hair back from her face and slides his hand down to cup her cheek. "It's almost over. I need to make some preparations before our next guest." He pats her cheek before standing upright.

Next guest? Isabella's focus blurs and the familiar wash of weakness spread through her body. "Please…"

"When you wake up you'll have a lovely surprise waiting for you. I promise." He pecks her on the forehead and leaves the room.

37

TOM

Traffic crawls through South Kensington and Tom curses the cab driver silently.

"You know," James says next to him. "It would have been faster if we took your bike."

Tom slides his eyes to James. "And ride nuts to butts with you?"

"Nuts to what?"

"Butts. Apart from that one time you had to move the bike for me... you will *never* ride it again."

"You're welcome for that, by the way."

Tom grunts and stares out the window. "Should have walked." He taps his knuckles against the window.

"It's like four kilometres."

"Stop talking, will you?"

"Although... he's taken us most of the way. If we got out here and jogged, I reckon we could get there in about ten minutes."

"Done." Tom leans forward. "We'll jump out here thanks." He throws money at the cabbie and gets out.

"You just gave him a forty quid." James slams the cab door shut.

"And?"

"Well, don't you think—"

"Have you ever heard of pain in the arse tax?"

"Ummm…"

"Because he had to put up with you babbling in the backseat. Pain in the arse tax. You owe me forty quid." Tom takes off at a fast jog. "C'mon. Keep up," he throws over his shoulder. The sound of James grumbling and puffing brings a smile to Tom's face.

Fifteen minutes later they stand outside the Ibis Hotel, both with their hands on their knees, gulping in big breaths.

"This place…" Tom swallows and straightens up, walking in a small circle with his hands on his hips. " Looks like a hospital."

"Try… running with a laptop… slung over your shoulder." James flops onto the pavement and puts his head between his bent knees. "My throat's drier than a nuns—"

"*Thanks* for that." Tom claps his hands once. "C'mon. You put us in the room next to hers?"

James nods as he gets off the ground. "Yeah. Room 2014. We need the key, obviously."

"Obviously." Tom walks into the foyer and James follows, slumping onto a plush sofa while Tom walks to the desk. He smiles at the girl reading from a printout and she drops the paper. Her cheeks turn pink. "Hi. Don't mean to be a bother…

my friend here." Tom jerks his head towards James. " Lost our room key when we went for a quick run."

She looks over at James and back at Tom. "That's what you wear when you go jogging?"

Tom looks down at his jeans and black t-shirt. *Think man. Think.* "Did I say run? I meant… wander. Anyway… I don't suppose you could give us a new key? Room 2014?"

She grins at Tom. "You're also very sweaty, as though you did actually go for a run."

"Yes, well it's rather warm out there." He looks out the front doors at the drab, drizzly day. "You know… when you're… wandering."

She holds a new room card out and gives Tom a little wink. "It's okay. Your secret's safe with me." She looks him up and down. "Pity though."

Tom blinks. "What? No. It's not—"

James appears beside him and gives Tom a slap on the back. "We good?"

Tom plucks the card from the smirking concierge and spins towards the lift.

James catches up and leans against the wall beside the lift. "I think I'm finally breathing normally again."

The doors open, Tom walks in and leans against the back wall. "You might think about a bit more cardio, James."

James snorts. "I get plenty of card…" He quickly closes his mouth. "I'm so glad you decided to shut the fuck up."

"I know you're sensitive about Mischa, Tom. But I'd never hurt her or disrespect her. I hope you realise that."

The lift dings and Tom pushes himself off the wall as the

doors open. "Yep, I do. I'd hang you over a pit of flesh-eating pigs by your ankles if you did." He saunters past James. "Not to mention I'm still on the fence about you two." He reaches the door to room 2013 and stops. The urge to shoulder barge the thing down passes, but he knocks on the door, anyway.

"Are you mental?" James hisses.

"Yep." Tom knocks again. Silence comes from inside, no muffled voices, no footsteps. Nothing. "Hello?" He presses his ear against the door.

"You're gonna scare her."

"Scaring her would have been me pounding on the door like I did with Ed. I'm just knocking. We could be room service for all she knows."

"Tom. I know you're on edge, but we need to regroup." James steps towards the door for their room. "Key?" He holds out a hand.

Tom scowls and tosses the keycard to him. "Stop making sense. It irks me."

"I get why you're not thinking straight. But luckily I am."

"You? Think straight?"

Inside the room, James kicks his shoes off and climbs onto the king-size bed. "Yes. I often do. You just don't notice." He pulls his laptop out while Tom goes to the window and stares out at the street. He rests his forehead on it and watches a man get luggage out of a cab. The glass is cool and for a moment it helps the dull thud in his head fade a little. "This has to work out, James." The adrenaline running through his veins makes it hard to stay still. He turns from the window and paces the room.

"I know."

"We have to get Iz back." His stomach tightens.

"I know."

He stops pacing and folds his arms, but taps his fingers against his biceps. "What are you doing?"

James' fingers fly over his keyboard while his tongue runs back and forth along his top lip. "I'm checking something…"

Tom bites the side of his mouth and takes a moment. "Which might be?"

"Well, I'm accessing the keycard activity for her room."

Tom grabs the chair from the desk and straddles it. "And?"

"And… she went in three days ago."

Tom waits, but James doesn't continue.

"And?"

"And… she hasn't used her room key again. Not once." James looks up with a furrowed brow. "That's kinda weird, isn't it?"

"Not if she's scared shitless or waiting for someone to come and collect her. Except that someone is dead…" Tom's brain does a happy dance. "But I'm not dead." He stands up and spins the chair on one of its legs.

"Huh?"

"I'm not dead."

"Correct."

"I could be the one collecting her. No… fuck it. I *am* the one collecting her." He drops the chair back onto all four feet and goes to the room door.

"But what if she's not in there?"

He stops with his hand on the door handle. "You just said she hasn't used her room key."

James slides the laptop off his lap and stands up. "Just... you need to stop and think for a sec. You're hell bent on getting Iz back and I get it. But what if you go storming in there and it all goes tits up?"

"Okay, first... never try to reason with me. I'd listen to Sylvie for advice before I listen to you. Second... if her room hasn't opened in three days... she's in there."

"I didn't say it never opened. I said she hasn't used her key. The service cards have been used. Not to mention the electronics on the door note every time it opens, from outside or within the room."

"A girl's gotta eat, James."

"Okay fine. What if she has a gun?"

Tom grins despite himself. "A gun?"

"It's not impossible. You go storming in there, she might shoot you dead. Then what good are you to Iz?"

"Well, I..." Tom purses his lips together. "She doesn't have a gun."

"Okay fine. Let's say she doesn't. What do you plan to do when you get in there?"

"Convince her to come with me."

"A girl on the run from... everyone? And she's just gonna come with you?"

"I can be very convincing."

"I say we wait a few hours and see if anything happens. See if any service keys get used, or anyone visits."

"Cool. We done with the fireside?" Tom feels behind him and grabs the handle of the door.

"What if someone got hold of a service key, went in there and took her? What then?"

Tom pauses. "Stop being logical, would you? I feel inadequate." He scrunches his eyes closed and rubs them with his thumb and forefinger.

"Well you *did* hit your head pretty hard, and you haven't slept properly in days and you're all emotional—"

Tom's eyes pop open. "I'm not *emotional.*"

"Okay." James holds both hands up. "Wrong word. But Martha told me—"

"You can stop right there. Martha isn't here. *Martha* has gone off for a little jaunt through London while I'm here, finding a kidnapped, trafficked school girl. *Martha* doesn't get a say. *Martha* had afternoon tea with my weirdo neighbour while I slept after being knocked out in an explosion. *Martha* can shut her mouth."

"I'm just saying, let's be rational before we go bursting in there half cocked."

"*We* are not half cocked. You... no doubt. Now... are we done?" Tom opens the door and walks backwards out of it.

Seconds later, Tom knocks on the door again. "Annika." The silence on the other side of the door sends prickles down the back of Tom's neck. "This is eerie as fuck," he whispers.

"It does feel strange," James says.

Tom knocks again. "Annika. I know you're frightened but I'm here to help you." *Fuck it.* "Aaron sent me." Tom holds his breath.

A trolley jangles behind them and Tom turns to find a hard

faced woman glaring at him. He bows his head slightly. "Ma'am."

She frowns and stops her trolley in front of Tom. *"Tum kya ker rahe ho?"*

"I can speak French, Russian and German… but she speaks Hindi." Tom sighs. "Friend." He points to Annika's door. "We are friends."

The woman waves her hand and moves towards the door. "No, no." She grabs Tom's arm and tries to pull him away from the door.

He yanks his arm back. "Listen… I'm worried about…" He takes a breath. "This is pointless."

"Let's go. We can come back later," James mumbles.

"Aap ab chhod do!" She grabs a feather duster from her trolley and whacks Tom across the body with it.

"Whoa, whoa…" He takes the feather duster and throws it halfway down the hallway. "Listen. I know you can't understand a word I'm saying, but I'm not *fucking going anywhere.*" He moves his face to within a breath of her and glares into her eyes. "Do you hear me?"

"Jesus, Tom. You've lost the plot." James tugs at his sleeve and Tom rips his arm away, ignoring James and glaring at the woman.

She holds his glare and reaches into her apron, pulling out a walkie talkie.

What am I doing? Tom steps back while the woman chatters into the walkie talkie. Tom holds his hands together under his chin as though in prayer. "I'm sorry. Very tired." He puts his hands up in surrender.

She lowers the walkie talkie from her mouth.

"We're leaving." He jerks his head towards the lift. "James c'mon. Let's go."

James motions towards their room. "But we're—"

"Let's go, James." Toms stalks to the lift and presses the button.

"I don't understand."

"I don't want her to know which room we're in. Use your brain, James. I'm sure you have one sloshing around in that pin head of yours."

"Oh, I see."

"And she's probably calling someone to cart us off somewhere as we speak."

"I would suggest that may have been on account of your behaviour…"

Tom nods and punches the lift button again. "You're right. But she's right there." The lift arrives, and Tom walks in. "She's in that room. And I need her, James. *We* need her."

"I get it. Let's take a walk and then we can go back—"

"James, we're gonna ride up and down in this lift for about ten minutes and then go back to the room. I'm not leaving this hotel without her."

"But what if the crazy maid lady comes back?"

Tom pushes James against the wall with his hand in the middle of his chest. "I *am not* leaving this hotel without her."

"Fine."

The doors open, but no one gets in. Tom's eyes rest on a trolley parked across from the lift stacked with plates and discarded food. He glares at a half eaten scone with jam and cream slopped on it and the hairs on the back of his neck stand on end. The doors go to close again and Tom slaps a hand against them to make them open. He walks out of the lift, still staring at the scone.

"Tom, you're really being bloody weird." James follows him out and stands beside him. "Why are we staring at someone's half eaten breakfast?"

Tom frowns and looks at James. "Martha hates scones."

"Huh?"

"They make her sick. All the flour. She can't eat them."

"Good to know… I suppose?" James shrugs.

Fuck.

38

ISABELLA

Isabella opens her eyes and focuses on a dark mass in the corner of the room. Her blurry vision doesn't clear no matter how many times she blinks, so she drops her head back on the pillow and closes them.

One, two, three, fou—

"Isabella? Are you awake?"

She opens her eyes again, settling them on the mass that now looks more like… "Martha?"

"Yes, Dear. Are you hurt?"

"Umm…" She struggles to move her body to see Martha properly, but the movement exhausts her and the fog enveloping her won't dissipate. "Not really." Her words again don't seem to come out the way she hears them in her head. "Sorry I'm… I'm a little foggy."

"Don't struggle to move, Dear."

"No, but… are you hurt? Where's… Tom? Is he here… too? Is

he okay?" She stops and swallows. "I feel like I'm... in one of those... weird dream sequ...sequences in a movie."

"I imagine you would."

"Why... Why aren't you... moving?" She squints, and she sees Martha but blurry around the edges. "Are you sitting... in a chair?"

"Indeed, I am. I'm tied to it, actually."

Isabella's heart beats faster than the rest of her body will move. "God, are you hurt? Where's... Tom?"

"Tom isn't here. I'm fine. I've been a prisoner of war, remember?"

Images of the scars across Martha's back; revealed to Isabella on their first meeting, float in her mind's eye. "What did he do to you?"

"Well, he gave me quite the black eye. I'm sure it surprised him when I punched him straight back."

Isabella snorts softly. "I bet. Supergran."

"I don't know that I was as deft as that time in Paris... but he thinks it's worth tying me to a chair now, so... I'll take that."

Urgency takes over Isabella and she pulls against her restraints. "But Martha... Where's Tom?

"He's.. working. Trying to find you, to be precise."

Isabella's gut plunges. "God, he must be worried... sick." She blinks as the fog seems to ease.

"Yes, he's not coping the best."

"Has he been drinking?"

Martha says nothing.

"Martha? Has he been drinking?"

"He thought you'd left him. Edward cleaned everything you owned out of the flat."

"He took all my stuff?" She slumps back on her pillow as tears gather in the corners of her eyes. "Tom must be beside himself," she whispers.

She sighs. "This is very inconvenient."

Isabella peers at Martha through her tears. "Inconvenient? Martha, what the hell is wrong with you?"

Martha whispers to herself, but Isabella can't make out the words.

"Martha!"

"Isabella, please… I'm trying to think."

Isabella slams her mouth shut and watches Martha. Her body is upright and rigid, though she appears to be gently rocking back and forth while she keeps whispering to herself. "You never answered my question."

Martha huffs and turns her head towards Isabella. "Dear?"

"Tom. Drinking. Is he alright?"

"He fell off the wagon but climbed back on swiftly. So please don't panic."

Isabella's muscles tense. "We need to get out of here."

"Agreed. Or at least you do. You must get out, Isabella."

"We *both* need to get out of here. Why would you not include yourself?" As she asks the words, she realises her clarity has almost returned.

"Well yes, of course, both of us." Martha nods to herself before fixing her steely eyes on Isabella. "We cannot let Tom find us here. Do you understand?"

"No Martha. I don't understand a damn thing."

The door to the bedroom opens and Edward walks in, stands at the foot of the bed and smiles at the pair. "Well, isn't this nice? The gals having a natter."

Isabella glares at him, clamping her mouth shut.

"You have me now, Edward. Why don't you let Isabella go?" Martha says.

He gives Martha an exaggerated, incredulous grin. "I thought you were smarter than that."

Isabella frowns. "Wait. He has you *now?* What does that mean? Why am I here?" Again, rage infiltrates her veins, and she pulls against the restraints, causing the bedhead to thud against the wall. "What the *fuck* is going on?" She pulls again, and the bedhead rocks.

Edward leaps across and grabs the bedhead to stop it from hitting the wall. "Look at you loosening the bedhead. I must fix that." He looks behind the bedhead and at one of the legs. "Yes... I'll tie that back to... there... and—"

Isabella drops her head back and screams.

Seconds later Edward's hand claps down on her mouth, and his nose pushes against hers. "You shut your pretty little mouth, or I slit Martha's throat. Do you understand?"

Isabella breathes heavily through her nose as Edward's hand stays pushed against her mouth. She stares into his eyes, giving her the same steely stare as Martha moments before. A chill frosts her blood.

"I asked if you understand?" Echoing Martha's words now as well. An invisible force grips her gut and twists. Isabella nods, and he slides his hand from her mouth. "There's a good kitten." He pecks her on the forehead and gets off the bed. "While I'm ecstatic, I have you here where you belong Martha, Isabella is just as important to complete the puzzle. Wouldn't you agree?"

"No Edward. I wouldn't."

He smiles at Martha. "You keep calling me Edward. Why?"

"It's your name, is it not?"

Isabella's gaze moves from Martha to Edward and back again. *What the hell is going on?*

"Wouldn't have been your choice, though. Would it?" He narrows his eyes at Martha.

"I doubt what I think matters."

Isabella flips onto her side again. "What are you both talking about?"

Martha keeps staring at Edward and says nothing.

"Martha?" Isabella thrusts her body to add an exclamation mark to her question.

"Yes, dearest Martha. Why don't you explain things? Or are you afraid life as you know it will never be the same again?" He walks to Martha and kneels in front of her. "Because it won't," he whispers.

"This is between you and I, Edward. Tom and Isabella have nothing—"

"*That's* where you're wrong. Tom has *everything* to do with this. And *she* means everything to Tom. You see?" He stands and brushes his clothes down with his hands. "Now, if you'll excuse me. I have a dining table to put together. I'll let you both stay gag free. But one scream, shout or anything smart and I kill one of you in front of the other." He motions a knife across his throat. "Capice?" He walks out of the room, slamming the door shut.

"You're trembling, Martha."

"Dear?"

"What's Edward talking about that has you so rattled? Don't try to tell me it's nothing. I'm not an idiot."

"As I said. We need to prevent Tom from coming here."

"Why would he come here? He doesn't know we're here or he would have come bursting in already. And why on earth would you not want him to find us?"

Martha chews on her bottom lip. "We need to get you out of here."

"Answer my question, Martha."

"I locked Edward up some years ago. It seems he's unhappy and wants to make things even."

"What does that have to do with Tom not coming here? And his name?"

"He's a fraudster, so he used many names." She stops and takes a breath, closing her eyes before opening them again and staring straight ahead, not looking at Isabella. "I want to get you to safety. And that's with Tom."

"But Tom can't come here according to you?"

"I'll get you out of here."

Isabella slams her head into the pillow. "God, Martha, you're talking in riddles and making no sense. Not to mention, how exactly do you expect to get me out of here? You're an amazing human being, but you aren't a magician."

Martha turns her head to Isabella. "We outsmart him. And you get out and keep Tom as far from here as you can."

"That's impossible and you know it. I've never heard you speak such nonsense. Keep Tom away? While you're here? With this psychopath?" Isabella shakes her head.

"It's… it's imperative." Martha's voice cracks. "Please…"

"Martha?"

"Please, Isabella. Edward is right. If Tom comes here, nothing will ever be the same again."

Isabella opens her mouth but no words come out, instead she watches as a single tear rolls down Martha's cheek. "Martha—"

A bang, followed by a loud crash, and the sound of splintering wood from out in the lounge cuts Isabella off. "Where the fuck is she?"

"Tom," Isabella whispers. She draws in a breath to scream but before she can get it out, a sickening crack followed by a groan sounds from the lounge and silence falls.

39

TOM

"Ugh…" Tom scrunches his face up and pushes both heels of his palms into his eye sockets.

"Wakey wakey."

The sound of Edward's voice sends Tom's blood pressure soaring, and he realises Edward is standing over him, holding what looks like a table leg. "You hit me in the back with a table leg?"

"Yes, and then I gave you a little love tap on the head. Just to be sure. I don't want to hurt you too badly… yet." He giggles.

Tom rolls onto his side and tries to ignore the throbbing in his temples and eyebrows. He takes a breath and launches himself towards Edward's legs, pulling him to the floor. The sudden movement sends nausea and dizziness spiralling through his body, but Tom's arms remain wrapped around Edward's lower legs.

"Not… smart…Tom." Edward thrusts and wriggles, getting

one of his legs free. He kicks out and lands his foot with a thump in the middle of Tom's chest.

Air whooshes out of Tom's lungs, and he crumples against the wall. While fighting away the urge to throw up and the splitting pain in his head, he evens his breathing and feels around the back of his trousers for his gun.

"Looking for this?"

Tom looks up into the barrel of his own gun. *Fuck.*

"C'mon Tom, sit on the sofa. You'll be far more comfortable."

He gets onto all fours and takes a moment before climbing onto the sofa. "Did you seriously whack me with a table leg?"

"I did. Quite fortuitous, my Ikea delivery came today, wasn't it?" He grins and sits in the armchair. "I managed to close the door again, although you've broken the frame." He sighs. "You could have just knocked."

Tom looks around the lounge. "Why are we in my lounge?" He looks towards his mother's antique desk, but it's not quite the same. "Wait..." He rubs the back of his neck and keeps taking in the bizarre scene before him. "Edward?"

"Tom?"

"Why the fuck is your flat a replica of mine?"

"Ahh... all will become clear soon enough. Now... I'm so very glad you dropped by. Albeit a tad early. Tomorrow night, Tom. Remember?"

Tom glares at him. "What?"

"Roast? But never mind, I'm sure I can cook this evening instead. Martha will be along soon, I imagine." He grins again, still pointing the gun at Tom. "It was quite lucky you had this in your waistband. Makes everything much easier for me. Though why would a fellow like you be carrying a firearm, I wonder..."

Martha! "Where's Martha?"

Edward widens his eyes and arches his brows. "Hmm?" Tom moves to stand up, but Edward wiggles the gun at him. "Uh uh. You stay right there. This is *my* flat. I make the rules here." He winks, still giving Tom his irritating, psychopathic grin.

Tom pinches the bridge of his nose and takes a full breath in. The pain in his head doesn't dissipate, but it gives him a moment of relief. "Edward, I really need to be somewhere else right now, so if you could tell me what the hell happened to Martha this afternoon. I'll get out of your hair and you can keep putting that table together." Tom opens his eyes and gives Edward a smirk. "Which I don't have in my flat, by the way."

"No. This is very true. I bet if we really turned this place upside down, you may find a couple of things that aren't... currently in your flat."

"Excuse me?"

A knock on the door makes both of them freeze and stare at each other.

"Edward?" Lorna's shaky voice floats through the closed door. "Do you have a moment?"

"Well," Edward whispers. "I guess you'll be on your very best behaviour, won't you Tom? Stay exactly where you are on that sofa, yes? I mean... I wouldn't want Lorna accidentally finding herself dead."

"You touch one hair on her head and I'll rip you apart."

He throws his head back and laughs as he walks to the door.

Holding his hand with the gun behind his back, he pulls the door open. "Lorna. What an absolute delight."

"You certainly sound cheerful, Edward. I was looking for— Tom! Oh my, I didn't know you were here. Another lovely surprise."

Tom does his best to give her a smile. "Lorna." *Get out of here.* "To what do we owe this lovely interruption?" He gives Edward a side eye before looking back at Lorna and smiling wider.

"Well, I was looking…" She walks towards Tom, staring at his face. "Tom… dear. What on earth happened to you?"

Shit. "Hmm? Oh, I fell… over."

"It must have been quite the tumble, dear. You've got a swollen cheek, and a cut chin… and above your left eyebrow. My goodness." She reaches out to touch his face, and he grabs her hand, giving it a squeeze.

"Well, I never do things by halves Lorna, you should know that by now."

"You are quite the daredevil with that motorbike of yours."

"Why don't you head off to your flat and have a nice cuppa? Ed and I are about to watch football."

"Ohh, I didn't know you're into the Premier League."

I'm not. "Love it."

Edward moves towards Lorna, staring straight at Tom with a grin playing at the corners of his mouth. It sends Tom's gut plunging, and he shifts in his seat to face Lorna, grabbing both her hands. "Lorna, head home, yeah? I'll check in on you soon."

"Yes, of course. But if you could keep an eye out for Pebbles?"

"Oh dear," Edward says. "Has little kitty gone missing again?" He pouts.

Something in Edward's voice creeps up Tom's neck.

"Yes, I haven't seen her for quite some time."

"Lorna," Tom says. "You go on home and I'll see if I can find her soon, okay?" *C'mon, go home for fuck's sake.*

"Yes, alright, well, I do have some knitting to get on with." She winks at Tom. "I'm making Pebbles a little blanket for winter."

"Well... isn't that the sweetest thing?" Edward sweeps a hand, ushering Lorna towards the door. "Don't worry Lorna. I have a funny feeling little Pebbles will turn up somewhere closer than you think." He gives her a little wave before shutting the door on her.

"What the fuck does that mean?" Tom swallows against the bile threatening to rise. "What have you done?"

Edward grins and walks to the kitchen. He reaches into the cupboard above the fridge and pulls out a shoebox. He brings it to the lounge and drops it on the coffee table in front of Tom. "Have a peek."

Tom lifts the corner of the lid and peers in, knowing what he's about to see. The furry, broken body of Pebbles greets him. He drops the lid and stands up, his body swaying a touch. His fists itch to beat Edward's face into a bloody pulp. "I knew you were a psychopath. You're insane, dangerous and frankly... I fucking hate you."

"I'm not overly fond of you, either." Edward raises the gun, so it lines up in between Tom's eyes. "Sit down."

Tom leans forward, resting his head against the muzzle of the gun. "Make me."

Edward slides his finger on the trigger. "That cat walked

around this block as though it was her own personal kitty litter tray. I did everyone a favour."

Looking into Edward's cold, hard eyes, Tom realises empathy doesn't live there.

"I twisted that mangy cat's neck without a second thought. I suggest you don't push me. You aren't really in any shape to win a fight today… as evidenced earlier. Am I wrong?"

Tom's head pounds as though nodding vigorously in agreement with Edward. Tom stares into Edward's eyes and steps back, sitting on the sofa.

"Good lad." Edward sits in the armchair again. "I must get that roast on soon or we'll never be eating on time."

"You haven't told me where Martha is yet."

"What makes you think I know?"

"She doesn't eat scones."

"Pardon?"

"She can't eat scones."

"Based on her dietary requirements, you think I've done something untoward?"

"One hundred percent. That and the fact you're pointing my gun at me."

"Hm. Maybe she isn't who you think she is, and she took off?"

"I know exactly who she is."

Edward's eyes flicker a moment before he leans back in the armchair and taps the gun on his knee. "Well, aren't you adorable when you're indignant?"

"A delight I've been told."

Edward gazes at Tom. "How different things could have been."

"What?"

Edward gives his head a shake and stands up. "Nothing. Maybe you make yourself useful and finish putting this table together for me?"

"How about you go fuck yourself?"

Edward opens his mouth as Tom's phone rings in his pocket. Tom slaps a hand against the vibrating phone. "Didn't check my pocket, huh?"

"Answer it."

"Answer it?"

"Maybe it's Martha." Edward snorts. "But obviously you'll get rid of whoever it is. You have a table to build. Put it on speaker."

"Obviously." Tom pulls the phone out and James' name lights up. He taps the screen and puts it on the coffee table. "James."

"Hey, so I've been monitoring the hotel room since you left. No one in, no one out. Not even services."

"Great."

"So, did you find Martha?"

Tom keeps his eyes on Edward as he speaks. "Not yet."

Edward raises his eyebrows and puts both hands up as if to say, *where could she be?* And it clenches Tom's jaw.

"Stay on monitoring that room, James."

"Yeah, I'll stay here. I can work on that other job while I'm hanging out. It's getting juicy."

"What is?"

"This other job. But I really shouldn't have said that to you. So…"

"Hey before you go."

"Yeah?"

"Can you call Mischa? Ask her to go home to her flat? Or yours."

"Huh? Why?"

"Just do it. Please."

"Fine, fine. You sound weird."

"You always sound weird. Gotta go, I'm about to watch Ghostbusters." Tom ends the call.

"Ghostbusters?" Edward asks, gesturing for the phone.

"Childhood favourite." Tom tosses the phone at Edward.

At the mention of the word childhood, Edward's face darkens. He takes the phone and with the butt of the gun he smashes it on the worktop. He nods with satisfaction before walking towards Tom.

Tom stands with every intention of wrestling the gun from Edward, but the stress his body has endured today has given him vertigo, and the room sways as nausea hits him again. He slaps a hand to his gut and takes a breath. "Jesus."

Edward stops in front of him and grins. "Feeling poorly?"

Tom glares through the dark spots dancing in his vision. "Fuck you." His legs wobble and he stumbles, falling back onto the sofa.

Edward pushes the gun against his temple. "Build the fucking table."

40

ISABELLA

"No, no, no," Martha whispers. "This mustn't happen. We need to end this."

Isabella glances at her from where she is tugging on her restraints, knowing it won't free her, and ignoring the shooting pain in her wrists and forearms. "No problem. I'm assuming you brought a weapon with you?"

"I didn't bring my handbag."

Isabella goes to chuckle, but the look on Martha's face swiftly changes her mind. "Martha. My point is… we are both tied to furniture. We both know that if we make a sound, he will kill one of us. Or maybe Tom."

Martha looks Isabella up and down. "How far can you move?"

"Not far. Why?"

"Because in my sock I have a small Swiss army knife, Dear."

"You *what?*"

"I said I didn't bring my handbag." She gives Isabella a wry smile. "Not that I wasn't armed with anything at all."

"Why didn't you whip it out earlier? When he was punching you in the face, for instance?" Isabella shakes her head.

"It all happened so fast. One minute he was groaning because I punched him in the nose. Next, I was on the floor with my hands tied and his knee in the middle of my back."

"Is he really that nimble?"

"He's not what you think he is, Isabella." Martha clears her throat and looks away.

"What is he?"

Martha says nothing.

"Martha? What is he?"

"Damaged."

Isabella waits, but Martha's gaze fixes on the wall opposite her and she says nothing more.

"Right, well… about this knife?"

Martha takes a breath and appears to come back from wherever she got lost. "It's in my sock. Which neither of us can reach." Martha shifts her body, twisting her torso with far more ease than a woman of her age should be able to. Her chair creaks at its joints with her movement and she jerks her entire body towards the right. The chair moves slightly. "There." She looks up at Isabella. "I'm going to get close enough to you so that when I tip my chair, you can reach my ankle."

"With what Martha? My teeth?"

"If you have to."

Isabella screws her face up and stares at Martha as she wriggles and jerks her body to get the chair inching towards the bed. "Have you lost your mind?"

Martha stops moving and stares down at the floor. "I need to stop this."

"Stop what?"

"Do you care about Tom, dear?"

The question catches Isabella off guard and she opens her mouth and closes it.

"It's a simple question."

"And one you know the answer to. Why are you asking me that?'

"Because Edward is going to hurt him."

"He already has Martha, or was that almighty crack of something hitting a body earlier in my imagination?"

"I'm not talking about physically." Martha takes a breath in and shuffles her chair another nanometre closer to the bed.

"Then what *are* you talking about?"

Martha keeps fussing with her chair, sweat dotting her brow line.

Isabella is more awake at this moment than she has been for days. "Explain yourself Martha. Because right now, you're scaring the shit out of me."

Martha stills in the chair and raises her chin. "Sometimes in life Isabella, we do things, make decisions we think are for the best, no, *are* for the best. But they don't always turn out the way we think they should. And as a consequence, they… they come back to bite us on the behind."

"What decisions? What are you talking about?" Isabella leans towards Martha, her voice a harsh whisper. "Did you do something?"

"Yes. And I thought it was for the best."

"What was it?"

Martha opens her mouth as the bedroom door also opens.

Edward shuts the door behind him. "No doubt you heard we have another guest." He walks further into the room, tapping something against his thigh.

"Oh my god," Isabella whispers.

"That's Tom's gun," Martha says.

"Well spotted Martha. Yes. Yes, it is."

"How the hell did you get that from him?" Martha glares at Edward.

Edward bends down in front of her so they are eye to eye. "Feeling conflicted are you?"

"Should I?"

Edward smiles. "He's being a very good lad, putting together my new table. I also cuffed him to the radiator, which is probably why he hasn't stormed in." He glances at Isabella. "In case you're wondering."

Isabella ignores the tingles in her nose. "He just let you tie him up, did he?"

Edward snorts and rolls his eyes. "Tie? I said cuff. I made him *cuff* himself to the radiator while I shoved his own gun against his temple."

Isabella pictures Tom's face, glaring at Edward the entire time, and it brings her a strange sense of closeness to him. It also brings more tingles to her nose and tears to brim in her eyes.

Edward's face falls, and he sidles to her and sits on the bed. "Oh, Kitten. Don't cry. It's almost over, I promise." He leans to her ear. "And then I can put you out of your misery." He strokes her face. "Not unlike poor little Pebbles. God rest her furry little soul."

Isabella blinks and silent tears tumble down her cheeks. "I'm not afraid of you."

Edward grins and looks at Martha, whose gaze is straight ahead, her skin a paler shade than usual. "She's a firecracker isn't she, Martha?"

Martha doesn't answer, continuing to stare into space.

Edward stands. "Well... I must get back out there and supervise the building of this table. It's imperative it's ready in time. Tata." He strolls to the door and stops to turn and wink at Isabella. "All over soon, Kitten. Oh and... one sound and Tom's dead." He leaves, closing the door behind him with a soft click.

"He's going to kill you," Martha whispers.

"Were you about to give me a knife or not?" Isabella sniffles and tries to edge as close to Martha as she can. "A few more shuffles should do it... Let's go." Knowing Tom is metres from her renews a spark in Isabella's chest.

Martha doesn't move. "I'll give you the knife." She shifts her eyes to stare into Isabella's. "But you mustn't kill him. Do you understand?"

"I'm sorry... what?"

"Use it to defend yourself and Tom. Do not kill Edward."

"I... I really don't understand."

"Take it and hide it under the pillow. Use it if you need to, but don't kill him. I really don't understand how much clearer I need to be, Isabella."

Isabella holds Martha's gaze. Determination rests behind her sharp eyes and it encourages Isabella to nod. *She always has a reason.* "Okay, Martha. Whatever you say."

Martha nods once and recommences her chair shuffle.

41

TOM

Tom sits, leaning against the wall and glares at the radiator Edward insisted he cuff himself to. He tosses an allen key and catches it with his free hand.

"You haven't got too far," Edward says as he walks into the kitchen. He grabs a rack of lamb from the fridge, already dressed and on a tray, and slides it into the oven.

"I've no intention of building your table."

Edward turns; his face blank. "But… what will we eat off?"

Tom leans forward and curls his lip. "I don't fucking care, Ed."

Edward sighs. "Remember that cute little kitty cat all dead and twisted in that shoebox?" He nods towards the box on the coffee table. "I'd really hate to repeat that on that old bag down the hall."

Tom stops tossing the allen key and glares at Edward.

Edward grins. "You know I will." He nods at the pieces of flat pack table scattered around Tom. "Best get building." He sits in his armchair and smiles at Tom.

Tom squeezes the key in his hand. He holds Edward's stare as he reaches for the closest table leg and the instruction booklet. *Fucking fine.* "So, is Martha okay in the bedroom?" he asks.

Edward's adams apple bobbles and he sits up straighter in the armchair. "Don't know what you're talking about."

Tom shrugs. "Because if you've hurt her or caused her any distress, I *will* feed your own intestines to you. Pass that packet of screws, would you?" Tom holds a hand out for the plastic bag next to Edward's armchair.

"Get it yourself if you're so smart."

"Well, I do appreciate you recognise my superior intelligence, I'm also tethered to a radiator at your request so…" He shrugs and claps his fingers against his palm. "Screws?"

Edward gives a dramatic sigh, picks up the screws and tosses them to Tom.

Tom catches the bag, glances at the bedroom door and back at Edward. "Great. Thanks."

"What makes you so sure she's in there?"

"Hmm?" Tom looks up. "Oh, I wasn't. Until you confirmed it for me. So… thanks for that."

"Confirmed it?"

Tom grins as though they're old friends. "Yep."

Edward shakes his head. "You're nuttier than a fruitcake."

"Martha?" Tom calls, staring straight at Edward.

Pink spots appear on Edward's cheeks, and he slowly smiles as no answer comes from the bedroom. "Well… I guess we can put that ridiculous theory to bed now."

"Or… she knows you have my gun pointed at me and won't risk answering." Tom picks up another piece of the table and concentrates on it, ignoring Edward but feeling his stare on the side of his face.

"In case you forgot, she's coming to dinner with us, too. Remember?"

"I do." He spins the allen key, securing the pieces of one leg and support, and moves to the next. "I assume you informed her of the new day and time of this meal?"

"Yep."

"Great. Pass me that bracket?"

"I'm not your assistant."

"No, but…" He jerks the handcuffed hand, making the cuffs jangle against the radiator, and shrugs. "You want your table ready for your fancy dinner, don't you?" Tom rests his free hand on the next table leg and raises his eyebrows. "Bracket?"

Edward huffs and gets off the sofa. He bends down to pick up the piece Tom gestured to. Tom grasps the table leg, swings, and smacks Edward in the back of the head.

Edward grunts and topples forward, just out of reach of Tom, the gun sliding across the floor into the kitchen.

He punches the floor as the gun stops well out of reach, and strains against the cuff knowing it's futile. Grabbing the table leg he hit Edward with, he reaches across the floor, but the gun is still too far. He throws the table leg at the wall, leaving a nice dent in the plaster.

"Fuck." Tom shifts forward on his backside and kicks out, just landing a flutter kick in the small of Edward's back. "Fuck!" Sweat slides down the middle of Tom's back as he shifts onto his stomach to get closer before Edward wakes up. *I need the key…*

Tom pushes himself to the limit of where his cuffed hand will let him and manages to hook his foot around the back of one of Edward's knees. He bends his leg and tries to pull Edward towards him, but the body weight is too much and he loses grip, his foot sliding off.

Tom groans into the floor. He tries again, hooking his foot around the same knee and pulling. Edward moves the slightest from the hips down, but the bulk of his body stays put. Tom punches the floor again, bends his leg and kicks Edward as hard as he can. There's no point other than to make him feel better, but it doesn't work.

As Edward moans and wiggles his fingers, Tom gets into a sitting position and leans against the wall. "Damn!"

Edward moans again and slowly pushes himself onto all fours.

Tom drops his head onto his shoulder and watches Edward gather himself. All his energy coiled in his body.

"Well," Edward says, getting to his feet and leaning forward with his hands on his knees. "Not your smartest move, Tom."

Edward disappears behind Tom into the kitchen.

Tom stares at the imitation antique desk across the lounge and twiddles the allen key in his fingers. His eyes wander back to his predicament and he focuses on the radiator. "Ed?"

"Tom?" His voice is above and behind him, still in the kitchen.

"How do you feel about your flat being flooded with rusty radiator water?"

Edward chuckles. "You can try."

"Maybe I will." He pulls against the cuff again.

A puff of air hits the side of Tom's neck and Edward's voice is right next to his ear. "It's a nice idea."

Tom jerks his head away from Edward and attempts to shuffle away. Edward slides his forearm against Tom's throat from behind and squeezes. Tom thrashes in an attempt to free himself but a short sharp sting hits him in the neck.

"What the fuck?" Tom grabs the back of Edward's head with his free hand but no sooner has he gripped his hair, a strange fog descends, slowing his brain. "What did you inject me with? Why is it working so fast?"

"Shhhh... You won't die. I'm not a complete sadist. *I'm* a pharmacist. I took an oath." He laughs at his own joke, releases Tom from his sleeper hold, and stands up. "And it's working because I got it straight into your blood stream. I know what I'm doing."

Tom swipes at his neck as his vision blurs. "What the actual... fuck is wrong with you." He blinks and squeezes his eyes shut before blinking again. Nothing improves his vision or the cotton wool filling his head. "I asked you what you... fucking gave... me."

Edwards crouches in front of Tom and puts a hand on his shoulder. "And I told you... you won't die." He takes a key from his pocket and unlocks the cuff. Tom's hand hits the floor with a thud. "C'mon Tom. Why don't you and go lie on the sofa. You're in my way here."

Tom allows Edward to help him to his feet, with every intention of flattening him the moment he's upright.

"There we go," Edward says, draping Toms' arm over his shoulder and leading him to the sofa.

Tom's feet don't cooperate, his body sways, and he stumbles against Edward. "Fuck this," he slurs.

"A little rest and you'll be awake in time for dinner." Edward drops Tom on the sofa.

Tom's eyelids droop as he slumps against the cushions. The hatred and fire in his chest is still there, but nothing is working the way it's supposed to. He swings at Edward, but instead of making contact, he tumbles forward onto the floor. He rolls onto his back and stares up at Edward's grinning face.

Edward peers down at him. "Well, if that is where you're most comfortable…"

42

ISABELLA

"I haven't heard voices in a while," Isabella turns her head towards the door of the bedroom and holds her breath. "Have you?"

"There," Martha says. "Are you ready, Dear? I'm going to tip the chair."

Isabella tears her eyes from the door and frowns at Martha. "Did you hear what I just asked you?"

"Yes, dear."

"Well?"

"Well what?"

"It's been like an hour at least and it's silent out there. Not a peep apart from some hammering and clattering around the kitchen."

"Okay dear, now I'm about to tip. So you need to get that knife... use your teeth if you must. Are you ready?'

Isabella stares at Martha, tempted to do one of those exaggerated double takes from an old cartoon. "What? Did you hear—"

"*Yes* Isabella. I heard you. I've listened to you fret and worry for the past goodness knows how long, while I plan how to get us all out of here with the least possible damage done. So if you don't mind… get ready to bite my ankle."

"*You* have a plan? Care to share?" Isabella shakes her head. "Least possible damage? What's with you?"

"Teeth. Sock. That's an order." Martha takes a breath and jerks her body to the right. The chair rocks and lands back on all four legs. "And again," she huffs. She throws her body towards the right again and the chair lifts. She closes her eyes and scrunches her face up, tipping her head in the direction she wants to go. The chair teeters before falling on its side, Martha still securely taped to it. She lets out a sharp yelp as her shoulder hits the floor.

"Martha, are you alright?"

"Yes, just get the knife."

The bedroom door opens before Isabella can get anywhere near Martha's ankle.

Edward leaps across the room and grabs Martha's shoulders, pulling her and the chair upright again. "Martha, Martha, Martha. You're going to hurt yourself."

She winces as Edward drags her chair back where it started. "Damn," she whispers. "*Damn it.*" Distress paints her face, and she doesn't look at Isabella.

"Where's Tom?" Isabella asks Edward, keeping her eyes on Martha.

"Having a rest. He has a big night ahead." Edward kneels behind Martha's chair and slices through the tape holding her hands together with a knife.

"A rest? You drugged him?" Isabella's heart squeezes. "You drugged him?

Edward brings Martha's hands to the front, her feet still taped securely to the chair. He looks at Isabella. "Yes but—"

Martha punches him to the jaw and he topples backwards.

"That hurt," he mumbles.

"He has a knife in his pocket." Isabella thrusts her body, her wrists seem looser than they were thanks to all the twisting and pulling. She yanks against the bedhead.

Edward gets to his feet and slaps Martha across the face before she can get her feet free. He grabs her hands and slaps handcuffs on her. "You're really trying my patience, Martha." He whips his head around to Isabella. "And you, I think you might need another little rest."

Isabella's stomach tightens. "No. Please, Edward…"

He storms from the room, leaving the door open. With nothing left to lose Isabella tips her head back. "Tom. *Tom.* Help!" Tears stream down her face and she watches as Martha sits in the chair, limp as a rag doll. "Tom!"

Edward walks back into the room with another bag of liquid. "He can't hear you, Kitten. So please shut your pretty little mouth before I shut it for you."

"Fuck.You." She grits her teeth while he secures the new bag to the drip. "*Fuck you.*"

"Yes Kitten, I'm a very bad man. But I don't have time for your carry on. I have a roast to finish. A table to set and rules to lay down." He finishes securing the bag but doesn't connect it to the cannula. "In fact… let's do the rules now."

"Rules? For what? You *fucking* psycho." Isabella writhes and thrusts, knowing that in a matter of moments, any ability to release her anger and pain will be gone. "I want Tom. And I want you to get the *fuck* away from me." She screams at him, with every ounce of breath in her lungs she screams and shouts and throws her head from side to side until she has no more fight left.

"Are you finished?" He sits on the bed next to her.

She drops her face away from him and closes her eyes.

"Right, well since we're all here together and everyone has finally shut up… I'll explain what I expect over the next few hours."

"What you expect?" Martha's voice crackles as she finally speaks.

Isabella rolls her head back to the left to watch Martha.

"Yes, Martha. What I expect." Edward crosses his legs as casually as if he were at a garden party and smiles at the pair. "Martha, you and I are going to have a lovely, civilised dinner with Tom. No doubt he will be stirring in an hour or so."

Isabella snorts. "As if you can be civilised."

Edward chuckles before slapping Isabella across the face.

The sting burrows into her cheek and she bites the inside of her mouth.

"Do shut up Kitten. I won't ask you again."

"Enough's enough Edward." Martha's voice has her authoritative edge back . "I'll do whatever you want. Stop hurting Isabella and Tom. Do you understand?"

Isabella blinks through the tears in her eyes and watches Martha. Colour has returned to her face and she glares at Edward. *She's back.*

"Finally decided to cooperate, have you?" Edward tilts his head.

"Yes. It seems my attempts to stop this are pointless. You have your plans and I can't stop them."

"Finally, you see sense."

Martha nods. "Yes. So leave Isabella alone now. She won't be a bother to you."

"No she won't. She'll be sleeping. I can't have Tom distracted, he has too much at stake." He grins at Martha. "Wouldn't you agree?"

Martha nods again. "I would. So what do you want?"

"I want you to remember I have Tom's gun. I will not tolerate any misbehaviour from you at dinner. You'll sit, you'll eat, and you'll participate in polite conversation. If you tip off Tom that Isabella is here before I'm ready to tell him, I'll come in here and shoot Isabella dead while she sleeps. Are we clear?"

Isabella's body chills. The force and finality in Edward's voice sends a tremble through her body and for the first time, terror reaches her in this dark room.

"Yes Edward," Martha says. "I understand." She shifts her eyes to Isabella and the hardness from earlier is gone. Reassurance from her gaze settles Isabella's tremble and she gives Martha the lightest of nods.

"A nice dinner," Edwards voice cuts back in. "You'll behave?"

"I'll behave."

Edward stands and claps his hands together once like a child on Christmas morning. "Delightful. You can set the table for me." He leans across Isabella and connects the cannula. He pecks her on the forehead. "Sweet dreams," he whispers. "I do hope this isn't the last time we get to speak."

43

TOM

Cutlery chinks together and a chair scrapes along the floor as though someone shifted it.

"Can I offer you some water?" Edward's voice tenses Tom's muscles even though his eyes want to stay shut. His brain sloshes in his head and he slaps a hand to his face.

"No, thank you." Martha's voice peels Tom's eyes open, and he squints across the room.

A fully laden dining table with a white tablecloth, a single white candle in the middle and three chairs stands where the pile of table parts had been. He struggles to sit up and both Edward and Martha turn to watch him from where they sit, at either end of the table.

"Ah," Edward stands and crosses the floor as Tom finally gets into a sitting position. "You're awake. I was starting to worry I'd gone overboard." He chuckles.

"Overboard?" His own voice sounds foreign to him and he shakes his head.

"Yes. I had to keep giving you shots to keep you asleep."

Tom looks past Edward at the table. He makes out Martha, sitting with her ankles crossed where the tablecloth doesn't quite reach the floor. "Martha?"

Martha looks at Edward, who gives her a nod. "Hello, Tom. Are you going to come sit with us?"

"What?" He leans forward. "Are you alright?"

"Perfectly fine, thank you." She picks up her water and takes a sip.

Tom looks up at Edward, who stands next to him with a sickly grin plastered across his face, and back to Martha as she places her glass back down. "Am I in some messed up twilight zone right now?"

Edward laughs and slides a hand under Tom's arm and attempts to lift him off the sofa with the hand not holding the gun. "Up you get. It's time for dinner."

Tom yanks his arm away from Edward. The force of the action disorients him and he falls forward to his knees on the floor. "Touch me again and I'll rip your face off."

"Tetchy." Edward gives his high-pitched giggle, grabs under Tom's arm again and gets down to his ear. "Get up. Sit at the table and have a delightful meal. Or I'll shoot Martha between the eyes. Capice?"

Tom pulls away from Edward and gets on his hands and knees before standing upright. He grabs the back of the armchair to steady himself as the room warps and spins like a bad seventies movie.

"That's the spirit." Edward gives him a shove to the back that would have landed him on his face if he hadn't been holding the armchair.

Tom shuffles to the table and sits in the empty place. He slides his eyes to Martha, and she meets his gaze, giving him a fleeting warning before looking down at her plate.

"Water, Tom?" Edward holds a jug in his free hand and nods towards an empty glass sitting in front of him.

"What's in it?"

Edward smiles and pours. "It's not poison. If that's what you're asking."

"You'll forgive me if I don't believe you."

Edward huffs and sloshes water from the jug into his own glass, picks it up and gulps. "Happy?"

The dryness in Tom's mouth from whatever drugs Edward shot into him wins the battle. He picks the glass up and gulps the entire contents. It helps his mind clear a little more and his senses are almost back to normal. He slaps the glass onto the table and glares at Edward. "Can we get whatever this is over with?"

"Whatever this is?" Edward pours Tom more water. "We're having a good old fashioned Sunday roast, Tom. All together." He puts the jug down and plants his elbows on the table, resting his chin on his hands. "Won't this be lovely?"

"It's not Sunday."

Edward rolls his eyes and picks up his fork. "Must you be so argumentative?" He smiles at Martha as he chews on a potato. "Honestly Martha, is he always like this?"

"I find it endearing," she says in a tone that conveys that she does *not* find it endearing and Tom should stop being difficult.

Tom stares at her as she pushes peas around her plate with her fork.

"Now, Tom," Edward says. "This is supposed to be a traditional Sunday roast. You know… the kind you would have had with your family as a child. I'm sure you and Martha had a few, did you not?"

Tom's head snaps to Edward. "What did you say?"

"Tom. Please." Martha puts her fork down and reaches across, grabbing his arm and squeezing it. "Do as he says." She squeezes again, a little too hard, before returning to her peas.

Tom clenches his fists on either side of the plate on the table and draws a long breath in. He looks around the flat, noting again how it's the exact same as his own down the hall. He glances at Martha, still pushing peas around the plate and back to Edward, who is dishing himself up a second helping of beans. "Ed?"

He puts the platter of beans down and raises his eyebrows at Tom. "Yes?"

"Have you ever seen that film, Single White Female?"

A clatter sounds, and Tom turns to Martha.

"For God's sake, Tom. Please. Don't make this harder than it needs to be." She throws her napkin onto the table and claws a hand through her hair.

"Harder than it… have you drunk the Kool Aid?"

Edward slaps his hand on the table, making the cutlery jump. "So."

Tom clenches fists tighter and stares straight ahead.

"Martha, Tom. Why don't we talk about some stories from the old days?"

Tom quirks a brow and turns his head. "The old days? What rubbish are you talking about?"

"He knows you grew up in my house, Tom."

Cold water plunges into Tom's gut, and he swallows.

Edward smiles. "Yes. And I think that's simply delightful. So... Martha, why don't you think back to Tom's childhood and have a conversation you may have had over a roast all those moons ago?"

"What? Why?" Tom shakes his head. "You're a damn loon."

Edward's face darkens, and he pounds a fist onto the table. "Because I *wasn't* there. Was I?" He moves his eyes to Martha and tilts his head.

"No. You weren't." She puts her fork down and clasps both hands together. "Okay fine. Tom—"

"No." Tom stands up, ignoring the residual fog in his head.

"Sit down, Tom." Martha's voice carries anger and exasperation. "I was going to recall that conversation we had about your childhood friend *Irina*. Remember her?"

The name gives Tom's heart a jumpstart, and it beats as though he's run a marathon. "What about her?" he whispers, lowering himself into his chair.

Edward claps once. "Excellent. Okay, now listen... have the conversation as though it were happening now." He picks his glass up and tilts it towards Martha. "And go."

Tom ignores Edward, his eyes stuck on Martha.

She nods once and shifts in her chair. "Well, you remember that dear girl, Irina, that you took to the movies when you were thirteen?"

Tom says nothing.

"Well, remember how she just disappeared one day, and you were so sad she hadn't told you her family was moving?"

"Oh, Tom. That must have broken your little heart," Edward says.

"Well, I heard recently that she had only moved a few houses away."

Tom's mouth dries again, and it has nothing to do with the drugs. "A few…"

"Yes. A few houses away. But you didn't see her because she became unwell and was in bed a lot. Very tired, all the time."

"I see," Tom's voice strains against the pain in his throat. "So she couldn't get out of bed?"

"Ah." Edward spears another roast potato and nods. "Sounds like chronic fatigue. How old was she?"

"Quite young," Martha answers, keeping her eyes on Tom. "Was very sad."

"Her father was a bit mad, wasn't he?' Tom balls his napkin up in his hand.

"Yes, come to think of it. Rarely let her out of that room. Kept giving her medicine, thinking it might help. But it just made her more bed ridden from what I understand."

"Oh," Edward taps the table with his fork. "I see what's happening."

Shit.

Tom looks at Edward, who stares back a moment before gazing at Martha.

"What do you see, Edward?" Martha asks.

"God complex."

Silence falls across the dinner table and Tom eyes his gun, still in Edward's left hand, his knuckles white with the grip he has on it.

"God complex?" Martha rubs her chin. "Go on?"

"Well, we see it a lot in the pharmaceutical game. People think they're doctors... can treat their family members better than the professionals."

Tom ignores Edward as he launches into an explanation about crazy parents and tries to calculate if he can kick Edward square in the crotch under the table, take the gun and... *Nope. Fuck it.*

Tom lunges forward, grabbing Edward around the middle, tackling him off his chair.

Edward wriggles and kicks out as Tom smothers him with his own body weight and grabs at his gun, still in Edward's hand. Edward flicks his wrist and Tom loses his grip. The gun goes off and plaster rains down on them from the wall they wrestle against.

Another gunshot rings out from behind all of them and Edward covers his head, dropping the gun. Tom grabs his gun and racks the slide, just to make sure but also to make a point.

"It's him. Martha, it's him." James' voice fills the flat.

Although Tom's head is still swimming in leftover sedative, he's renewed at the possibility, no, probability of Isabella being in the bedroom. Tom pulls his knee back and crunches it into Edward's crotch.

Edward's knees recoil against his chest and he curls into the foetal position, howling like a wounded animal.

"It's *him* Martha," James points his gun at Edward's curled up body.

Tom scurries from the floor, suddenly feeling like he could take on an army, and joins James in pointing his gun at Edward.

"Calm *down*, James. I know." Martha stands up and lowers a hand towards James. "I *know*."

"You know he's Jared?" James asks.

"Jared?" Tom looks between Martha and James.

"Well, well." Edward grunts and rolls onto his back, his face practically purple. "Aren't you a clever little fella?"

Tom squeezes his temples with his thumb and forefinger. "Who the fuck is Jared?"

"Jared Miller. Got out of prison three years ago after serving time for killing his mother with a shovel while she slept."

"Haven't you done your research? Although you stuffed up one minor detail, dear lad—"

"Edward. Stop." Martha's voice cuts through the chaos and Tom watches as she moves to the sofa to sit. "Please stop."

Tom observes Martha for a moment as she sits and grasps at her stomach as though she's about to be sick.

"She's right Edward," he says, turning back to the crumpled heap on the floor. "No one gives a shit what you have to say."

Edward laughs, though it's laced with a grimace. "Don't be so sure."

Tom kicks Edward to the crotch again, and he folds in half, howling into the floor.

"Another satisfying crunch," James says.

"Indeed." Tom nods as the pair of them stand over Edward, their guns trained on his head. "James?"

"Yeah?"

"Thanks for turning up."

"No problem."

Tom turns to find Martha staring at the blank television. "Martha?"

She lifts her chin and finds Tom's eyes. "Get Isabella out of that room."

"Wait, what?' James looks between Martha and Tom as Edward groans on the floor in front of them. "Tom?" James kicks Edward in the temple and he goes quiet.

"Good shot." Tom shoves his gun into his waistband where it belongs and grabs a roll of tape from the coffee table. "Tie him up. We aren't finished yet."

James takes the tape. "She's here?"

"She's here."

James nods. "Take your time. We aren't going anywhere."

Tom leaps across the lounge room and shoulder barges the bedroom door open. He flicks the light on and all the breath leaves his lungs.

Isabella is tied to the bedhead, a cannula in her hand. She's asleep.

He jumps onto the bed, drops to his knees and unhooks the quarter full bag. He drops it on the floor and unwinds the tape from her wrists, wincing as the raw, blistered skin underneath is exposed. "I'm sorry... I'm so sorry," he whispers.

She moans softly but doesn't move as he gently brings her arms down from above her head.

Tom sits against the bedhead and pulls her onto his chest. He rests his lips on top of her head. "Take your time," he whispers.

44

ISABELLA

I sabella becomes aware of warmth against her cheek and nuzzles into it.

"Iz?"

A deep voice seeps into her ears and the warmth against her cheek vibrates softly.

"Are you awake?"

She pulls a breath through her nose and stretches an arm out, hugging the warm lump she's leaning against. *My arm hurts.* The skin around her wrists burns and she scrunches her eyes up before slowly opening them onto a fully lit, blurry room.

"Hey..."

A warm hand strokes down her face from her temple to her chin and cups her face. She pushes her face against the warm hand. It's a place she's been before. *Am I still out?*

She forces her eyes to open again and she blinks, realising it's a body she's lying against. Her heart jolts and she pushes against the body and tries to sit up. "Get away from... me." She pushes again and uses her other hand, folded under her own body to try and sit up.

"Iz, it's me. Hey." His hand is still curved around her cheek and chin. "You're safe."

Tears flood her eyes, and she pushes against his chest to look up at him. The pain in her wrists is electric, but she doesn't care. "You found me." Hot tears roll down her cheeks.

Tom smiles at her and rubs the tears from her face with his thumbs. "You doubted me?"

"No." She flops against him again and his arms wrap around her. "Is.. is he dead?"

"Not yet." Tom's muscles tense under his shirt.

Isabella presses a hand against his chest. "I need to see him. Is he here?"

"He's in the lounge. Hopefully trussed up like a Christmas ham."

"Hopefully? Who... who else is here?"

"James and Martha."

She settles against his chest again. "There's something... something between Edward and Martha."

"Like?"

"It's like they've..." She stops and licks her lips, her mouth dry. "It's... like they met before. But Edward taunted her... about you. I don't know... I don't know. It was just weird."

"He has the entire flat set up like ours."

Isabella attempts to sit upright. Her core muscles are sluggish and her joints scream to stop moving. "God," she whispers, trying to shuffle to the edge of the bed.

"Where are you going?" Tom's voice is edged with a smile.

"I want to go out there."

"Of course you do." Tom gets off the bed and stands in front of her. "Shall we?"

Isabella takes his hands and tries to stand. Her knees buckle and her ankles shoot pain through her legs. She drops back onto the bed. "Give me a second."

"Iz, let me carry you."

"Carry me? No... Tom, I don't need you to... I don't need you to carry me. I'm..." She stops and takes a breath as dizziness hits her. "I'm perfectly capable of walk... walking."

I know you are. But he pumped you full of god knows what for days. Just let me—"

"*No.*" She shuffles her backside to the very edge of the bed. "I'll walk out of here. I just need a few tries."

"Iz—"

"I will *walk* out of here."

45

TOM

E dward turns his head as Tom and Isabella walk into the lounge. He's slumped in the armchair, tied by the wrists and ankles while James trains a gun in the middle of his chest. "Ah, Tom. Come back to join the party?" Edward's voice grits Tom's teeth and he punches Edward in the nose as he passes the armchair.

Edward squeals like a teenage girl and it gives Tom a moment of enjoyment.

He lets go of Isabella's hand. "Iz, go sit down."

She stops in front of Martha, bends down and grabs something from Martha's sock and comes back to Edward.

"Iz, what are you doing?"

She flicks open a tiny pocketknife. "I just need a sec with Edward."

Go nuts. Tom steps back.

Edward smiles at her. "Hello Kitten. I know this all seems a little strange, but you'll be back in the right spot soon. I promise." He winks.

She leans over Edward, grabs his jaw and points the tip of the knife in his cheek.

Something in Tom's stomach flip flops. "He doesn't deserve a number, Iz."

"He's not getting one." She drags the knife down the side of his face, not making a cut, continues down the middle of his chest and stops over his heart. "I don't know if I ever told you, but I'm quite nimble with a blade. Did you know that?"

Edward snorts. "I'm sure you are, Kitten."

A millisecond later, Edward hollers and jerks his body back and forth. "Are you fucking insane?" The knife sticks out of his thigh.

Tom doesn't miss the slight whimper from Martha, and he raises a brow at her.

Isabella pulls the knife from his thigh. "I missed your femoral artery on purpose, in case you were wondering. I'm far more precise when I want someone dead quickly as opposed to..." She turns and looks at Tom. "Drawn out?"

"I intend to hurt him a little."

"Lovely." She wipes the blade on Edward's shirt, hands it back to Martha and sits at the end of the sofa.

"It's just a minor graze," Edward says. "What's a little blood?"

Tom's fists clench and he glares at Edward, imagining all the ways he intends to torture him.

"Please Jared, just let them leave. I'll stay." Martha says.

The fuck? "Why did you call him Jared?"

Martha presses her lips together and closes her eyes. "Because that's his name."

"I never thought this day would come," Edward says.

Martha stares stonily back at him. "Neither did I."

"Have you missed me?"

"I have thought of you often."

Tom squints at the pair of them. "What?" His fists unclench and he holds his hands out in question.

Edward grins. "This *will* be entertaining.Though I was hoping we would have this conversation over dessert. I made a lovely spotted dick..."

"Edward, will you shut the fuck up?"

Edward snorts. "Have a seat Tom. You'll need to sit down for this."

Tom grabs Edward's face and presses his gun against his temple. "You have got to be the most infuriating human I've ever come across."

"Tom. Stop."

Tom turns and peers at Martha. "Stop? After everything he's done to you?" He looks across at Isabella. "And Iz."

"Take the gun away from his head. Please."

Tom glares at Martha, and she holds his gaze until he moves off Edward. He goes to the imitation antique desk and leans against it. "So what the fuck's going on?"

"You really should probably sit down, Tom," James says, nodding towards the sofa next to Martha.

Ignoring James, Tom holds both hands up in question. "I'm

waiting." *To end him.* Edward giggles and Tom's blood curdles at the sound. "You're creepy as fuck. You know that?"

Edward blows Tom an air kiss, and blood trickles from his nose.

Tom's blood pressure shoots through the top of his skull and he leaps across the room, pulls Edward to the floor and straddles his chest.

Edward's eyes widen, but a smirk stays on his lips. "What are you gonna do, Tom? You know... if we were brothers, our mother would claim this isn't a fair fight."

"Lucky we aren't even remotely *fucking* related, then. Isn't it?" Tom pulls his fist back, but Martha grabs his arm.

"Tom. No more. Stop." Martha grabs both his shoulders and pulls him away from Edward.

Tom falls onto his backside before scrambling to his feet. He towers over Martha, but she doesn't move back. "Are you kidding? He's tortured Isabella for days, kidnaped you and made you eat fucking lamb and you're telling me to stop? You've killed men for much less."

"I have. But this is different."

Edward laughs again from the floor. "Let's give him the good news, Martha. I wanted to make it special, but I suppose this will have to do."

"Jared. Please." Martha's voice falters and she clears her throat. "No good can come of this." A tear runs down her cheek and drips onto her blouse.

Edward snorts. "You gave up the right to ask anything of me. Remember?"

Tom's ear prick. "What?"

Martha sits on the sofa again and folds her hands in her lap.

Tom sighs. "Get this over with Ed, before I shoot you dead."

Isabella smiles at him from the other end of the sofa.

"Will someone please sit me in my chair so Tom and I can be eye to eye?"

James, Isabella and Tom stare at him, none of them move.

"I'm not saying anything until I'm in my damn chair."

James yanks Edward under both arms and drops him in his chair. He leans into Edward's face. "This isn't necessary. Think about it. Maybe we can get you into a psych hospital somewhere instead of prison?"

The fact James knows something about this complete shit show Tom doesn't irks him more than it should. "He's not getting any favours from us." Tom pulls the coffee table across and sits directly in front of Edward. "Speak."

"Tom, I really think—"

"James, I really think you need to get the fuck out of the way." Tom curls his lip. "Get Iz some water."

"But I—"

"It's fine James. It's done now." Martha's voice is meek and Tom has to turn and look at her to make sure it's she who spoke. "I'm sure Isabella would love some water. Isabella?"

"Thanks James, I would."

Tom locks eyes with Isabella, and something in her gaze unsettles him. "Do you know what this is about, Iz?"

She shakes her head. "No. But… I'm starting to get an idea." She glances at Martha, who bows her head and fiddles with her hands in her lap. Tom looks between the two women a moment before turning back to Edward.

"The floor is yours, Edward." Tom slaps both hands on his knees. "Well?"

"I want what you took."

"I've taken nothing from you."

"You took my place." He shuffles in his chair, his hands still secured behind him.

"Your place where?"

Edward looks at Martha. "I think it's got more impact coming from her."

Tom doesn't turn around, somehow knowing that whatever comes next, he won't like.

A heavy silence descends on the flat, and Tom's neck prickles.

"Jared Miller is my son."

Tom's ears ring and the room tunnels. He gives his head a shake. "Pardon?"

"Take it in. It's big news." Edward's voice sounds a million miles away as Tom gazes back at Martha, suddenly not recognising her face.

"Why don't you have kids of your own?" Tom looked up from his maths homework as Martha pottered around the kitchen.

She stopped drying a dish and looked out the window for a moment. "Well?"

Martha walked to the table and sat across from Tom. "Well Tom, I can't have children."

"Why not? Did something happen to you?"

"Some women just can't. And I'm one of them."

"Does that make you sad?"

Martha fiddled with the salt and pepper shakers in the middle of the

table. "Sometimes. But if I had children of my own, I may not have had
room to help you. So maybe it worked out for the best?"

"Maybe."

Martha patted his hand and stood up.

"I'm sorry, Martha."

"What for?"

"Asking why you don't have kids."

Martha smiled. "Unnecessary."

Tom shrugged and leaned over his maths book.

Tom peers at Martha. "You lied to me?"

"I didn't lie so much as—

"You *didn't* lie?"

"I was protect... I'm sorry."

Tom blinks and stares at her. He moves next to her on the
sofa, still gazing at her, unable to look anywhere else. *Who*
are you?

"I have some nifty papers that explain everything in the
cupboard above the fridge. Maybe your little mate can get
them?" Edward jerks his head back towards the kitchen.

James pulls a folder down from the cupboard and brings it to
Tom.

He drops his eyes to the offering and takes them. He reads the
top of the first sheet. *Barnardos.* Tom gulps in air as the walls
close in around him and he swallows, shaking his head. "No.
I'm..." He drops the papers and looks at Martha.

"I need to expl..." She inhales and watches Tom. "Can I
explain?"

"You can try." Tom swallows, his throat not cooperating. He

slides away from Martha, towards Isabella and she puts a hand on his back.

"Wait a minute, wait a minute. I feel I deserve the first explanation. So why don't we start at the beginning? Mumsy?"

Tom watches this scene before him unfold without seeing it. *This has to be a joke. Has to be.*

"Or maybe I should start?" Edward narrows his eyes at Martha.

Tom grabs both of Isabella's hands and covers them with his own. He wants to wrap his arms around her and run as far away from this place as he can.

She squeezes his hands, and he looks at her. Her eyes say everything. *Let her explain.*

"So, Tom. Here's the thing. This… woman here. This highly decorated, respected woman." He stops and eyes Martha. "Yes, I did my research on you. She threw me away. She gave birth to me and *threw me away.*" He glares at Martha. "Isn't that right?"

"I saw it differently."

"Oh! Oh I'm sorry. You saw it differently, did you? Please go on… I'm simply dying to hear how *you saw it.*"

Tom shifts on the sofa, and Isabella rests her head on his shoulder.

Martha closes her eyes a moment before opening them and looking not at Edward, but at Tom.

"I was twenty years old. I wasn't in a relationship. And I was starting my career in the Royal Navy. I had nothing to offer a child."

"So you threw your child away." Edward says, as though she just solved the most obvious of riddles.

"No. I gave you to someone who could give you the life you deserved."

"Ha! Life I deserved. Do you know what that life consisted of?" He sneers at her. "Do you?"

"I do not."

Tom sits stock still, watching this conversation unfold and having nothing to say. *She lied for twenty-three years.*

"They adopted me because they couldn't have children. Or so they thought. Then one day when I'm six years old. Bam! Mumsy gets knocked up. And before I know it, they have this baby that they love more than me."

"I doubt they—"

"Don't you tell me what they did or didn't feel for me. How would you know? You *weren't there!*" Spittle gathers at the sides of his mouth. "I was *nothing* to them when that girl arrived."

"Your sister."

"No. She wasn't my sister. We don't have the same blood. Do we? Martha? You and I, however…"

An electric volt hits Tom in the gut, and he jumps from the sofa. "Stop!"

Edward freezes and turns his face to Tom. A smile curls his lips upward and he nods. "Sorry, Tom. Did I forget how all this must be affecting you?"

"Your concern is touching. It's quite clear you want to take my place in the world."

"*My* place. You are in *my* place, Tom. I'm merely taking back what's mine." He grins at Isabella. "And *who* is mine."

Tom clenches his jaw. "She isn't a possession for you to take, Edward."

"My fucking name is Jared." Edward shouts. "That's the name Mumsy over there gave me."

Gave him. Tom squeezes his eyes closed and pushes a palm against his face.

"Are you happy, Tom? Are you happy living a life that was never meant for you?" Edward seethes from his armchair.

"I'm fucking ecstatic." Tom sits on the edge of the sofa again and puts his head in his hands. "I have no idea what to do with this," he whispers.

"Might I suggest sitting next to Mumsy?" Edward flicks his head. "She looks forlorn."

"Are you alright?" Tom asks her without looking in her direction.

"I'm more worried about how you are."

Tom snorts.

"Now, Mumsy—

"Why are you doing this, Jared?" Martha's voice is even and flat.

"I've been wronged, Martha. By you and Tom. The system. Everyone."

"I never wronged you. I did what was right."

"From the age of six, I was ignored. Punished for things *she* did wrong. My so called father left. And my mother didn't give a hoot about me. Is that what was best for me?"

"I wasn't to know—"

"Well, now *you'll hear it*! All of it. And I'll finish by telling you of the work of art I made of her dead body before I fed her tongue to the two pitbulls down the road."

Tom curls his lip and swallows. "I'm going to kill you, Edward. Make no mistake. You're dead."

Edward giggles. "That's cute." He looks at Martha. "Was he always so adorable?"

Martha's face remains expressionless as she stares back into Edward's cold eyes. "Always."

Edward winces and sucks a breath through his teeth. "Ouch. That hurts."

Tom's jaw clenches. "You hurt Isabella."

"She asked for it. Smart mouth she's got."

Tom grins as adrenaline pumps through his blood. He lunges forward and grips Edward around the throat. He pushes his thumb and index finger into the soft spots under his jawbone. Tom squeezes harder as Edward's eyes bulge and he squirms, unable to pull Tom's hand away with his own taped behind his back.

"Tom!" Martha's voice cuts through the mist surrounding him and he releases the pressure.

"You tied her up." Tom swings his gun into Edward's mouth and smashes his front teeth.

Edward cries out. Blood and teeth spill from his mouth, and he digs his chin into his chest.

"Tom, please. Stop." Martha jumps from the sofa and grabs Tom's arm with both hands.

Tom shrugs Martha off, and she falls back onto the sofa. "Don't." He shoots a warning look and turns back to Edward.

He squeezes the gun and smashes it into Edward's already broken, bloody face. Edward howls in agony. Tom fists the collar of Edward's shirt in his hand and pulls him up off the armchair.

Edward half hangs, half totters on his tied together feet.

"You drugged her." Tom throws Edward onto the floor.

Edward squirms and thrusts his hips in an attempt to move away from Tom and gets nowhere. Tom kicks him in the ribs and a satisfying crack accompanies Edward's moans as he curls into the foetal position.

Tom leans down so his mouth is close to Edward's ear. "But you know how I knew you were a psychopath, Edward?" He shoves the gun against the side of Edward's head. "You left fucking moving boxes in the stairwell for three god damn weeks."

Edward frowns and looks up at Tom through his bloodied face. "That makes me a psychopath?" His words come out slurred and squeaky.

"Absolutely." He jams the gun into Edward's knee and is about to fire.

"Tom. Don't!" Martha's voice sounds a million miles away, but Tom drops his finger off the trigger.

He grabs Edward's jaw and twists his face, squeezing harder. The jaw buckles and moves under his fingers. He slams the gun into it and it drops further, hanging from Edward's face at an unnatural angle.

Edward moans and cries, trying to roll himself away from Tom.

"Enough! Tom, stop. Please. Stop." Martha's voice is loud and urgent. "Don't hurt him anymore."

Edward's cries fill the room in a disturbing cacophony of pain.

Tom turns his head and squints at her. He looks at Isabella, whose hand is against her chest and she's breathing heavy breaths. He closes his eyes a moment and takes a breath of his own before opening them and addressing Isabella. "Am I scaring you?"

She shakes her head. "No."

He slides his eyes to Martha. "You?"

"No."

"Then?"

"Please don't hurt him anymore."

"Why?"

She hesitates, dropping her eyes to her lap a moment before raising them to him again. "Because every time you do, a tiny piece of my heart feels it."

Tom's vision mists, and he lowers the gun.

Edward is still writhing on the floor, whimpering into the floorboards. His mouth drips of blood and broken teeth.

Tom wipes the back of his forearm across his mouth. He looks over at Martha and Isabella again. "I want to kill him."

Isabella stands up. "So do I. But…" They both look at Martha, sitting with her hands clawing into her knees, her eyes glued to her son.

Her son.

Tom's gut lurches and he grits his teeth. He grabs Isabella's hand. "We're going home now. I'm done. You need to rest." He nods to James. "Can you organise for this piece of shit to be picked up?"

"Yeah, yeah, of course."

"What about Martha?" Isabella whispers.

"I'm sure she has some thinking to do."

Martha stands. "Tom, I—"

"Goodnight." Tom walks to the door, not acknowledging Martha again.

"It'll be okay Martha," Isabella says as they pass her.

He stops and turns to Edward, broken and beaten on the floor. "Isn't sibling rivalry fun?"

46

TOM

Tom opens his eyes and focuses on the ceiling. His arm is around Isabella, hugging her to him, her bare chest against his. She is breathing long, even breaths across his skin and he drops his lips to her head. She stirs, but stays asleep.

He slides out from beneath her and lays her on the pillow. He pulls tracks on and goes down the stairs of his mother's house and into the kitchen, flicks the kettle and scoops three overloaded scoops of coffee into a mug. *There isn't enough this morning.*

He turns and observes the lounge room, and his eyes fall to the phone he bought at a service station on the way to Avebury, still on the coffee table. He pours water into his mug and sits on the sofa, picking the phone up and switching it on. He leans back and closes his eyes. Pings sound and he counts them as they break the silence of the morning.

Twelve.

He checks the screen. Six missed calls from Martha and one

text. Three calls from Abbie and two from James. He clicks on Martha's text.

I need to speak to you.

Tom raises his eyebrows and throws the phone back on the table. He takes a sip of coffee and grimaces as it slides down his throat. *Three scoops was maybe too many.*

A hand runs through his hair and down his neck, and Isabella sits on his lap. "I can smell your coffee from upstairs."

"It's awful." He leans across her and puts the mug down.

Isabella points to his phone. "You turned it on."

"Yes. And now I'm turning it back off."

"Leave it. You can't ignore her forever."

"Sure I can."

Isabella sighs. "Hey, I never asked, what did you tell Lorna?"

"I told her Pebbles must have run outside and got hit by a car."

"God, the poor thing. Was she okay?"

"I told her I buried her in the garden near the snapdragons. So she has a place to visit."

"You're a softie, Tom Grant."

"But?"

"But… you need to speak to Martha."

He drops his head back against the sofa and closes his eyes.

"I'm gonna go shower." She goes to the edge of the lounge. "Oh, by the way…" She turns. "I googled and found a meeting in Avebury. You can go to one tonight." She points at him and retreats up the stairs.

Tom sighs and scrubs his hands through his hair. "Fine," he whispers to himself.

He walks to the kitchen and dumps his mug in the sink. He stares out the window at the fields beyond. The phone rings and he scrunches his face up, ignoring it. *Dammit Martha.* He waits until it stops before going to check the screen. *Her.* A message pings to let him know a voicemail waits. He dials in and listens. He hears her sigh out a breath before hanging up. His gut twists and he sits down, staring at the phone.

Martha raised her hand and Tom flinched. She peered at him as she pulled a cup from the cupboard.

"Tom?" She handed it to him. "I was just reaching to get you a cup."

"I thought..."

"You thought I was going to hit you?"

"No." He bit his lip. "Yes."

"What for?"

"You don't need a reason. Do you?"

"Who told you that?"

"Rick. He said he's in charge of his house and can do what he wants. And this is your house..."

Martha gestured for Tom to sit down and they sat face to face at the dining table.

"Tom, I will never strike you. Do you understand?"

"What if I deserve it?"

"When would you possibly deserve it?"

Tom shrugged and ran his finger around the top of the cup.

"Tom look at me."

Tom looked up into her face, her eyes were intense and direct.

"Do you trust me?"

He shrugged again.

"I'll never hurt you and I'll never lie to you. Do you understand?"
Tom nodded.

"Do you trust me?" she asked again.

"Yes."

"With my life," Tom whispers to himself. He goes to the back door, grabs and axe and goes outside.

One fresh pile of firewood later, Isabella slides her arms around his waist and rests her head on his back. "I love it here."

"So we can stay a while?" He turns to face her.

She fiddles with the button on his polo shirt. "You can't hide from her forever."

"I'm not hiding."

Isabella widens her eyes and purses her lips.

"I'm *avoiding*. Not the same."

Isabella rolls her eyes. "You're impossible."

"Wanna walk through town? Get food?"

"Sure."

Tom smiles.

"After you call Martha."

His smile drops. "Iz—"

"Good chat." She turns and walks inside.

Tom closes his eyes and massages his forehead. "Fine." He goes inside, pulls his phone out and scrolls to Martha's number. His thumb hovers over the call button as his throat closes up. *Get a goddamn grip.* He presses call and waits.

She picks up after one ring. "Tom."

"Hi."

"I was worried about you."

"Why?"

"Well... everything that was said."

"Said? Not much was said, Martha. Except by Edward, Jared... whatever you want to call him. He had a lot to say."

"Yes. I think we should have this conversation face to face. May I come to the flat?"

"Since when have you had to ask to come to the flat?"

"Since yesterday."

Heavy silence lingers between them a moment before Tom clears his throat. "We aren't there."

"I see. You're in Avebury?"

"Yes."

"For how long?"

"I don't know."

"Maybe next week then?"

"We'll still be here."

"Tom—"

"You know, I don't feel like there is really much else to say."

"There are things I need to tell you."

"Are they truths? Or lies?"

Martha doesn't say anything.

"I've never lied to you, Martha."

"I know."

"I expected nothing but the same in return from you."

"It wasn't as simple as..."

Tom waits a beat and nods to himself. "Right. Listen I have to go. Wood to chop, milk to buy. Chat soon." He hangs up before Martha can speak and drops the phone on the table.

He takes a deep breath and leans back in the chair, staring at the ceiling.

The floorboards above him creak and he walks up the stairs, taking them two at a time. He wanders into the main bedroom. Isabella is hanging clothes in the wardrobe. Tom leans on the doorframe and watches her.

She turns back to the bag on the bed and looks up at him. "That was quick."

"Not much to say."

She folds her arms and gives him a lopsided grin. "On the contrary, Tom. I think you both have *a lot* to say."

He walks into the room, pulls her onto the bed with him and strokes her hair as she curls against him. "Not over the phone."

"Ok, that's fair." She leans up and looks into his face. "So when?"

"When I'm ready." He gives her a pointed look. "I called her. That's what you asked of me and I did it. Can we not talk about it anymore?" His phone rings from downstairs and his body tenses. "For the love of—"

Isabella pushes her mouth against his and he forgets about the phone. Seconds later, Isabella's phone rings from the bedside where she left it. She moves to go to it and Tom holds her against him. "Not yet."

Isabella sighs against his face. "Tom…"

"Give me one day. Yeah?"

Isabella grins. "One. One only."

"Fine." He leans down and kisses her mouth. "I have plans for the moment."

Tom stands at the kitchen sink the next morning and stares out the window at the back gate and the couple of large grey standing stones that sit in the fields beyond, scattered like abandoned building blocks.

Isabella appears next to him and rests her head against his arm.

Tom turns and tilts her face up. "Let's walk."

Isabella nods, grabs his hand and pulls him towards the backdoor.

The air outside is crisp and clean and the afternoon sun warms Tom's back as they wander towards the very fields he was just looking over.

"How long can we stay here?" Isabella turns and walks backwards in front of him.

"Forever?"

"It's a nice thought. Bit far from the warehouse, though."

"Exactly."

They reach the back gate, and Isabella leans against it and folds her arms over her chest. "When we get back to the house, we should probably turn our phones back on. It's been a bit long."

"And?"

Isabella rolls her eyes and grins. "And... *you can't avoid her forever.*"

Tom reaches around Isabella and unlatches the gate. "C'mon. Let's go sit out there."

"You're impossible Tom Grant."

"Yes."

She pecks his mouth. "But I still love you."

"Tom! Isabella!"

Tom spins around and squints at the figure walking towards them. "Are you fucking kidding me?"

"What's James doing here?" Isabella grabs Tom's hand, squeezing it.

"No idea, but he's fucking right back off again." Tom walks and meets James halfway across the garden. "What are you doing here?"

"Well, I've been trying your phone every hour since last night."

Tom's gut tumbles. *What's happened?* "Why?"

"It's Martha. I think she might really need you."

Tom swallows through the arid desert his throat has become. "Is she hurt?"

"No. Not physically, anyway."

Tom rolls his eyes. "Then what is it?"

"Edward was found dead in his hospital cell last night."

Tom stares at James' face as Isabella grips his hand tighter. "How?"

"Bedsheet…" James makes a noose gesture around his neck.

Well, fuck.

Tom motions towards the house and the three of them walk inside to the kitchen.

James looks around. "Nice place. I never would have picked you for the type."

"So where is she?" Tom slumps into a chair at the dining table and picks his phone up.

"I can only guess she's at her house? She won't answer calls, but her phone's on."

Isabella sits next to Tom. "She's waiting for you to call her."

A stabbing pain hits Tom in the chest and he stands up. *Not over the phone.* "I need to go to her."

Isabella lets a rush of air out and stands up. "Go. She needs you. Go."

James stands. "I'll leave too. Sorry—"

"I'm not angry at you, James. Calm down." Tom scans the worktop and spies his keys. He snatches them up and looks at Isabella. "Iz?"

"I think you should go alone."

He bites his lip and gazes at her. "Okay." *You're right.*

"I'll stay here and chop firewood." She grins.

Tom pulls her against his chest. "I'll be back later tonight."

"Okay."

Tom tightens his arms around her and kisses the top of her head. "Bye." He turns and James is standing behind the chair he vacated, rocking on his heels. "Stay and have some coffee, James. It's a long drive for a five-minute chat."

"Oh. Umm... thanks?"

Tom grunts and stalks out the door.

———

Tom cuts the bike engine at the top of the street and stares at Martha's house. He rolls the bike down the road and parks it three houses away. He walks around the back of the house and climbs the few steps to the back door. Peering through the window, he spots Martha at the kitchen table. Her back is to him, but she rests her head in her hands.

He walks into the kitchen and plonks his helmet on the worktop.

"Tom." She doesn't look up.

"Yes." He sits across from her and waits.

She takes a deep breath, her shoulders rise and fall. She drops her hands and looks up into his face. Her eyes are puffy and tired.

"You look terrible."

"I haven't slept."

Tom watches her and says nothing.

"Jared is dead."

Tom nods.

"You know that. That's why you're here."

"Have you eaten?"

Martha shakes her head.

Tom nods towards the teacup in front of her. "How long have you been staring at that tea?"

"I don't know." Her voice is raw and hushed.

Tom stands and flicks the kettle on. He throws bread into the toaster and leans against the worktop. Martha puts her face back in her hands and sighs heavily. The aroma of toasting bread fills Tom's nostrils, and he stares at the ceiling.

"Have some marmalade." Martha slid a plate in front of him.

He dragged his eyes from the floor to the plate and poked the toast with his finger. "I'm not hungry."

"It'll make you feel better."

"I don't want to feel better."

"Why not?"

Tom shrugged. "It's too hard."

"*Do you think your mother would want you to feel sad on her birthday?*"

"*No. But...*"

"*But?*"

"*She isn't here.*"

"*No. But I am.*"

The toast pops up and Tom slathers marmalade on it and slides the plate in front of Martha. He turns back to the kettle and pours water into her teacup with a fresh tea bag. He pours one for himself into a mug and sits across from her again.

"Are you alright?" Tom taps his mug with his index finger.

"I don't know."

"How did you find out?"

"He listed me as his next of kin when they processed him."

"Psychopath."

"He knew he was going to do it."

Tom nods.

"And he wanted me to have to face it."

"You identified him?"

"Yes."

"But you'd only known him for a day."

"I'm his mother."

A knife plunges into Tom's gut and twists. He leans forward in the chair. "How could I forget."

Martha's face pinches, and she coughs out a sob, bowing her head. "I don't understand why it feels like this."

"Because he was part of you."

"He was a stranger to me."

"He was your son, Martha. You share his blood."

A tear rolls down her cheek, and she swipes it away and looks up at the ceiling.

"The second my mother took her last breath, I knew. I'd fallen asleep next to her on the bed, hugging her arm. My eyes popped open, and I looked at her face." He stops and clears his throat. "I was sound asleep, but I knew the moment she left. Because she was my mother."

The pair sit in silence for eons, sipping tea and looking everywhere but at each other.

"I'm sorry, Tom."

"I know."

Martha sips her tea. "I never intended to keep it from you."

"But you did."

"I thought I was protecting you."

Tom squeezes the handle of his mug. "From what?"

"I didn't want you to think that if it got too hard, I would send you away."

"Why would..." Tom shakes his head. "I wouldn't have..." *Would I?*

"You have no idea, do you?"

"About?"

"You were traumatised when you came to live here."

"No, I wasn't."

"Yes, Tom. You were. It took me weeks to have you feel comfortable enough to open the fridge and get yourself a snack."

Tom swallows and drops his eyes to the table.

"If I raised my hand, you thought I was going to hit you."

"Not every time," Tom mumbles.

"I didn't want you to feel insecure."

"You could have explained it to me." Tom's heart rate rises, and he grits his teeth. "It would have been handy to know he existed. *Before* he turned up out of the blue and went all *Single White Female* on my arse." Tom goes to the sink and leans over it.

"I wanted to tell you. Years passed and every time I thought about explaining…"

Tom turns and raises an eyebrow. "Go on?"

"I… I didn't know how. And then you left to join the cadets, and I… figured it was better left unsaid. I never imagined he would…"

"Move in down the hall, kidnap Isabella… tie her up… hurt her…" He grinds his teeth. "*Touch* her?"

"I'm so sorry," she whispers into her hands.

"The thing is… none of that's your fault. He was insane. Do you understand? Insane. And it's not because of you. You aren't to blame." Tom takes a breath and rubs his face. "I trust you more than anyone in this world, Martha. Do you know that? No person since my mother has ever won my trust the way you did. But you've lied to me the whole time. Right from the beginning."

Martha nods. "Yes. And I've felt sick about it for twenty-three years."

"Don't you see? You had twenty-three fucking years to tell me. What if he'd never found you or me? Would you be telling me?"

"Well, I—"

"Let me field that one for you. The answer is no. You wouldn't." Tom stands again and wanders the kitchen with his hands interlaced behind his head. "Why did you take me into your home?"

Martha looks up. "What?"

"Why did you take me into your home?"

"You needed a safe place to live… I wanted to help you."

Tom drops his arms by his sides. "Was I some sort of opportunity for redemption?"

"Redemption?"

"Yes." Tom sits in his original chair across the table. "I know all about guilt, Martha. I know how it feels and I know it eats away at you no matter how much you try to put a plaster over it or ignore its insistence. And you grasp at any opportunity to make that all-consuming guilt go away. To make up for whatever planted it in the first place."

Martha stares into his eyes and says nothing, but her face is barely hiding her pain. "Is that truly what you think? That I used your circumstances to make myself feel better?"

"I don't know," Tom whispers.

"Why did you come here today?"

"Why?"

"Yes. You rode two hours from your home to come to me today. Why?"

"Because, you needed me." The second the words leave Tom's mouth, he squeezes his eyes shut. *Fuck.*

"Now you understand."

———

"Tom?"

Tom looks up at Martha standing in the doorway of his old bedroom.

"You've been sitting in here for an hour."

Tom looks around the small room. His room. "I'm thinking."

"About?"

"Everything."

"I see."

"What do you think would have happened to me if you didn't take me in?"

"I don't know." Martha walks in and sits next to him on the bed.

"You gave me a private school education, let me play sport, took me on trips."

"Yes."

"Made me eat vegetables. Made me do my homework."

"Of course."

"Had you not found me, I'd probably be some kind of drug dealer."

"You're far too intelligent to have become a drug dealer."

Tom shrugs. "So… I owe a great deal to you."

"You don't owe me anything."

"I beat your flesh and blood to within an inch of his life."

"Yes."

"How did that make you feel?"

"Conflicted."

Tom nods.

"But you didn't kill him."

"No. But I would have."

"Why didn't you?"

"Because of you."

They sit in silence and stare ahead at the same wall.

After a few moments, Tom stands. "I think I'm done."

"What do you mean?"

"I quit."

"What?"

"I'm out."

"No..."

"I can't do it anymore. I want to just... I need a break. From all of it." *And from you.*

"You don't need to leave."

"Yes. I do. I need to rest and go to meetings and... chop wood."

"Tom— "

Tom pulls her into him and hugs her.

She squeezes him. "Can you forgive me?"

He drops his arms. "We're family."

EPILOGUE

Tom stretches out full length on the sofa in front of the crackling fire and closes his eyes. His phone rings and he fumbles around the floor next to him to pick it up. "Hello?"

"Tell me. Are you wearing those god awful explorer socks and some hideous lumberjack shirt?"

He smiles at the sound of Isabella's voice. "The socks yes, it's snowing out. I wouldn't be caught dead in a lumberjack shirt and you know it."

She laughs. "Yes true." She pauses. "I miss you."

"You're still coming home tomorrow, aren't you?"

"Yes, of course... I only get a few days here at Mischa and James' place before they get sick of me."

Tom flops back on the sofa and rubs his eyes. "I still can't believe they're living together."

"I still can't believe you aren't over it yet. It's been three months."

"Just make sure Sylvie keeps James in line."

"Hmm. I'll try. Anyway listen, I'll be there first thing tomorrow morning when you wake up."

"There's half an inch of snow, Iz. You won't be here first thing."

"Please… where I come from, half an inch of snow is nothing. But the way everything grinds to a halt at the slightest mention of snow here, I guess you're right. I'll be there as soon as I can."

"Or… you could always find a job around here and never have to disappear for days on end again…" He winces and waits for her response.

"We still have trafficked girls to intercept. It didn't stop because you up and left you know."

The edge to her voice makes Tom sit up. "I know. I'm sorry."

"You could always… I don't know… come back?"

Tom snorts. "First of all… no. And second of all, we don't have a flat there anymore. And I refuse to stay in James' place."

Isabella grunts. "You're a pain in the neck, Tom Grant."

He grins. "Love you."

"Yeah, yeah… see you in the morning." She ends the call and Tom chuckles as he drops the phone on the floor and lies back on the sofa.

The phone rings again immediately, and he slides a hand across the floor to find it while his eyes are closed. "Forget something?"

"Ah, Tom Grant. I knew there was more to you than meets the eye. Tell me… how is Irina?"

Tom grips the phone. "Benita."

ABOUT THE AUTHOR

Samantha Adair lives on the Northern Beaches of Sydney Australia with her family and golden retriever.

When she isn't writing, she can be found in her favourite coffee nook reading a good book or nattering with friends.

Sam has most recently been a Finalist in the 2021 The Wishing Shelf Book Award and a Silver Medalist in the 2022 Global Book Awards.

ALSO BY SAMANTHA ADAIR

Blood Orphan

Deadly Deceit

Motherland

Rough Seas